THE
RELUCTANT
FORTUNE
TELLER

THE RELUCTANT FORTUNE TELLER

KEZIAH FROST

PARK ROW BOOKS

PARK
ROW
BOOKS

Recycling programs
for this product may
not exist in your area.

ISBN-13: 978-0-7783-1281-9

The Reluctant Fortune-Teller

For questions and comments about the quality of this book, please contact us at CustomerService@Harlequin.com.

ParkRowBooks.com
BookClubbish.com

Printed in U.S.A.

To my children and grandchildren:
may you always honor your snowflake nature.

THE
RELUCTANT
FORTUNE
TELLER

CHAPTER ONE

Six of Clubs:

Your current difficulties may seem
unresolvable. Do not despair. A solution is
on its way. Beware of the motives of others.
They are not as they seem.

The Intervention occurred on a morning in early May. Norbert Zelenka was not expecting it.

Before the doorbell rang, Ivy had been regarding Norbert with a tenderness he had never known. He was serving her breakfast, and could not be sure if the love in her eyes was in fact for him, or for the breakfast. He hoped it was for him. Ivy was a four-pound white Chihuahua, bequeathed to him by his aunt Pearl. In all his seventy-three years, he had never before been the focus of such intense affection. It gave him a new feeling, and a new feeling is a rare thing at seventy-three.

Norbert considered himself a fortunate person. In his life, he had been truly loved by two people: his aunt Pearl—in her peculiar, distracted way, and his beautiful wife, Lois. Both were gone from this world now, though, and he was left alone with Ivy, who loved him as only a dog can love. Although

many people in his situation would have considered themselves lonely, Norbert was blessed with a gift for appreciating all that he had been given in his life, and all that he still
had. It would have been an easy task for him to name a dozen
things for which he was grateful: he lived in a beautiful tourist town on Lake Ontario; he enjoyed his hobby of oil painting and watercolor; he had a garden all his own to tend; and
his health was still robust.

He also was grateful for his happy routines. He had been
about to have his midmorning snack of four crackers with
peanut butter, breaking off a minuscule piece for Ivy. After
that, he would ask Ivy if she wanted to go for a walk, and she
would indicate with all her might her answer in the affirma-
tive. This is what they did every morning.

But now the doorbell had rung, and it unsettled him. He
was not accustomed to interruptions to his routines.

Because the doorbell seldom rang—in fact, it never rang—
the clang of it caused Ivy to become hysterical.

Norbert, running a hand over the half ring of white hair
that remained at the back of his head, glanced around his bungalow, hoping that it was presentable (it was) and that whoever was outside would not want to come in. (They would.)
Norbert's home was small, orderly, and exactly to his liking.
When Norbert first saw the house eight years ago after retiring and leaving Buffalo, the Realtor had exclaimed, "This has
to be the tiniest house in Gibbons Corner!" Norbert liked it
that way: small and manageable.

Feminine murmuring drifted in through Norbert's windows, and he decided it must be a pair of church ladies who
intended to force their way in to pray with him. There was
certainly no one else he knew of who would visit him un-
expectedly. Norbert was no good with forceful people, especially forceful ladies. They never heard his protests. However,

he couldn't just pretend he wasn't home. That would feel dishonest. He would be compelled to open his door at last, and he would have to be firm and send them away.

But first, he would need to calm Ivy. She was still trembling and creating a nerve-shattering racket. Norbert shook the spray bottle of water at her and said, "Quiet, please," which was her command to stop barking. Ivy went silent, as if operated by a switch. Putting back her enormous ears, she retreated under the coffee table, and rested her tiny white head between her diminutive white paws.

Tugging at his lavender button-down shirt to straighten it, Norbert opened the door. Before him in the unseasonably sweltering heat he saw three slightly damp artists. He knew them all: women he saw almost every day at the Gibbons Corner Art League and Gallery. But he had never seen any of them on his doorstep before.

All three of them were his age or older. They were known in town as "Carlotta's Club" and had been friends with each other for decades. Their leader, Carlotta, was always running something, and at present she ran the Art League. Norbert, on moving to Gibbons Corner, had begun classes there, and he had even become a member, attending faithfully, hoping to find some structure for his days and possibly discover a hidden talent. He had even wondered if he might make new friends. He hadn't really *expected* to make friends, though. He had never made them before.

Blinking into the bright morning, Norbert regarded the women who had come, inexplicably, to his door. One was tiny and gave off a sparkly feeling; her eyes were very blue: Margaret Birch. Birdie Walsh was the one with reddish hair and freckles; she always wore flowy hippie clothes and had a permanently far-off expression in her eyes. And the leader of the trio was the intensely smiling Carlotta Moon: slim, stylish and white-haired, with eyebrows thinly drawn.

"Good morning, Norbert!" chorused the Club.

"Why are you here?" is what Norbert wanted to ask, but didn't.

At the Art League, as everywhere else, Norbert felt invisible. He tried to be noticed by being thoughtful, but perhaps he wasn't very good at it. The only thing he could think to do was bring fresh *kolaczkis* every day from Gloria's Bakery, and offer them to everyone. These special Polish pastries, covered in powdered sugar and containing a fruit filling, were irresistible and caused the takers to glance up at him and say "Thanks!" as they passed. He used them as a conversation piece with gallery customers and Art League members, instructing them in the pronunciation of the delicacy: "Koh-latch-keys," he would say slowly, but people really only wanted to eat *kolaczkis* and not learn hard Polish words.

On his doorstep, Birdie and Margaret exchanged glances.

Carlotta tilted her head at Norbert. "Were you going to invite us in, Norbert, or just smile at us?"

Norbert had a habit of smiling in all situations, but especially when nervous. It was a very inconvenient habit to have at funerals. Funerals made him very nervous.

Norbert, pinkening, said, "What a nice surprise! Come right in, please! Welcome!" But they were already coming in, and as people usually did, talking over him.

"Oh!" sighed Margaret, the short, sparkly one. "We walked from Carlotta's house! It seems like we're getting the dog days in May now! Eighty degrees! This has to be a record! It will be refreshing to get out of this awful heat." She broke off when she saw the open windows and then Norbert's damp forehead. It was a few degrees warmer inside the little 1920s-style bungalow than it was outside.

Norbert's Social Security check did not stretch to cover luxuries such as air-conditioning, so he went without—usually not a problem in upstate New York, except for this unusually hot day.

Norbert bustled about, offering cold water to his guests and asking them to sit down, please, and make themselves at home. He said a few more times that this was a nice surprise, hoping that it would be.

The ladies brought in the vaguely flowery fragrances of powder and perfume. That was nice.

Ivy ventured out of hiding when Norbert sat down at last, and he set her in her basket by the window, hoping she would feel a breeze from Lake Ontario. From her safe perch she turned her head from one intruder to the next, growling softly. Norbert had already introduced her to them all, as he brought her to the Art League each time he went. She even had her own basket to sleep in at the Art League, and everyone stopped by to tell her she was a lovely dog and to pat her apple-shaped head. It was quite a different feeling, however, for both Norbert and Ivy, to see these people in their home.

After courtesies and pauses, remarks on the unusual heat wave, exclamations on the divine aroma of lilacs coming in through the window screens, the little group sat in silence for a moment.

Margaret sipped her water and remarked on how refreshing it was.

Carlotta cleared her throat and launched into the reason for the unexpected visit.

"Norbert, we always thought you volunteered at the food pantry at St. Edmund's."

Norbert crossed his thin legs and felt his big toes pushing through the holes in his beige socks. He hoped that his visitors wouldn't notice where his shoes were separating at the soles.

"Why?" asked Norbert, coloring slightly. "I never said

so." This was true: Norbert was temperamentally incapable of lying, unless it was for someone else's benefit.

"No, you didn't. But of course we've seen you going in. It's a small town," added Carlotta, straightening. "We can't help seeing our friends going around town."

Norbert was surprised and pleased that Carlotta had, even indirectly, referred to him as a friend. But he was wary of what might be coming next.

Birdie leaned forward, her dangling earrings jingling softly. "I saw you yesterday, Norbert, crossing the street from the church—with a cardboard box of food. You were taking it home."

"And so," added Margaret, her eyes gleaming, "we're here to find out how bad you've got it, and to help you out."

Norbert's eyes widened behind his thick lenses. In a leap, this conversation had gone from embarrassing to mortifying. These women had come to announce that they knew he was poor, and even worse, they were going to offer him money. He glanced at the door and wondered how he could get them out, or, failing that, how he could escape himself.

At seventy-three years of age, after having worked as an accountant for forty years, Norbert's cupboards were empty except for dog food, peanut butter, rice and beans. Whatever food he had, he picked up at St. Edmund's food pantry twice a month. For variety in his week, there was a free spaghetti dinner at the church every Friday night. He always wrapped the garlic bread to have the next day. He often had to choose between buying food and paying utility bills. It was a continual juggle to keep the lights on and the water running. After all his years of work and responsible living, Norbert did not even own the little house he lived in.

Norbert's secret was no longer a secret. He thought of protecting himself by telling the ladies that he was a "private person." But was he? People generally didn't try to find out anything about him, so he didn't know.

"There's really no need for you to be concerned," he said, looking from one interested face to the other.

How long had it been since he had had a real conversation with anyone? Ages. It had probably been with his aunt Pearl, before her death six months ago. Was that possible? It felt good to have company, but there was his routine to get back to. He didn't want to offend the Art League ladies, but Ivy would be expecting her walk. He needed to send them on their way.

"Thank you very much," he said. "I, uh, thank you for coming, and I won't hold you up any longer."

Carlotta pursued: "Are you able to pay your bills?"

Norbert was shocked at her frankness and simply looked at her.

Carlotta stared back at him and pressed, "Or not?"

The misery on his face answered her question. Even his eternal smile extinguished itself.

The sympathy on the three faces of the Club was more than he could bear. Before he would allow himself to show tears in their presence, he made a stab at saving his self-esteem.

"I made a good living, all my life, as an accountant. I was careful with my money, always. I invested well. I had quite a bit saved for my retirement, if you want to know."

They did.

"How much, Norbert?" asked Margaret, her blue eyes bright.

Norbert lowered his chin. He did not want to appear to be boasting. "It would be over two million, all together."

"'It *would* be'?" Birdie encouraged him.

"It would be, if I hadn't, you know..."

Three pairs of eyes were trained on Norbert, willing the truth out of him. And although it was painful to admit his weakness, there was something so spellbinding about being the center of attention for once in his life. Three people were waiting to hear what he would say next.

"I, uh, well, I gave it away, I guess."

Three ladies sat back in their chairs and regarded him without blinking. Carlotta spoke: "You gave away two million dollars?"

"Well, not all at once, of course. It happened a little at a time, over several years."

Carlotta demanded, "Well, who on earth did you give it to, Norbert?" And it didn't sound like a criticism, but more like a lament.

Really, his financial information was none of their business. Their curiosity about it was very strange, to begin with. They were asking him questions that people simply don't ask, especially of people who are not intimate friends or family members, and they seemed to expect answers. The word "boundaries" came to mind. He hesitated, deciding first that he would put an end to their questioning, and then deciding that he didn't want their attention to end. He was beginning to feel interesting.

Norbert fixed his eyes on a large oil painting that hung over the couch on which Margaret and Birdie were sitting. The painting was of three Native American men on horseback, riding across the plains, and was signed simply, "Norbert."

He didn't want to meet their eyes while he spoke.

"I gave sums of money to people who needed it more than I did, and I guess I just did that a few too many times. A cousin's nephew needed money to go to medical school. Of course, he dropped out later... A coworker's daughter wound up being a single mother with no job... A neighbor wanted to start a business—well, that didn't work out, and then he moved away... My aunt Pearl needed her house made handicapped-accessible, with a ramp for the front door, a special bathroom, and an elevator to take her to the second floor… Let's see. Oh, then another neighbor—"

"Enough!" Carlotta held up her hand. "Are you a bank, Norbert? A scholarship program? A one-man social service agency?"

If Carlotta had not stopped him, he would have gone on to tell them about what happened to his wife, Lois, and that was truly something he did not want to be reminded of, let alone discuss.

Birdie pushed in, "Compassion, Carlotta. Compassion. Isn't that why we're here?"

Margaret, seeming to change subjects, said, "Your aunt Pearl, she's the one who left you Ivy, isn't she? And you were very involved with your aunt's care."

"Why, yes." Norbert had not realized that anyone had ever heard him talk about Aunt Pearl—or anything else, for that matter. "Aunt Pearl raised me. I'd always go when she called, and even when she didn't. She frequently needed something in the house fixed, and I enjoy fixing things. I did all her yard work. I'd organize her stacks of mail into files, pay her bills, drive her to her appointments. We were very close."

From the window, Ivy let out a shuddering sigh and a yawn.

Margaret pursued, "That's nice… Did she happen to…leave you anything else—I mean, besides the dog?"

"Actually," said Norbert, "it turned out she had more money than anyone ever imagined. She lived very frugally, and I always assumed she was just scraping by. That's why I paid to have her house remodeled. But I guess she didn't want to touch her, uh, 'nest egg.' Which was considerable." Norbert glanced toward the window where a hot breeze was wafting over Ivy and into the warm living room. "But she didn't leave it to me."

Norbert ran his moist palms over his trousers. "She left it all to my cousin in California."

"After all you did for her?" asked Margaret, clearly disappointed in Aunt Pearl. "Why?"

"Because she thought I didn't need any money."

Carlotta tilted her head at Norbert, in lieu of asking the obvious question.

"Because I made her believe I was well-off. I didn't like to give her a false impression, but I had to. Otherwise, she would have insisted on paying me for helping her. I couldn't take her money."

Norbert thought, but did not add, *After Lois was gone, she was the only person left who truly loved me.*

Carlotta took charge.

"We're not here to pry into the past," she began, ignoring the fact that they had all been doing just that. "We're here to see what can be done now."

"I couldn't possibly accept your money," said Norbert, eyes wide.

"We weren't going to offer you any!" exclaimed Carlotta, eyes wider.

An awkward silence ensued.

"First of all," Carlotta resumed, "what have you tried, or thought of trying, yourself, to make money?"

Norbert had, in fact, been trying and thinking of trying many things over the past year, as his situation had become increasingly grim. Eight years retired, he was unable to get anyone to hire him as a consultant. He made a few dollars a week working in the Art League's frame shop, but it wasn't enough. He thought he'd do well in a job in one of the stores—Gibbons Corner and nearby Edwards Cove had a plethora of touristy shops and bookstores, but none were hiring. He thought of bartering: for example, in exchange for getting Ivy's teeth cleaned—important maintenance for a small breed dog, as his aunt Pearl always told him—he could clean kennels, file and make calls for the vet. But the ponytailed veterinarian smiled and shook her baby face at him, saying that she employed paid staff to do all of that. He would even mow lawns, but the fifteen-year-olds had that market cornered. He sold his television and then his car, and found he didn't miss them much; it was easy to get around Gibbons Corner without a car, and there was a bus to Edwards Cove. At the food pantry, he heard some people in line talking about selling plasma, and making twenty-five dollars twice a week. After just one week, that would earn him enough to pay a monthly water bill. But at seventy-three, Norbert's plasma was apparently too old. You had to be sixty and under to sell your life's blood. And it seemed his kidneys had also passed their freshness date and could not be sold for cash.

After Norbert finished his list, Carlotta nodded. "Very thorough and creative," she approved. "So you are, shall we say, at a dead end. You have no further options for generating cash flow." Carlotta glanced at her friends, and then, folding her arms, settled her eyes on Norbert. "You are clean out of ideas."

Norbert could not contradict her. He was smiling his default smile.

"That's what we thought."

Norbert looked from one intent face to the next.

"That's where our idea comes in."

Carlotta seemed to be waiting for Norbert to ask.

Norbert reflected. He had known these women from a distance for eight years. They had never noticed him until now. Suddenly, they had come into his home, torn the veil of secrecy off his poverty, and were ready to offer him, if not money, then something else. Advice?

This was an odd turn of events. He was used to *giving* help—in the form of money, only. No one ever wanted *his* advice, of course. He did try to offer his advice whenever he could, but no one seemed interested in his words of wisdom. People had always been glad to take money from him, however. Giving money had made him feel significant, because people certainly treated him as someone very significant before the check was cut. Afterward, though, they tended to drift off. Noticing the financial crisis of another and offering aid had always been his department. He wasn't sure how to handle being on the receiving end of help for his own money trouble.

Norbert pushed his glasses, which were sliding in sweat, up toward the bridge of his nose. Birdie drained her water glass and Margaret dabbed at her brow with a tissue. My, but it was hot.

"You have an idea? About how I can get cash flow?"

"That is exactly what we have," replied Carlotta, apparently determined to wait again. She obviously would say nothing more until Norbert asked for the idea.

Norbert took a deep breath and exhaled. Why did he feel that he needed to be very careful just now? He was enjoying the ladies' attention and was even willing to postpone Ivy's walk so that this fascinating experience could continue. But there was also something else. In the back of his mind, a muted warning began to sound. He looked into the eyes that were observing him so closely, willing him to go ahead and ask the question.

"So," said Norbert. "What, uh, what's your idea?"

CHAPTER TWO

Queen of Diamonds:

A charming woman with a deep
need for control. She is always involved
in some intrigue. In youth, flirtatious;
in old age, commanding. She can be
a strong ally, but beware of falling into her power.

Carlotta's Club had begun at the dawn of time—or so it seemed now—as a Wednesday afternoon Mothers Coffee Klatch. As their children grew, the Club developed an abiding passion for literature, and met in the evenings to discuss the classics. For a couple of years in the '70s, it was an astrology-numerology-tarot-palmistry club; Carlotta, through a distinctive combination of inspiration, charm and force, then led the Club through a psychology and self-development phase in the '80s; for a few years in the '90s, they focused enthusiastically on the study of guardian angels. Then they moved on to being a wine-tasting club, but pulled back hastily after some embarrassing incidents they immediately and collectively chose to forget. When their peers began to dedicate themselves to bridge, they became the No-Bridge Club, which involved thinking games and puzzles, and they all felt brighter-than-average for a long time.

There were also several years during which they did crafts, such as candle-making, soap-making and origami, teaching themselves as they went. When they moved on to sketching one another, it seemed only logical to have everyone take some drawing classes. Almost immediately, the Art League became the new home of the Club, and older members of the Art League watched this influx of energy with passivity, expecting the zealots to clear out in a short time. However, the Club had come to stay. By now, it had been occupying the Art League for seven years.

Many members of the Club had come and gone over the decades, some of them moving away, others passing away, and several running away from the group's manic energy. Some had stormed away, complaining of Carlotta's bossiness, but that was envy, pure and simple.

Lately, Carlotta had been sensing the Club's restlessness, which was always her cue to come up with a new direction. Just as Carlotta had become aware of the need for a new idea, Birdie had seen Norbert leaving the food pantry. And in Carlotta's creative consciousness the new scheme formed itself: take the murmuring, watchful, ghostly Norbert—that odd, solitary man who was always trying to advise people who never took any notice of him—take him and his problem, and make a project out of him.

He had said something odd to her one day at the Art League. They had been painting side by side, and she had been thinking of her granddaughter, Summer. The young woman didn't seem to be having any fun in life, and Carlotta was pondering how she might remedy her granddaughter's lack of social connections, when Norbert murmured, "Let it be."

"Excuse me, Norbert?"

"Hmm?"

"What did you say?"

"Did I say something?"

"You said, 'Let it be.' At least, I think that's what you said. What do you mean by that?"

"Oh. Yes. I did." Norbert adjusted his thick spectacles and peered at her.

"Well? Let what be?"

"Oh, well, sometimes…don't you find you can do too much on a painting? You have to know when to stop and let it breathe. Give it a day or two and come back to it, do you know what I mean? Just…let it be."

She had wondered for a moment if he were reading her mind. But it was just a coincidence. In that moment, however, she'd seen in her teeming mind's eye an image of him as a psychic. It amused her. This retiring, unexceptional man, a psychic! A fortune-teller—that would be even better! She could see him sitting in a tent and wearing a turban, saying, "Cross my palm with silver and I will give you the answers you seek." She smiled at the ludicrousness of it. Then she thought back to the days when she and the Club—more numerous in membership in those days—had studied card reading. It had been all the rage. It was nonsense, of course. Birdie and Margaret had taken it seriously, and Carlotta had enjoyed her own skepticism as proof of her superior intelligence. But nonsense or not, they'd all had fun with it for a time.

And suddenly, just as easy as that, the connection was made. The Universe just laid things out for her like this all the time. The Universe and her inspired mind, working together.

Carlotta considered herself an artist in more than the Gibbons Corner Art League-sense. She thought of herself as an artist of life, with human beings as her medium.

Carlotta would run this project, as she had so many others, for the amusement and benefit of the Club. Keeping them entertained was her responsibility, and she took it seriously. She was always thinking of them.

A few days before the Intervention, Carlotta called the Club to her house for a meeting. After presenting the problem, as always, she would ask for her old friends' suggestions. As always, she would listen to them with polite attention. And as always, the best suggestion would be her own, which she would present at the end, something no one else would have thought of, and that would be the idea they would go with.

With her usual uncanniness, Carlotta had correctly predicted the Club's enthusiasm for the Norbert Project.

"We could have a fund-raiser!" offered Margaret, her face alight.

Birdie thought not. "Oh, no, Margaret. That would shame him publicly."

"It's a really nice thought, Margaret," amended Carlotta. It was vital to take care of everyone's feelings—especially Margaret's. She could be touchy. "Let's keep brainstorming, shall we?"

Birdie, looking dreamily off into space as if receiving inspiration from beyond, offered a dangerously good suggestion: "We could buy up all his paintings that are hanging in the gallery. At above selling price. Anonymously. And as he keeps painting, we could keep buying."

Margaret turned to Birdie with interest.

Carlotta was quick to strangle this infant idea in its cradle. "Norbert would never believe that suddenly all his wolf etchings and Native American paintings are in high demand. He'd try to find out who was buying them. No," said Carlotta, wrinkling her brow with pretend concentration. "Good effort, Birdie, but I don't think it will work."

Margaret contradicted, "Well, *I* think it could work."

Margaret shrugged and looked at Carlotta, who pressed her fingertips together in the manner of one who is concentrating deeply.

After a few beats of silence, Birdie said, "Couldn't we just give him the money? That would be the easiest solution. If the three of us put our heads together, we can just give him what he needs for rent and utilities. Honestly, we'd never miss it."

"Speak for yourself," said Margaret.

"Teach a man to fish, Margaret," admonished Carlotta, with one manicured finger raised. "Teach a man to fish."

Margaret, as often happened, was having trouble keeping up. "We're going to teach Norbert to fish?"

Carlotta took a deep breath. She was so patient with Margaret; it was a credit to her.

Birdie and Margaret took turns straightening each other out when one of them got muddled. Birdie supplied, "Carlotta is quoting an old adage. What she means is, we should help Norbert get started generating his own income, so he can be independent."

"But," puzzled Margaret, "wasn't that *your* idea? To let him make money on his own paintings?"

"Yes," replied Carlotta kindly, "but we already decided that way won't work."

After a perfectly timed pause, Carlotta said, as she had so many times before, "Hey! I have an idea!"

"No," said Norbert. "I couldn't possibly be a *fortune-teller*. I—"

Carlotta drowned out Norbert's protest: "Oh, Norbert, open your mind. Don't be a fuddy-duddy. And stop saying 'fortune-teller.' Say 'psychic.' It sounds more legitimate."

"But there's nothing legitimate about it! I'm sorry, but it's a silly idea."

"What's silly?" Carlotta was speaking loudly, as if raising her volume made her ideas more reasonable. "This will solve all your problems. Your bills will be paid in no time. The money will *keep* coming in. There isn't a psychic in Gibbons Corner—or in Edwards Cove. And it's the beginning of tourist season."

Margaret chimed in: "That's right, Norbert. You could just do it for the tourist season and quit, if you don't like it. People will pay you—almost whatever you ask! Twenty dollars for twenty minutes. That's what they charge in Buffalo. We've all seen psychics and card readers over the years. People get their fortunes told for fun. It will be part of their vacation entertainment."

"It would be wrong."

Birdie, gazing with intense attention at Norbert, murmured, "Wrong? How, wrong?"

"It would be a lie. I don't lie. I never have."

Carlotta was quick to counter: "Sure you do! You lied to your aunt Pearl when you told her you had money."

Norbert recoiled. "That was for her own benefit."

Carlotta retorted, "And so will this be for people's own benefit. Oh, Norbert! You will give such *enjoyment* to people. You will calm their fears if they are worried. You can help them find the right path in life. And...and so on. It's sort of like being a psychologist."

"But I'm an accountant. I am not credentialed to be a psychologist. Or a psychic."

Carlotta, as if armed with superior knowledge, made a sweeping motion with her hand. "There *is* no credentialing for a psychic. And *anyone* can be a psychologist."

There was a silence as the group seemed to consider this assertion.

"Oh, there's nothing to it. You just listen, and then you give advice. Nothing easier," Carlotta insisted.

Norbert had always wanted to be helpful to people. It was pleasant to picture himself in a role where he could calm people and give them advice. But, no, this was a crackpot idea.

"I don't believe in psychics."

Carlotta quipped, "You don't need to believe in psychics. Your customers do."

"But that's wrong."

"Norbert," said Birdie, trying another approach. "You are naturally intuitive."

Norbert frowned. "But I'm not."

"But you are," insisted Birdie. "You told Margaret one day that her painting of petunias in a pot would sell—and it sold two hours later. When the phone rings at the gallery, you always predict who it is or what they'll want, and you're usually right. You asked me one day what I would do if I won the lottery, and that day I found a fifty-dollar bill in my pocket."

"I was only making conversation," Norbert defended himself. "I wouldn't have the first idea how to tell fortunes."

"Which is why," said Carlotta, pulling a paperback from her classic black purse, "we have brought you this!"

Norbert took the book with the tips of his fingers. He read the title out loud. "'The Cards Don't Lie,' by H. M. King."

Carlotta sat back and watched him with glittering eyes.

"We would help you, Norbert," said Carlotta. "The three of us have about 239 years' worth of lived experience. Including you, it's about 312 years of lived experience!"

"Stop!" said Margaret. "You make us sound like vampires."

Carlotta ignored her. "Think about it—we have access to all our combined wisdom. We know human nature, human longings and human dramas. We know the trouble people get themselves into, and how they could avoid it. We know what people need to hear. We'll train you and support you to—" and here she put her hands up and drew them apart, as if highlighting a slogan she saw in the air "—*serve humanity through fortune-telling.*"

Margaret, all aglow, added, "We'll practice with you!"

Norbert looked around at the eager faces pressing in on him. "Why are you doing this?"

Margaret giggled. "You're the psychic. You tell *us.*"

"Margaret, shush. We just want to help you, Norbert. You and Ivy. It's as simple as that."

Something told Norbert that it wasn't.

CHAPTER THREE

Ten of Hearts:

You have a special gift
that you have kept hidden,
perhaps even from yourself.

Although Norbert told Carlotta, Birdie and Margaret that he
did not believe in fortune-telling, the Club left the book with
him. They said, "Think about it. You may feel differently in a
week or two." Carlotta knew that ideas take time to incubate.
She also knew, with the certainty of a soothsayer, that this
idea would take hold in Norbert's soul in a very short time.

A week after the strange meeting at his house, the book
still rested, untouched, on Norbert's coffee table.

One breezy summer day, Norbert and Ivy were digging in
the backyard. Norbert was working in his vegetable garden,
and Ivy was digging a few feet away, in solidarity. Every once
in a while they stopped their labor and contemplated the joy-
ous industry of squirrels, rabbits and birds in the small, lush,
green world of their picket-fenced yard. Norbert had always

loved the outdoors, and during his youthful years in Boy Scouts he had learned how to identify birds by their songs. He stopped and listened to a robin's repertoire, and it made his heart lighter. Norbert's aunt Pearl had been a gardener, and he thought of her as he tended his plants.

Aunt Pearl's garden had been a pleasure for everyone to behold. No one would have imagined the mess and clutter inside the gardener's house. No one was ever let in.

The kids used to make fun of Norbert's aunt Pearl. They said she was "weird." That hurt him, because he loved her, and she was his.

Norbert had been an only child. He had no memory of his father. His mother died when he was four years old. It was her sister, his aunt Pearl, who had raised him, and it was with her he had his sense of belonging. Toward her, he felt a mixture of love, loyalty, gratitude and shame. Shame because she was different, and brought him unwanted attention.

Aunt Pearl was a tall old lady. In Norbert's memory, she was always old. Her foursquare home in Buffalo was crowded with piles—piles of clothes, piles of papers, piles of books, and in the kitchen, piles of dishes. She could never sort things out. She was an anxious woman, and she tried to work out the snarls and confusion in her mind through repetitive monologues that Norbert listened to with patience. She was always overwhelmed by life. Yet she was kind to him, and made him feel helpful and smart and indispensable. He loved her. He knew that she loved him, too. She was generous to Norbert and regarded him as an astonishing little boy; she was glad to have charge of him. Yet she often seemed to lose sight of him in the unmanageable details of her life.

When she remembered his presence, she would sit him down and talk with him, as if he were her own age. He liked that. He sensed that she had a great need to be listened to, and he felt a sense of importance when she spoke to him. She told him family stories, her own childhood memories, and about the books she read.

She also told him many times that he was "born with the caul," or as she sometimes said, "the veil." As a child, Norbert had pictured an actual veil over a baby's face, something like the white netting that a bride wears. This bewildered him. Aunt Pearl laughingly cleared up his childish confusion by clarifying that, no, it wasn't a real veil; it was in fact "just remnants of the amniotic sac." When she instructed him on what that meant, he was even further disturbed: "It means you're very special, Norbert. It means you have second sight."

Norbert had taken his glasses off and squinted his eyes. What could she possibly mean? He could hardly see at all, without his glasses.

"It means you can see into the future."

Norbert put his glasses back on and turned away, sensing instinctively that this was another form of strangeness, for a boy who felt excluded and strange already. He didn't want this gift.

He was the boy not chosen for teams. He was the boy who didn't have a pal to sit with at lunch. He didn't know why. He felt he was unpardonably different from the others, and he wanted so much to be just like the rest. It would be an answer to his prayers to have a gift like extraordinary strength, or sports ability. But the "gift of second sight"? No, thank you.

Norbert loved his aunt Pearl, but he hated that she told him about the caul, and that she expected him to perceive things that were hidden from others. Because the fact was: he could. He did sometimes seem to guess things about people and even predict some things that would happen in the future. He would often have a sense of foreboding just before Aunt Pearl would discover she didn't have enough money to pay the utility bills. He always knew who his teacher would call on just before the student's name was called. But such things could always be explained with a rational understanding of intuition, or even coincidence.

Instead of pursuing the paranormal, he pursued math. Norbert loved math because everyone gets the same answer. Math is rational. Math is not weird. To pursue a career in accounting, reasoned the young Norbert, is to be conventional and realistic, like other people.

Aunt Pearl, often in moments of crisis, would wring her bony hands and croon, "Oh, Norbert, you have the gift. Tell me—what's going to happen?"

But he had only looked at her sadly, offering no predictions to calm her anxious heart.

Norbert rested the shovel in the dirt and wiped his brow. It was restful for him to work in the yard with Ivy, his only living link to Aunt Pearl, and to watch the hyperactive squirrels doing acrobatics high above in the trees. The teeming rabbits leaped and stopped, leaped and stopped, apparently under the impression that they were camouflaged. Watching them made him happy. Using his muscles and working with the earth made him happy. The world of nature and animals, where he could blend in and be a part of things, gave him peace.

The Club, bursting into his home and telling him he could be a fortune-teller, gave him the opposite of peace. Had they seen this strangeness—this intuition—in him? And why were they interested in solving his money worries? Of course, he would love to relieve his financial stress...

But...fortune-telling?

Norbert and Ivy sat together after gardening, Ivy waiting patiently for a tiny lunch and Norbert sorting the pile of bills he could not pay. He tried to get a sense of mastery over his situation by organizing the pile according to due dates. They were all past due. He noticed that his breath was shallow, and tried to breathe more deeply, because he had read in *Reader's Digest* that this would reduce stress. Should he pay the electric bill, or the sanitation? His dentist had been waiting the longest, and Norbert most wanted to pay that bill because it was more embarrassing to owe money to a person than to a utility. Norbert looked at Ivy, as if she might have a perspective to offer. Her trustful eyes met his, and he was stricken with guilt: he had no way to pay for a dental cleaning for her. He knew that Aunt Pearl, even in her disorganization, had had Ivy's teeth cleaned annually. Norbert had never been totally responsible for another being before, and his financial inadequacy weighed on his heart.

Seeking escape from anxious thoughts, Norbert reached for the book on his coffee table—the one left by Carlotta and her Club.

The Cards Don't Lie by H. M. King

This is a guide to cartomancy, a traditional and revered method of divination, or fortune-telling, dating back to the fourteenth century in Europe.

In this book you will find all that you need to begin telling fortunes using ordinary playing cards. As your skill develops, you may do card readings for amusement and even profit. Read on to learn the meanings of all the cards and the spreads you may use for various purposes, depending on the needs of the person having the cards read—to whom we shall refer as "the querent."

Begin by committing to memory the card meanings, and by practicing on your own to gain confidence.

Everyone has psychic ability, otherwise known as intuition, however latent it may be. You will see as you read the cards for yourself and your friends that your intuition will gather strength quickly, and you will recognize its particular voice within you and be better able to work with it. Keep in mind that the card meanings given here are to be used only as a general guideline. Most often, your intuition may "whisper in your ear" in a figurative sense, and you will follow your own prompting as you tell your querents what is "in the cards" for them.

Always remember that your querent is depending on your reading for clarity and guidance, and that the reader who approaches the deck with an awareness of the sacredness of this work will have the most accurate results and the most loyal following.

CHAPTER FOUR

Four of Clubs:

Popularity You may not be aware
of others' regard for you. You are liked
more than you suspect.

Norbert looked forward to Carlotta's oil-painting class every Tuesday night. He got a little bit of notice and even occasional praise for works he created from photographs out of old *National Geographic* magazines: bears, wolves, owls and Southwestern landscapes.

The studio was on the second floor of the Art League, a large space with north light and a paint-speckled wood floor. Norbert, Birdie and Margaret attended Carlotta's class session after session, and were sometimes joined by others in the community. Birdie's watercolor class was Wednesday afternoons, but her class did not have the draw of Carlotta's. That was because Carlotta was actually a very good painting teacher.

On this night, three weeks after the Club's visit to his house, Norbert offered advice to the adolescent Liam, who was painting a giant bloodshot eyeball. He observed as Liam frowned, raised his brush to the canvas and drew it back uncertainly. He knew what Liam wanted to do, and that he didn't know how to do it.

"Believe it or not, the realism is all in the shadow. Now, what you need to do is paint a line of shadow just under that upper eyelid—"

"Mrs. Moon," whined the ginger-haired fifteen-year-old, "I have a question."

"Yes, Liam," said Carlotta, coming to the boy's canvas.

"This eyeball doesn't look real."

"Ah," said Carlotta, "that's because you've forgotten the shadow. See, that will give you that bit of dimension that you need. Just a line. Here, look at my eye and see if you can see the shadow—or better yet, go to the mirror, and look into your own eye. You'll see. These are the things we don't notice, until we become painters."

Liam, standing before the wall mirror, exclaimed, "I see it!"

Norbert smiled and turned his attention to the young mother, who was painting "The Snow Child" to hang in her daughter's fairy-tale-themed bedroom. He saw how she could make the painting better, how she could intensify the winter sparkle of it.

"You know," said Norbert, "to give the scene some dimension, you could have a branch just in front, with icicles hanging from it. Or even a giant snowflake showing that microscopic pattern that snowflakes have, you know?"

The young mother smiled, the way she probably smiled at her child when she was too busy to listen.

Norbert felt himself being watched and turned to see Carlotta looking at him thoughtfully. It gave him a shock. It was not a kind look, but a piercing one. Sometimes he wondered how deeply she could see into people.

"Who was it who said," proclaimed Carlotta, "'Distrust unsolicited advice'? I believe it was Aesop. Yes, I'm sure it was Aesop."

Norbert knew that remark was directed at him. He took no offense. Smiling, he turned his attention back to his own canvas. He was used to having his comments disregarded. People tended to look right past him. When he spoke, people spoke over him. When he made a suggestion, he was ignored, only to hear someone else make the same suggestion and be cheered for it. Many times in his life, Norbert had been led to wonder if he existed at all.

Norbert cleaned his brushes and carefully stashed his wet canvas, and returned to the framing area downstairs to finish an order. He was straightening the mats and putting away blades and Windex as Carlotta, Margaret and Birdie came down, admonishing each other to be careful on the stairs and snapping back at each other, "Be careful yourself!"

They stopped to pet Ivy and say good-night to Norbert.

"Penny for your thoughts, Norbert," said Margaret. "You seem pensive, eh?"

Norbert, surprised, looked up. The Club had not been inquiring into his inner workings since that morning at his house. He had been feeling less invisible among them, but it seemed they had lost interest in his economic hardship.

"Actually, I was thinking about snowflakes."

"Snowflakes?" Margaret turned toward the window. "It's almost June! Well, it's New York. Anything is possible!"

"Something they taught us in school," Norbert remembered. "Mrs. Applegate, in fifth grade. I remember it was the last day before Christmas vacation, and Mrs. Applegate let us cut snowflakes out of paper, you know, like kids do, and she said that if you look at them under a microscope, no two snowflakes are alike. Each one is unique."

Birdie and Margaret listened with soft expressions as Norbert recalled his childhood memory. Norbert could see himself in that classroom at Central School in 1953, struggling to get the glitter and glue off of his fingers, and he could see

Mrs. Applegate with that improbably blue-white hair that older ladies of that time seemed to have, and he felt her kindness and her wonder. The silver glitter, before he'd touched it, had been so lovely; it made him happy just to look at it. But as he'd applied the glitter to his snowflake, things went sadly wrong. The girls all seemed to have the knack of it. The teacher would want to hang theirs up on the window. Even the boys were all doing better than he was. But Norbert's snowflake had been a misery to behold. The glue and glitter had gummed up on his fingers and formed little gray blobs that stuck sullenly to his snowflake, his desk and his sleeves. Mrs. Applegate had said, "Well, snowflakes are just like you in that way, boys and girls. Each one is unique. There isn't anyone else in this entire world like you, with your special gifts. Each one of you can do something that is just yours alone, something that you will do better than anyone else. Your job in life is to find that thing. Find your snowflake nature!"

Norbert had felt excited to think that he had something special about him, and he wondered what it could be. As he'd rubbed his fingers together and watched the dried glue drop on to his pants, he knew that his special thing wasn't making snowflakes.

"I guess it was looking at that snowy painting just now that made me think about snowflakes. And whenever I think about snowflakes, I think, *I have to find my calling.* My teacher all those years ago, telling us we all had something special in us… I believed her. I didn't know that the uniqueness of snowflakes is a cliché. I didn't know that it was later proved to be untrue. Now we know that snowflake patterns actually do repeat. At the time, I wondered what unique gift I had hidden away, that I would find in time. But now I look back on my life and realize, I never did find my special thing. I guess maybe we don't all have a snowflake nature." Norbert's nervous smile widened, and he laughed a little, to let them know he didn't mean to be taken seriously.

"Oh, but you do!" said Birdie, in her smooth, breathy voice. "Your teacher was talking about the Daimon that Socrates wrote about. There is a voice, or a leading, or a prompting. As you listen to it, it gets stronger. It tells you, go here now, try this next, talk to that person today. And as you follow it, you grow into who you really are. And that's why we are here!" Birdie seemed elated to impart this philosophy. "We are here to grow into who we are!"

Norbert waited for Birdie to finish, but apparently she already had.

Margaret said, "This whole conversation is a little too deep for me, if you want to know the truth. 'Find your snowflake nature. We are here to grow into who we are.' What the heck! My late ex-husband had a saying—'Don't think too much.' That's the one I live by. Well, ta-ta!" Before leaving, she grabbed the last *kolaczki* out of the bakery box on the counter. "One for the road, as they say!"

Norbert watched his dinner rise toward Margaret's lips.

Margaret took a few steps, and then turned back and replaced it in the white box.

"Oh, please take it!" urged Norbert. "It will just go to waste."

"Oh, no," said Margaret, widening her blue eyes. "I've got to watch my girlish figure."

Norbert chuckled to cover his relief.

Birdie began walking to the door after Margaret, but stopped and hesitated, in the attitude of one listening intently. Norbert didn't hear anything. She turned back to him and said, "You will get a sign, Norbert." Her eyes crinkled as she smiled.

As the door closed and the chime sounded, Norbert said into the empty gallery, "A sign?"

CHAPTER FIVE

Three of Spades:

Health concerns.
You may need to see a doctor.

Norbert did receive a sign, sooner than he expected.

It had happened on a simple walk that lovely morning. It was the same walk that he and Ivy took every fine day. He'd attached her wee harness (Aunt Pearl had always emphasized how delicate Chihuahuas' necks are, and that they must only ever be walked with harnesses, and not collars). From their little white stucco house, they strolled one block south to the downtown area, where Ivy attracted attention like a celebrity, and Norbert, as her escort, basked in her reflected glory. People would ask him questions about her ("Is that a Chihuahua? How much does she weigh? What's her name?"), and Norbert would feel proud to have such an interesting friend.

But this walk was to prove disastrous. They were meandering down Ontario Boulevard, approaching Main Street, when a mother and child came out of the bank.

The little girl, blinking in the bright sunlight, shouted, "Oh, look! A puppy!" and had come skipping toward Norbert and Ivy.

The mother called after her, "Wait, Angelina, wait!" But Angelina did not heed. Her mother came running, calling with some anxiety, "Ask first, Angelina, ask first!"

Angelina disregarded her mother's ravings, as if accustomed to dealing with such lunatics. Without so much as a how-do-you-do to Norbert, the child squatted and reached for Ivy. Ivy danced and wiggled, welcoming the little girl. Norbert was quick to explain the Doggie Rules, which he always had on the ready for children.

"You may sit on the ground and pet her like you're doing now, and be very gentle. You may not pick her up."

"I know I know I know already," roared Angelina, not deigning to look at him. "I know all about dogs. I'm an animal expert."

Norbert did not have much opportunity for interacting with children. He was sometimes shocked by their behavior, and more shocked by their parents' tolerance of it. He reflected that today's children were so woefully full of self-esteem; he wondered what would become of them.

Angelina's mother had caught up by now and was smiling at Norbert, as if to share with him a mutual enjoyment of her daughter's charm.

And then, against his instructions, Angelina stood up with Ivy in her arms. As Ivy lurched to lick Angelina's face, the child reacted in surprise by loosening her hold, and at the same time Norbert reached forward—but he was too late.

Norbert stood waiting in the small antiseptic room with growing dread. There was a discreet knock at the door, and in came the baby-faced vet, Dr. Jennifer Adams, DVM.

"Hello, Mr. Zelenka." She shook his hand. Hers felt surprisingly strong, paired with her face. He hoped that she *was* strong and smart and capable and would save Ivy.

"Ivy's doing well. I've given her pain medication and she's resting. Here are the X-rays."

She ran her pinkie finger along the shadowy image of Ivy's right hind leg.

"As you can see, she has a fracture—unfortunately not unusual in Chihuahuas. They're a fragile breed. Much more fragile than cats."

Dr. Adams laid out the options for Norbert. She could pin the fracture. This would be the best option. Or she could put Ivy's leg in a cast, which would stay on for six to twelve weeks.

Norbert felt a squeezing sensation at his heart. He wanted to turn back the clock and prevent the accident. He wanted to feel the delicate weight of Ivy in his arms, stroke her fur and take her home.

"How much—?" he began. It was so difficult to have to ask the question. He wanted to say, "Pin it," and not worry about the cost. But the truth was, he wouldn't be able to pay for this visit, let alone either of the options.

Dr. Adams gave a soft sigh, and Norbert wondered if she was judging him.

"To pin it will cost $2,000. The cast option will cost $550."

Norbert looked down at his shoes, where they were separating at the soles, and then out the window at the perfect day, which he and Ivy had been enjoying just half an hour before. Dr. Adams followed his gaze to his shoes, and looked back up at his incongruously smiling face.

He was ashamed of his shoes, and more ashamed that he was powerless to help the one being who loved him and relied on him. He felt inferior to this young veterinarian, who could probably support her pets and pay her bills. The humiliation of this moment stung him. He would not cry. He continued to smile.

"We can do a payment plan," she offered. "You can take a few minutes. Ivy's just relaxing, and she's not in pain right now. I'll send Stacy in to explain the payment plan to you, and then you can decide."

As he listened to Stacy's explanation of the payment plan, Norbert found himself considering a pair of elementary school–level word problems, which could be written like this:

If a fortune-teller earns twenty dollars for a twenty-minute reading, how many readings will he need to do to earn two thousand dollars?

Answer: One hundred.

And if that same fortune-teller can do five readings in one day, how many days will it take him to do one hundred readings?

Answer: Twenty.

CHAPTER SIX

Nine of Clubs:

A period of study and hard work
is indicated, if you are to advance in your aims.

"Close your eyes, Norbert, and just relax. That's right."

Birdie had an open book—*We Are All Psychic*—on her lap. She was dressed in a long, flowy dress and sandals. She always had a mysterious air about her, as if wrapped in vapor, and listening to the music of distant spheres. Norbert had heard her friends laughingly try to get her attention on many occasions, calling, "Hello, hello, Earth to Birdie. Come back from spirit-land!" And Birdie would start and bring her focus back to the group again. He had observed her over the years and often had the impression that she had some deep secret. She was an unusual lady, and Norbert was curious about her.

Across the table from Birdie, Norbert sat with his hands resting on Ivy, who was dozing on his lap. Norbert's attitude toward the arcane had reversed itself ever since he'd brought Ivy—and the veterinary bill—home from Dr. Adams's. Ivy was now "pinned" by the veterinarian and in perfect form, to the great relief of Norbert—and the Club, as well. Her teeth were also sparkling clean, as the vet had scraped the tartar off them while Ivy was anesthetized for the leg surgery. All that remained of the dreadful accident was the vet bill, still to be paid, in installments. The Club considered themselves qualified to give "psychic lessons," as they called them, because, as Carlotta noted, they had "studied this stuff in considerable depth in the '70s." They'd had fun with astrology, pendulums and mind-reading games, as well as card reading. Carlotta, always brimming with confidence, was convinced that once she'd learned a bit about something, she was qualified to teach it. And the Club lined up behind her, whatever she set her mind to. Norbert sensed that they filled important needs for each other. Carlotta provided the need for adventure and belonging, while the Club provided her with the assurance that she was the leader who would always be important and needed. He enjoyed watching them all together.

"Now," intoned Birdie, "let your shoulders drop, and just *feeeeel* the *lovely* velvety darkness behind your eyelids. Bring your awareness to the area on your forehead between your eyes. This is your mind's eye chakra. The poet Rumi says, 'Close both eyes and see with the other one.' You will, in the coming days and weeks, feel a growing awareness of what others are thinking and feeling."

Carlotta interrupted: "Oh, Birdie, stop being silly."

Norbert didn't think it was silly. He thought it was very pleasant, receiving all this special attention from Birdie while Margaret and Carlotta looked on, all offering opinions at once on how his fortune-telling career was to begin.

Carlotta took a much less metaphysical approach.

"Think of it this way, Norbert. You are just reading people, and you are a natural at that. Anyone who has been as quiet and observant as you have must be good at sizing up what people are all about."

Norbert started. What did Carlotta see, when she looked at him? While he had been observing others, she had been observing him. It gave him an uncomfortable feeling.

"Psychics are successful," continued Carlotta, "because they understand one thing—the human brain is constantly looking for relationships. Your customers will remember everything you guessed right, and they will forget all the misses. This is because people look for patterns and connections. And also, because they *want* you to be right. Never underestimate that last part."

Carlotta seemed to be enjoying her professorial role. She was dressed in cream and black, the picture of taste and professionalism. Norbert couldn't help admiring her.

"As it says right here in *The Cards Don't Lie*," Carlotta went on, running a mauve fingernail across the text, "'Much can be gleaned by observing the querent's posture and attitude. Notice how your querent approaches the cards. Does he shuffle only as briefly as possible? You have someone who is anxious to get to the point. Likewise, the querent who sits on the edge of his chair is anxious. The person who cuts just a few cards from the top of the deck really doesn't want to do the reading. Either he is afraid of the answer he will receive, or he is afraid of psychic processes. If his arms are crossed, he is defensive—or else skeptical.'"

"Oh, Carlotta," sighed Margaret, like a bored child, "Norbert can read all this later, when we're not here. Couldn't we just *practice*?" Margaret was wearing a navy dress with white polka dots, belted at the waist. She liked to repeat that polka dots looked good on petite women, and she wore them often.

Margaret grabbed the deck of cards from the table and, nodding to Carlotta, said, "'Learn by doing,' right, Carlotta?" as she split the deck and noisily let the two piles fold into one another.

"Well, if you're all so eager to skip the basics," said Carlotta, with an aggravated sigh "Norbert, you will just have to study some of this on your own."

"There's no problem there. I enjoy studying," replied Norbert.

Carlotta glanced at the rows of *Reader's Digest* magazines in his bookcase and pressed her lips together. Norbert suspected her of being a reading snob.

Norbert set Ivy in her basket in the windowsill, where she huddled, shivering in the gentle June breeze.

Carlotta was not about to allow Margaret to initiate Norbert into the dark arts. She would do it herself. She grabbed the cards from Margaret. "I'll read for Norbert," asserted Carlotta, getting down to business. Handing him the deck, she commanded, "Shuffle."

Norbert took the deck and shuffled slowly.

"Am I supposed to concentrate on something?" asked Norbert. Carlotta smiled to herself; Norbert wanted to do it right.

"Oh, yes," recalled Carlotta. "Think about a question you have, or an area of your life for which you need guidance." She turned to her old friends. "Funny how it all comes back, isn't it?

"As you shuffle, I want you to stop and hand me a card, shuffle again, then hand me another one, and I will stop you when we get to the seventh card," said Carlotta, and her friends nodded approvingly.

Yes, this was how they did it forty years ago, when Birdie was thirty-three years old, and Margaret and Carlotta were in their forties. The years rolled back, and they felt the old excitement for the occult returning to them. What a good time they had had, consulting the deck for insights and answers as they read for one another. In the intervening years, those interests had been put aside for intellectual pursuits, crafts and finally fine art. Carlotta had never let them stay with anything long enough to get bored with it. But now that card reading was cycling back for them, they met it like an old friend. It had given them hours of fun.

Carlotta received the cards one by one from Norbert and placed them in the "Horseshoe Spread." When all seven cards had been placed on the table, Carlotta took the deck from Norbert and began his reading.

"Believe it or not, I still remember some of these. Let's see. At the top of the horseshoe, we have the Jack of Clubs. Margaret, would you look that one up?"

Margaret had already flipped to that page, and her bright eyes were skimming. "Oh! 'Jack of Clubs—an unremarkable or dark-eyed man'! Norbert! That's *you!*"

Norbert smiled.

Carlotta said, "Eight of Clubs. That's a business card, I remember…"

"Yes! 'Eight of Clubs—you have a business opportunity. Whether you should accept it or not is unclear, and will depend upon the cards closest to the Eight of Clubs.'"

Carlotta started, "Well, *whatever* the cards say—"

"Ohh!" sighed Margaret. "Look! The Nine of Hearts! Remember the Nine of Hearts? That's the best card in the deck! We always wanted to get that one!"

She opened quickly to the page: "'The Nine of Hearts signifies that your deepest wish will be granted, and in addition, you will receive benefits beyond your deepest wish.'"

"Oh, my!" said Norbert—pleased, in spite of himself. Norbert wondered what his deepest wish might be. Might he one day find his "snowflake nature"? Even in his seventies?

"Now," said Carlotta, "those three cards at the top of the

arc are the ones that most closely touch you. The other four cards show important factors that influence your current situation. Here we have the Queen of Diamonds. I remember that's a strong-willed woman, isn't it, Margaret?"

Margaret turned the pages. "'Queen of Diamonds. A fair-haired woman. Or, alternatively, a controlling woman or a flirt, or one who interferes in the affairs of others.'"

Everyone looked at Carlotta.

"I am *not* a flirt," she protested.

"Then," put in Birdie, tactfully turning everyone's attention from the Queen of Diamonds, "you have the Four of Clubs. That's another good card. Popularity, isn't it, Margaret?"

"'Four of Clubs—the querent enjoys growing popularity. He is undoubtedly more well liked than he realizes at present. In the coming times, he will experience a widening sphere of influence.'"

"Well, Norbert," said Carlotta, "do you see how it's done?" She made a reach for the cards, to gather them up.

"Wait!" exclaimed Margaret. "There are two more cards to read!"

"Well, I don't think it's necessary to read them all. Do you?"

"What do you mean?" said Margaret, laughing. "'It's not necessary to read them all,'" she repeated. "Aren't the customers going to expect Norbert to read them all? Come on."

Carlotta bit her lip.

Margaret was already reading aloud. "'Six of Diamonds. Financial security. The querent has the opportunity to earn a satisfactory income and will find that money comes to him more easily now.'"

Birdie encouraged, "Well, that bodes well for your current enterprise, doesn't it, Norbert?"

"It certainly does!" said Norbert. "Margaret, are you really reading what it says in the book? It's kind of unbelievable, how it all fits so perfectly."

"Of course I am, Norbert. You'll have the book here to study for yourself. It's always like that—uncanny. I can't remember why we ever stopped reading cards! It's amazing!"

"But," said Norbert, "there is one more card."

They all fell silent, contemplating it.

It was the Nine of Spades.

Birdie said, "Oh. Isn't that the…?" She stopped.

"The what?" asked Norbert, his eyebrows raised, looking around at the three ladies.

"The disaster card," said Margaret in a quiet voice.

"Oh, fiddlesticks," said Carlotta. "This is why I wanted to read the book, together, in order, so you would get the full context, and not get worked up about individual card meanings. Now you're all confused, and *I* have to straighten you out.

"First of all, the whole card-reading thing is just for entertainment. I think you're forgetting that. Remember, Norbert? You don't believe in psychic things? If the cards seem to 'fit,' as you say, Norbert, it's because the meanings are general, and could fit for a lot of people.

"Second of all, you always have to consider the spread as a whole, and each card's influence is mitigated by all the other cards that appear with it." She pointed at the cards on the table. "The ones that have the greatest influence are the ones closest to the face card that represents the querent."

"That is true, about noticing which cards are closest to the querent card," assisted Birdie. "The Nine of Spades is way down at the end of the horseshoe, far away from the Jack. So maybe it's a disaster that you will see for a customer, and not one that will happen to you."

"Or," said Carlotta, "it could be that if you don't take the business opportunity, there will be a disaster. That's what *my* intuition says."

Norbert's pleasure had faded. "You are saying there will be a disaster? And that it's a disaster that *might* not happen to me? But that means that it *might* happen to me, then, doesn't it? What kind of disaster?"

"Oh," said Margaret, "now I do remember why we stopped reading cards."

A spirit of dismay passed over the Club as they recalled old scenes better left forgotten. It had all started out so exciting, with the Nine of Hearts promising everything everyone wanted, and had ended with the Nine of Spades bringing the Club crashing down. There had been card readings that had upset certain people because they hadn't come true, and other card readings that had upset certain other people because they had. There had been some nastiness about who was more psychically gifted than whom, and there'd been a mighty spiritual competition between Carlotta and a former Club member. All of it was very disagreeable. Several members of the Club had left, claiming that Carlotta was "a bossy, negative energy field." The Club, however, rose again, through Carlotta's sheer force of will, and she took the remaining loyal members on through decades of adventures. Margaret and Birdie still remained after all these years. They loved and trusted Carlotta. If she thought it was safe to return to telling fortunes, that was good enough for them.

CHAPTER SEVEN

Two of Spades:

We are all carrying our own sorrow.
Be kind.

Summer Moon met her grandmother Carlotta for a late lunch kitty-corner to the Art League, at the Mexican Cantina on Quaintance Court. They each looked forward to breaking bread together at least once a week. Summer knew that her grandmother found her youth enlivening, and Summer was often entertained by her grandmother's machinations. It was a sublime afternoon, and they sat at a Talavera-tiled table on the sidewalk, surrounded by petunias, marigolds and softly pulsing cumbia music. A two o'clock lunch meant that they would get a table without waiting, and not be surrounded by people.

There was no one left on earth that Summer loved more, and no one she teased as constantly. It was Gramma who had raised her from the age of fifteen, from the night it happened. Nearly ten years ago.

"So!" began Summer. "Tell me all about your new project. What is your Club up to now?"

Carlotta clearly enjoyed the effect her words had when she answered, "Oh, well, we are in the process of creating a psychic."

Carlotta told Summer every detail of Norbert's financial problem, Ivy's accident, and the Club's benevolent interest in helping him.

Summer marveled. "Whoever would have thought of such a solution?"

"It was all very natural," said Carlotta modestly. "Creative inspiration always is, you know."

"I love how you find a way to help this guy out, while at the same time providing entertainment for the Club. So tell me more about these so-called 'psychic lessons.'"

Carlotta basked in her granddaughter's admiration, like a lioness in the sun. Summer's enthusiasm was very gratifying.

"Gramma, this is so cool. I'd love to have my cards read! I'll go see your psychic—you know, just out of curiosity. Where is he setting up shop?"

"Oh," said Carlotta with intentional mystery. "I have a very special place in mind for him. But first things, first. We are putting him through a rigorous course of study before we will allow him to read for the public. Once he shows that he has learned enough, I'll see that you get a complimentary reading.

"Now let's talk about *you*, dearie. How are things in your life these days? Enjoying your summer break?"

"Yep!" Summer shone her happy-girl smile at her grandmother. She had no reason to tell her grandmother that she spent the sunny summer days alone, in her apartment with the shades drawn. "But I'll be happy when school starts, too. I can't wait for the first day of class. I know I'm so lucky, to have a job that I love. What does Aunt Birdie always say? 'Gratitude is the secret to happiness'? It really is, isn't it?" Summer studied her grandmother's face, to be sure she was buying the happy story. She seemed to be. She always did.

"No young man in your life right now?"

Classic Gramma. She's hoping for a scoop. She'll be disappointed.

"No one serious," Summer answered coyly. *No one casual, either, for that matter,* she added mentally.

Summer pushed a chip around the guacamole bowl.

"Gramma, it's the ten-year anniversary coming up."

Her grandmother regarded the blue sky over their heads, as if checking for rain.

Summer felt the barrier go up. There was no way Gramma was going to let her talk about this. Not in public. Not in private. Not anywhere, and not at any time.

"Summer, you're biting your lower lip again. Do stop. You know it makes a scab, and then you chew on the scab, and it never heals. Why do you persist in gnawing at yourself? You're such a pretty girl."

"Okay, Gramma. I bite my lip. Thanks for pointing that out."

When the waiter came to take their order, Gramma lit up as if he were the one person in all the world she most needed to see right then.

The waiter was James Barnett, a guy Summer had gone to school with. Of course. You couldn't go anywhere in this little town without running into people you went to school with. They had the obligatory conversation, comparing notes about who from their class was doing what and living where.

Gramma chose the bean burrito, and Summer, the veggie burrito, "no cheese, no sour cream." James hurried off to put their order into the kitchen.

Summer caught Gramma looking calculatingly at her, and

knew she was wondering what might have passed between her and James.

Nothing, Gramma. Nothing at all.

"Did you and James ever—?"

"No, Gramma."

"Because he seems quite smitten with you."

"Hmm. You're basing that on how he asked me for my order? Or on the way he placed the silverware on the table?"

"Oh, Summer, you know I just worry about you."

"You mean you think I'm lonely."

"Well, you *don't* seem to get around much. As far as I can tell, you're practically a hermit, except for work."

"Thanks, Gramma. I'm a hermit with a bloody lip. Any more compliments?"

"I'm only saying that a young and pretty girl like you should be enjoying life."

Summer bowed her head for a moment to stop herself from glaring at her revered ancestor.

"So, about my mom and dad."

Gramma looked around distractedly.

"There are things about that night that we never talked about—"

"Do you need to see a therapist, Summer? I'll pay."

"You already sent me to a therapist right after it happened, remember?"

"I do remember you wouldn't talk to her. Well, it wasn't the right time—it was too early. Or she was the wrong therapist, perhaps. Find another one."

"Gramma, I want to talk to *you*."

"Of *course*, Summer. You know you can talk to me about *anything*. You and I have a very close relationship, dear."

Summer closed her eyes and reminded herself to breathe. Gramma wasn't going to make this easy. But this time, she would not give up. The secret pain in her heart was threatening to engulf her completely, and before it did, she needed to make her confession.

"I never told you, Gramma… I'm…I'm guilty."

Gramma cut her off. "You feel guilty. I understand. But you shouldn't. Don't feel guilty. It was an accident. It wasn't your fault."

Gramma's eyes filled with tears. She applied a napkin and seemed to be forcing the tears back into her eyes again.

Summer's stomach clenched with remorse. Gramma had her own burden of grief for her lost son, her lost daughter-in-law.

"I'm sorry, Gramma. I'm so, so sorry."

Gramma lowered her head to rummage through her purse and pull out a lipstick and a small mirror. She expertly applied the color and compressed her lips. She turned her face from side to side, peering at herself. Summer knew from experience that this was how Gramma pulled herself together. Summer watched her, preparing to have a bright smile on her face when her grandmother would snap the compact closed and look up again as if everything were normal.

CHAPTER EIGHT

Seven of Diamonds:

Your relationships deepen
and your connections grow stronger.
With understanding comes friendship.

After the first psychic lesson at Norbert's house, the Club had continued coming, one professor of the paranormal at a time, to instruct Norbert and to allow him to practice card reading. They found that the ratio of all three (sometimes violently disagreeing) ladies at once to one novice was a bit of an overload. Therefore, they staggered individual visits. This system allowed time in the intervals for Norbert's independent study of the books: *We Are All Psychic, Positive Affirmations and Visualization, Read People Like a Book* and *The Cards Don't Lie.*

Following the old adage that practice makes perfect, Norbert, nearing the end of his tutoring sessions and independent studies, was to prove himself to the Club by doing a twenty-minute private individual reading for each of them, just like the readings he would do for customers.

★ ★ ★

Margaret came for her reading after lunching at home with her enormous black-and-white cat, Myrtle. Myrtle, from a sunny window ledge, had watched without regret as Margaret left. Myrtle preferred to have the condo quiet. Margaret tended to hum, whistle, talk out loud, and ask Myrtle for her opinions, which Myrtle preferred to keep to herself.

Margaret marched with her customary energy—chin up, chest out, shoulders back—the two long blocks from her place to Norbert's. Margaret walked everywhere, whenever the weather was decent, and the more she walked, the more energized she felt. On a golden-green day like this, what could be better than to be striding along the streets of Gibbons Corner?

The trees on either side of the street formed an arch over the road, and the birds were calling and singing merrily.

She was looking forward to her card reading with girlish anticipation. Norbert had been working studiously to become a fortune-teller, and really, this was one of the most fun projects Carlotta had ever come up with.

Norbert opened the door to her firm pressure on the bell. Ivy, who had been barking madly, fell silent at the sight of Margaret. Ivy was used to her comings and goings ever since the psychic lessons had begun. She really was a dear little dog, so petite—she reminded Margaret of herself.

"Norbert," exclaimed Margaret, stepping in swiftly. "How are you? What fun! Now, I want to make one thing clear before we begin. I want you to tell me only *good things*. I am eighty-seven years old, though I don't believe that myself. How could I be eighty-seven? However, it seems that I am, in fact, eighty-seven. At my age, it's not wise to get one's fortune told. What good news can there be in my future? Nevertheless, I want you to *find* some good news, and leave out the bad. I won't even look at the cards. I'll turn around and just listen. Do we understand each other?"

"The customer's always right, Margaret," agreed Norbert. He was smiling as usual. His home had a sweet, homey cottage-y feel to it, with its florals and lace. Margaret appreciated its feminine charm, although she was surprised a man would feel at home here. She knew he was a widower, and wondered if his wife had picked out the flowery upholstery and the rose-covered china in the breakfront.

Margaret sat with her back to Norbert. She heard Norbert's voice, gentle-soft, as if he were speaking with great concern and concentration.

"I see a woman, shrewd and sensitive, and with her, I see strife between people who love each other."

"Norbert! What did I tell you?" Margaret tried to stomp her foot, but it did not reach the floor. "If you don't come up with something good right now, I am leaving."

"Ah, but right here, I see the potential for healing."

"Go on."

"Ah… Do you know who this sensitive woman might be? Someone very close to you?"

Margaret sighed. "That's my daughter Vivian. I called her this morning. Today is her sixtieth birthday… Norbert, can I tell you something in confidence?"

Norbert assured her that she could.

Margaret had never told the Club about the depths of her estrangement from one of her three children. There are things you just don't tell your dearest friends.

Margaret turned around in her chair to face Norbert. This was not a conversation she could have facing the wall.

Norbert listened to the contents of Margaret's secret heart-ache, the version of her life that her best friends didn't know. Margaret had not been a good mother—that's what her daughter Vivian maintained. Margaret had never wanted to get married in the first place, but in 1952, there was nothing else she could do on reaching the advanced age of twenty-three. If she'd been Catholic, she could have become a nun. But unfortunately, her family was Methodist, and in the '50s, no one changed religions—at least, no one that Margaret knew. The morning after her marriage, she realized she had made a terrible, irreversible mistake. She then had three children, as one did. She had loved them, truly, but she had never wanted to have them or raise them. She didn't know what was wrong with her. She struggled against her nature for as long as she could. She pretended to feel what other mothers seemed to feel: unrestrained love for house and home. But all she wanted was to be independent, single and free. She stayed with her husband until Mary, her youngest, was eighteen. While Mary and Gary seemed to harbor no ill will, Margaret's eldest daughter, Vivian, had been nursing rage against Margaret since she was a teenager.

"Norbert," said Margaret, "I tell her, 'Vivian, dear, I can't even remember any of this anymore. You're going back to the 1960s, for Pete's sake!' And she says, 'For you it was just the '60s. For *me*, it was my one and only goddamn childhood, Mother.' Every time I talk to her, I'm stunned. I feel so awful, Norbert. I just don't get this—this *therapy generation*. Why does she want to hold on to blaming me for the past? What can I do about it now?"

Norbert and Margaret sat in the little white house and talked.

One of the most generous things one person can do for another is to just listen intently.

Margaret emerged from Norbert's house believing she could mend her relationship with Vivian. Norbert had shown, through the cards and his careful listening, that Margaret and Vivian were very close to beginning to build a bridge.

As soon as she returned home, Margaret called Vivian; she got her voice mail. She left a message:

"Vivian, dear, it's Mother. I've been thinking… I'm sorry. Please call me back. I love you."

Birdie's reading was scheduled for the afternoon, and she had been happily anticipating it all day. Through the weeks of psychic lessons, Birdie had grown in appreciation of this quiet and modest man. There was something about him that made her feel that there was more to him than Carlotta and Margaret suspected. Norbert, thought Birdie, was the real McCoy.

She arrived after lunch, jingling faintly as she walked in. There were bells on her ankle bracelets, and her light red hair was wrapped gypsy-style in a pale green scarf. Ivy, always a one-person dog until now, had come to adore Birdie over the past few weeks of intensive lessons. Birdie held Ivy in her arms and accepted her kisses while Norbert studied the cards. The Queen of Spades was at the top of the horseshoe. All the rest were face cards, as well.

Norbert wrinkled his brow and rested his chin in his hands.

"Stumped, Norbert?"

"There's no card here talking of events. It's all face cards—nothing but face cards. It's all personalities. I haven't seen this before."

Birdie smiled expectantly.

"Not everything is in books, Norbert. What comes to you?"

"What comes to me? Well, just a question. Who are all these people?"

"Yes, who are they? What comes?"

Norbert's eyes went round and round the horseshoe, from one face to the other. He glanced up at Birdie, questioning.

"You don't need a hint, Norbert. Receive it as it comes, without judging or critiquing. I know you are hearing it."

Norbert started. "Hearing it?"

Birdie said nothing, letting Ivy settle on her lap and drop off to sleep.

Norbert looked down.

"The Queen of Spades is you, I feel—subtle, sensitive and perceptive. Normally, with all these face cards, I think I would tell the querent that they are surrounded by people, and will be going to social events, and be meeting new friends, all that sort of thing. But something stops me from saying that. That would be wrong here."

Birdie wasn't going to provide any more help.

"It's the oddest thing, but since you said 'hearing it'… A word keeps repeating over and over in my mind. I don't want to say it, because it's silly. But it's as if I can't think of anything else to say. It's stopping me in my tracks."

Birdie was waiting.

"Spirits."

Norbert shook his head. "I can't believe I just said that. But that's the word that keeps going around in my head, like my mind is stalled there and it won't let me say anything else. All these face cards are…spirits that are all around you."

The mantel clock ticked as Birdie rested her beringed hand on Ivy's sleeping body. Norbert shifted in his seat. Had he made a mistake?

"Norbert," said Birdie at last, "you have seen in your cards something that Carlotta and Margaret have not seen in me in all the years they've known me. I can share very little of who I am with others." Birdie lowered her voice confidentially as she spoke, although there was no one but Ivy to overhear. "When I was a child, my parents thought I had imaginary friends. They would hear me talking when they thought I was alone. But I was talking to my friends, the spirits. Later on, they discouraged it. They didn't want to see the part of me that talks to entities. And I am going to have to ask you to join with me in keeping this one secret. My friends could never relate to this side of my life. Carlotta has been a good friend to me, Norbert. She has always included me, while others have considered me...different. But she can never know about my life with spirits. She would want to make me her next 'project.'"

"Wait," said Norbert. "You're not saying that you actually see and talk to dead people?" Norbert was doubting her honesty and her sanity. It was one thing to memorize card readings and pretend to tell fortunes. It was a very different thing to have disembodied "friends."

"All the time," answered Birdie. "My house is full of them, my garden is full of them, and they come to me wherever I am." She seemed so calm, as if she were talking of ordinary things.

"Wait," said Norbert again. "Are you like those medium-people on TV?" Norbert had seen them, and thought they were full of baloney.

"Not at all like anyone on TV. This is a gift that is conditional, Norbert. Anyone who uses it for financial reward or to get attention will lose it. The famous mediums don't really have it. If they ever did, the gift left them when they decided to cash in on it. I never, ever, want my spirit friends to stop talking to me. That is why I don't discuss it."

"*Why* do you like to have spirits talking to you?" asked Norbert. He thought that if he ever saw a spirit, he would make an immediate appointment with a doctor.

"Because they have always been my friends, Norbert. They look out for me, they are interesting and caring, and they give me messages all the time."

Birdie was a beautiful and gentle person, with a soft and lilting voice. Norbert knew she was not lying; he was humble enough to consider that he might not know everything there was to know about so-called "spiritual" matters—or anything else in this world or beyond it. Maybe Birdie was what they call "the real McCoy."

"You should be the one setting up as a psychic—not me."

"No, Norbert. I told you already. This is not a gift to be used for profit. *You* are safe, using *your* gift to tell fortunes, because you are doing it to help Ivy and to help others, not to make yourself grand. And you *do* have your own gift."

"Me? I have no gift, Birdie."

Birdie smiled and shook her head at Norbert. "Then how do you explain the reading you just gave me?"

Norbert hesitated. "Explain it? How can I explain something like that? I can't explain it. I'm an accountant."

Birdie seemed to be listening to a far-off music.

Norbert shifted uneasily in his chair. Speaking to himself as much as to Birdie, he said, "Just because I don't have a ready explanation for it doesn't mean I'm psychic."

"Well, Norbert, while you've been trying to figure it out, I've been aware of a spirit presence here in your home." Birdie looked over Norbert's shoulder. "I've been seeing a tall old woman walking back and forth here, trying to get my attention." Birdie's eyes were darting from left to right to left again, as if seeing someone walking the length of the dining room behind Norbert. "She has been giving me a message for you. She has been pulling a white veil over her face. She says, 'Remind Norbert—he was born with the caul.'"

Norbert turned around quickly, half expecting and half fearing to see the spirit of his aunt Pearl. Of course, there was nobody there.

Norbert was troubled in his mind after Birdie left.

He picked up Ivy from her window basket and paced around his dining room, thinking. If, even for a moment, he could believe that Birdie did see his aunt Pearl, did that mean that loved ones who passed on were right here, among us? Did that mean that Lois could be right here, observing him, caring about him even now? He didn't know what to think.

He looked at the chairs where he and Birdie had been sitting moments before and played the reading back in his mind. He saw himself pointing to cards and talking about spirits. It was incredible. It was ludicrous. Fortune-telling was nothing but pretense. Everyone should know that. And yet he had found himself seeing things, saying things that had nothing to do with him. Nothing to do with what he believed and knew to be fact. He was getting carried away with this game. He was not a person prone to getting carried away. The very thought of it made him uneasy.

Fortune-telling was all lies and nonsense. Certainly.

But if it was all lies and nonsense, how was it that he had been able to see something in Birdie that her oldest friends had never seen?

His accountant, rational self emerged, and the card-reading, intuitive self withdrew. Intuition. What was it? Intuition was nothing more than observations collected unconsciously.

We all notice and file away in our subconscious minds hundreds of things we are not even aware of. In moments of need, that information can be accessed. It is what some people call "intuition." There is nothing mystical about it.

He was sure that was true. Could that explain what had just happened?

The fact that he couldn't explain it just meant…well, it just meant more data was needed.

Certainly he had heard the others laugh at Birdie and say she was "away with the fairies" or "off somewhere with her Ouija board." He must have filed that away, and it rose to the surface during her reading. Yes, that fit well with what he knew of intuition. People just absorbed information that they didn't seem to be paying attention to, and that information came up as so-called ESP and premonitions. There was nothing to it. There couldn't be. Not in his world.

CHAPTER NINE

Six of Spades:

Grief.
Allow a full expression
of your grief through mourning.
Be kind to yourself.
Grief is hard work.

In the golden late afternoon light, Carlotta rode her bike to Norbert's house and put the kickstand down on the walk before his door. At eighty, she may have been the oldest bike rider in town. While some of her contemporaries were giving up driving cars, Carlotta was holding her ground: swimming, gardening and using her muscles every day.

She approached Norbert with the same intention she approached everyone and all of life: to maintain her position of power.

She was not about to let Norbert read her cards.

"Let's be practical, Norbert, and make sure you know all the cards by heart. I'll hold them up one at a time, and we'll go through them like flash cards."

She pulled the top card from the deck and held it up to test Norbert.

"Now, isn't that interesting?" commented Norbert, a crease deepening between his eyebrows.

Carlotta glanced at the card she was holding.

"What's so interesting? It's the Queen of Diamonds."

"Yes. Exactly. A forceful and powerful woman. Isn't that the card that represents *you*?"

"You may call me powerful. You need not call me forceful. I did not come here to be insulted." Carlotta smirked, to let Norbert know she did not take any of this seriously.

"I just find it interesting that that is the card you picked up first. I mean, what are the odds?"

"Norbert. It was the card on the top of the pile. Let's not get carried away here."

Norbert looked at the Queen of Diamonds as if hoping to find a theorem on the card to explain this apparent coincidence.

"Of course, Carlotta, you know I don't believe this stuff any more than you do. But…"

"But what?"

"But. Well. Would you mind? Would you mind just turning over another card or two? I mean, just to show that your pulling the Queen of Diamonds was purely random, that there's nothing to it. Because there couldn't be. Could there?"

"Norbert, stop rambling." Carlotta touched the top card and drew her finger away. "Oh, fiddlesticks. Just go ahead and do a practice reading, if you must. Just hurry up with it. I don't want to ride my bike home in the dark." Carlotta handed her seven cards to Norbert, one at a time, and watched his long fingers take each card and place it in the horseshoe. Norbert was so focused and solemn, as if the fate of the nation rested on his interpretation of these playing cards. He was a hoot.

He looked at the cards for a moment, and then up into Carlotta's eyes. She looked more deeply than she intended into his brown magnified ones. She had never noticed before that his eyes were very dark, deep and strangely hypnotic. She found herself wishing, in spite of herself, that all of this hocus-pocus could be real, and that Norbert could tell her something that would mean something.

"Carlotta," began Norbert. When he spoke, his soft voice was compassionate. "Carlotta," he said again. He cleared his throat and paused. "I see...I see deep darkness and suffering in your past. You keep it all locked up. You carry so much... so much pain in your heart."

Carlotta, caught off guard, was now silent. Her breathing went shallow as she waited to hear what Norbert would say next.

"Loss is indicated here by the Six of Spades...

"And the Jack of Spades appearing in the same spread with the Six indicates the loss of a very dear one. These cards are to the left of the querent card, the Queen of Diamonds. So these losses are in the past."

Norbert looked up quickly to see Carlotta's face pinched with pain.

Carlotta remounted her bike with a mixture of unpleasant emotions: reawakened grief, discomfort with feelings that were better left buried, and resentment of Norbert for seeing her vulnerability.

She would have liked to think that Norbert was faking it, that he had already known she was a widow, and must have heard about the deaths of her son and daughter-in-law in the accident ten years before. But he wasn't faking it. She knew the card meanings as well as he did. Their intensive study sessions had refreshed her memory of them.

Why the Jack and Six of Spades had appeared in her spread, she couldn't explain, nor did she try. Carlotta did not possess that type of curiosity. What was troubling her was Norbert's intrusion into her feelings.

His sympathy was unwelcome. Who was he, a practical stranger, to look so intently into her soul and talk to her about her private pain—pain she didn't even look at herself? It was a violation, that's what it was. She felt vaguely ashamed. She would just have to pretend that that reading had never happened. And if he knew what was good for him, Norbert would do the same.

Carlotta pronounced Norbert "graduated from psychic lessons."

CHAPTER TEN

Queen of Diamonds
accompanied by
the Ace of Clubs:

When these two cards appear together
in the spread, intrigue is indicated.
A conniving person is working to influence events.
Keep your eyes open.

At the end of June, Carlotta set up the arrangement at the aptly named Good Fortune Café on Main Street. The manager and owner, Hope Delaney, just happened to be Carlotta's niece. Carlotta simply popped in one afternoon and worked her own magic.

The shop was empty of customers, and Carlotta, standing at the counter with her order of herbal mandarin tea and lemon cake, led Hope into the anxiety-ridden narrative that was seldom off her lips these days, about the impossibility of competing with the increasing presence of corporate cafés. Not that any of those were allowed in the downtown area of Gibbons Corner, but just outside of town was a huge sprawling mess of franchise stores and sandwich shops, drawing away too much of the attention of the eager-to-spend tourist crowds.

"Oh, Hope, I know, I *know*! I have been racking my *brain*, trying to think of a solution to bring in more customers for you."

"That's nice, Aunt Carlotta," said Hope, smiling. "I wouldn't expect you to know—"

"Oh, but I have an idea!"

Hope laughed, "I shouldn't be surprised! You've always been the Queen of Ideas, Auntie. *And* the Queen of Energy! What's your idea?"

"Well! I was thinking, you need to offer something that the chain places don't offer—something that they *can't* offer. 'What could that *be*, Carlotta? What could that *be*?' I asked myself. And then the inspiration came!"

Hope put her elbows on the glass counter and leaned forward.

"You know how my friends and I used to go, years ago, to Buffalo to have our cards read, just for fun? Sometimes these card readers are in a restaurant or café, and you just go in and get your reading, and then, of course, you stay and order something to eat."

"Ah! That's not too bad, Auntie. I had my cards read once—when I was on vacation in North Carolina. I could see how that would work here. And it would be kind of cute, because of our name—the Good Fortune Café."

"Oh! You're right! I never would have thought of that," prevaricated Carlotta. *"Lie" is such an ugly word.* "Now, the way it would work is, customers would directly pay the fortune-teller, who would keep the payment. Your benefit would be that the customers come in for a reading, and then spend money here before or afterward."

"That sounds fair enough. But I'd have to find someone who can read cards. And not a kook. Someone who's not going to freak people out by telling them they're gonna die, or something."

"Exactly! Getting the right person is crucial!" agreed Carlotta.

"So I don't know how I'd ever..." began Hope.

"I think I've found the right person, Hope! There is a gentleman at the Art League whom I have known for years. His name is Norbert Zelenka, and it turns out, he has impressive psychic abilities—*and* he reads cards!"

"Seriously?"

"Seriously."

"How do you do it, Auntie?" marveled Hope. "Well, first, I'll have to let him read for me, to see if he's any good. Now, don't tell him anything about me. Let's see what he can pick up with his psychic abilities!"

The list that Carlotta dropped off at Norbert's house had enough convincing details to hoodwink her open-hearted niece.

For a young woman who had been deceived and badly treated by a procession of unworthy young men, she was shockingly trusting. Poor Hope didn't have a drop of cynicism in her. She'd be putty in an amateur fortune-teller's hands. Carlotta loved Hope dearly and would never use her credulity against her. She would use Hope's credulity for her own good.

The list Norbert was to memorize read thus:

1. *Tell her she needs to break up with her boyfriend. His name is Rudy. Say you see a man whose name begins with "R."*

2. *Tell her Rudy will never marry her, and he's not good enough for her anyway.*

3. *Tell her there is a wise, fair-haired older woman in her life, to whom she should always listen. She'll know you mean me. (If not, help her to guess.)*

4. *Tell her that after she breaks up with the loser, she will meet another man who will be good to her and make her happy, but she will only meet him after she breaks up with Rudy.*

5. *Tell her that her business will improve soon, or if not, she should begin exploring other options.*

6. *Tell her she will begin feeling more energy after she loses fifteen pounds. She should eat more fresh vegetables.*

Norbert received the paper, folded into quarters, but he did not open it. He pitched it directly into the recycling bin while Carlotta was stepping away down his walk. If he had come to the point of telling fortunes for a living, at least he had not come to the point of cheating. No, he would read the cards for Hope, as he had so recently learned to do, and let that make or break his opportunity to become a professional psychic.

The customers who would come to him—should he go forward with this desperate plan—would not arrive with written lists from their aunts. Either he was able to do a convincing reading with the cards alone, or he was not.

It was "do or die."

He felt a little thrill.

CHAPTER ELEVEN

Ace of Diamonds:

The power of the magician

Within you, there is a powerful force.

It is time to tune in to it, and let it be your guide.

The Aces all signal various types of power to transform

lives. Whether this power is for good or evil depends on

the nature and intention of the possessor of the power.

Norbert had never entered the Good Fortune Café. Living frugally, it was not within his budget to frequent such a place at this point in his life. But he could see Carlotta's influence in the decor: original paintings of scenes that could be in France and a miniature iron bicycle hung on the wall. The sound system played old French standards by artists such as Jacques Brel and Édith Piaf, alternating with what Norbert assumed must be popular current music.

Hope dropped down in the seat across from Norbert, with a heaviness that would befit a much larger woman. She seemed out of breath, as if she had been climbing stairs. It was 4:00 p.m., two hours after closing at the Good Fortune Café. A tourist, peering in through the plate-glass window, tapped and pointed to the door. Hope did not even rise, but only shook her head and pointed to her watch. She turned her attention to Norbert.

"My aunt Carlotta says you really are a psychic," said Hope. "You don't look like one," she added frankly, and then amended, "but then, I don't know what a psychic looks like," and gave a little weary laugh, to show she was being friendly.

Hope put a yellow legal pad and pen on the table. She was going to take notes. Never before had anyone taken notes on what Norbert had to say. He felt an odd mixture of pleasure at the respect that her note-taking implied, and fear that she would soon see he had nothing noteworthy to tell her. It was a daring thing he was doing, and he had not lived a very daring life up until this point. There was a thrill in the daringness of it. There was also a sense of shame, that he was about to be exposed as a fraud. That would be awful. No, he must not be a fraud, and he must not let this woman down. She, like everyone, had problems and questions. He must pay attention to her and he must help her. Paying attention to people was his strong suit. He had been doing that all his life.

She looked at him, as if expecting him to begin.

Norbert took a deep breath, preparing himself to read the cards, not for someone who was in on the scheme that he was pretending to be psychic in order to take care of himself and his dog, but rather for someone who actually believed he had some special ability to tell the future. In this moment, he was stepping away from one kind of a life and into another.

Hope looked to be in her forties, with her blond hair in a braid and pinned in a circle on top of her head. She looked like a grave Scandinavian child, her face round and soft, and one hand resting over the other on top of the legal pad. Something about her hands, lying still on the table, caught his attention. An observant person can see a lot in a pair of hands. He noticed there was a bluish tinge around her fingernails. Hadn't he once read something about this in Reader's Digest?

"Well, I'd love to have you read my cards, Mr. Zelenka. Please make it a good reading," she added, smiling with only one corner of her mouth. "It's been a rough couple of... decades."

As she shuffled the deck and handed him cards, Norbert focused on Hope and on her wish for a "good reading." As he tuned in to her, he forgot himself. For a self-conscious man, this was a delicious feeling. Norbert lost awareness of himself just as he did when he was painting his canyons and blue skies, his wolves and his bears. He was entering into another's context, not his own, and he found it very natural.

Watching her shuffle and choose cards, Norbert saw that her shoulders rounded forward, and her eyes, which should have been bright, were dull. He got the impression that "Hope" was an incongruous name for this discouraged woman.

Together they looked at the horseshoe spread.

Norbert began by recalling the memorized meanings of each card, by now solidly lodged in his brain.

"The Queen of Clubs. That card is you." Norbert hesitated. He was about to begin naming the qualities of the Queen of Clubs, while closely watching her face to see if he was on the right track, changing his course if he wasn't. He was nervous as he heard himself reciting the book meaning, thinking how false he must sound. "A kind woman with an open heart, a loyal one who loves other people very deeply."

Hope gave a laugh that sounded more like a sigh.

"Loyal! Oh, yes, I'm loyal, all right. My aunt would say I'm a little too loyal. I like being queen of something, though. I'm the Queen of Clubs. Hooray."

Hope didn't seem to notice that he was speaking by rote. She was focused on the reading, and hoping to get something out of it. Norbert relaxed slightly.

"Okay. What do you see for me? How about my relationship? Do you see it going anywhere?"

Norbert realized easily, *If she has to ask* me, *then no, obviously not.*

"I'm sorry," said Norbert. And he really was. "I know this isn't what you want to hear, but no. No, it is not going anywhere."

It felt audacious to make a definite pronouncement like this on something he knew nothing about. At the same time, the answer to her question really was obvious. She had given it to him herself. Norbert thought of the passage in his cartomancy text that insisted that all querents have the answers to their own questions; they just don't know how to access that information on their own.

Hope pressed her lips together and gazed at the cards. Norbert felt his message slam into her heart, and he wished he could say something to comfort her.

She said in a soft voice, not looking up at him, "He's going back to his wife, then, isn't he?"

And Norbert could see and feel the pain, the mess and the futility of what people do to one another, and of what Hope had accepted and regretted. He wondered how long it had been going on, and the feeling came to him that to have such an impact, it must have been years.

Hope pulled her chin up to face Norbert. "Well, then, Mr. Zelenka, is there any *good* news here?"

Norbert tore his eyes from Hope's and searched the horseshoe. He would find "good news" for this young woman; he would encourage her. He would make up for the pain he had caused by reflecting back to her the truth she had been avoiding. And there before him, like a gift, was one of the cards that had been in that first reading that Margaret had done for him: the Six of Diamonds.

"Well, yes, Hope, there *is* good news." Norbert, his brows raised and his eyes wide, said, "This Six of Diamonds here tells of financial security. You're going to see that money now begins to come to you easily."

"Really? Well! That would be a first! I'd love to believe *that!*"

Norbert noticed how quickly she believed the "bad news," and how automatically she deflected the "good news."

That led him forward in the reading. "You have been pessimistic, I feel, some might even say negative, for a long time. Pessimism blocks blessings, you know." Norbert was thinking of assertions in the books the Club had assigned him. "Now, you will find that as you become more positive in your thinking, good things begin to happen more often." Norbert saw the look of entrenched discouragement in Hope's face. "Of course, positive thinking doesn't guarantee a carefree life—not at all—but it does remove the blocks that are of your own making, you see." Norbert found a little Norman Vincent Peale philosophy was returning to him as he spoke. He hadn't thought of *The Power of Positive Thinking* in years.

"There are two things I want you to do," said Norbert. He did not notice what an assertive statement this was for him. He was only aware of Hope, and what she must do to make her life better.

"The first thing is, I want you to change the things you say to yourself. Become aware of your automatic thoughts. You have been discouraging yourself without knowing you were doing it. You discourage yourself by saying negative or self-critical things in your mind. Now, write down these statements." And Norbert dictated: *"My life is a gift... I attract loving and sincere people into my life... I enjoy success in my business... I love and honor myself as well as others."*

Hope, obedient as a schoolchild, wrote the statements in

her round, chunky lettering. Why was she writing down the words he dictated? Simply because he had agreed to play the role of fortune-teller? In wonder, he watched her write.

Norbert's heart was touched. He had rarely had his advice heard, let alone accepted. It gave him an odd feeling, to see her follow his command and begin writing. He thought, *Is this what it's like, to have one's advice heard?* He felt a heady sense of self-worth.

At last he had the chance he had always wanted, to be the one with the answer, to be the help that others needed and sought out. This young woman before him might improve her life, and it would be because of him. The thought gave him courage to go on, giving more directions. He tried now to speak with authority.

"I want you to write these sentences several times a day and also repeat them in your mind, and allow yourself to really feel them, as if they are true—until they become true for you."

Hope nodded.

"What's the second thing?" she asked.

Incredible. She was making this so easy for him. He cleared his throat and proceeded.

"I want you to make an appointment to get a physical. I feel that there may be something in your lung or heart area that needs checking out—nothing for you to worry about, but just to be sure, get it looked at."

Hope put a hand on her chest, where her breath was continuing to flow in and out shallowly.

"Nothing to worry about?" She laughed, "Well, of course I'm worried now. I did say to my aunt Carlotta, I don't want a psychic working here who is going to tell people they're dying. That would be bad for business," she added, arching an ironic eyebrow. "So, Mr. Zelenka, let me think about bringing you on board here. But in the meantime, you can bet I'm making a doctor's appointment, like you said."

Suddenly Norbert had become worth listening to, for the first time in his life.

CHAPTER TWELVE

Four of Spades:

Begin on the new path that
destiny has laid before you.
Your calling is to serve others.
To trust in your calling is to receive blessings and gifts.

"You should have stuck to the list, Norbert, and not gone and invented things," Carlotta scolded.

Carlotta had dropped by Norbert's house to give him a piece of her mind about scaring her niece.

"I didn't invent things. And I threw out the list without reading it."

Carlotta narrowed her eyes and regarded this heretofore quiet man. He was beginning to show a stubborn streak. She didn't know which assertion to attack first.

"Why would you dispose of the list? I don't believe you. You told her to break up with Rudy—you wouldn't have known to do that unless you'd read the list."

"I don't know who Rudy is. I just answered her questions as I felt the answers come."

"BS, Norbert! BS!" Carlotta rarely used this term, but really, the situation called for it. "I'm delighted she broke up with that poor excuse for a boyfriend, finally, and I suppose I have you to thank for that. But you should have left well enough alone! You invented a health problem for the poor girl. She's only forty-five. There's nothing wrong with her heart! You've scared her to pieces. She's getting an echocardiogram right now—because of you! For nothing!"

"I'm sorry, Carlotta, if it's for nothing. But I just noticed a bluish tinge to her fingernails, and—"

"Where, Norbert, do you get your authority to diagnose heart problems?" huffed Carlotta.

"From *Reader's Digest*," answered Norbert.

Carlotta's eyes widened in an exaggerated show of disbelief.

Norbert didn't know what Carlotta had against *Reader's Digest*. It really was the most interesting publication. Norbert had been a loyal subscriber for years. What he loved best were the survival stories. He read with avid attention about how to extricate oneself from all the endless, awful things that could happen to a person, and as he read, he mentally rehearsed so that he would be ready: "How to Save Yourself If You Are Attacked by a Bear," "How to Survive a Tornado," "How to Save Yourself from Choking If You Are Alone," "What to Do If You Are Caught in a Fire," "How to Survive If You Are Buried Alive." Norbert read with quickening pulse, clammy hands and a thrill of excitement. Of course, none of these awful things had ever happened to Norbert, because he was a careful person. Being careful, he thought, should reduce one's odds of needing to know such strategies.

But life is very strange, and one never knows.

A few days after her reading, Hope called Norbert to thank him.

"Your reading may have saved my life, Mr. Zelenka. It

turns out I do have a heart issue. Who knew? So now I'm on meds to improve my heart function and to 'make oxygen more freely available to my body,' as the doctor says. I hadn't realized how low my energy was until I started the medicine."

Norbert rejoiced with Hope on the phone.

Before hanging up, Hope said, "I'm looking forward to featuring you at the café. So, what kind of a schedule do you want, and when would you like to start?"

Norbert and Ivy went straight to the Art League to share the news with Carlotta, Birdie and Margaret that he had "passed the interview" and that he "had the job." Of course, Carlotta would already know.

The Club cheered him, feeling that his success was theirs, as well.

"Norbert," said Carlotta, "it appears you were right about those bluish-tinged fingernails. I may have been just a little... judgmental, shall we say?...about you and your, ah, *medical journal*. So...well done! Very well done!"

"You'll be telling fortunes for customers now, Norbert. How does *that* feel?" asked Birdie.

"Well, uh, let's see," said Norbert, actually pausing and trying to discern how he felt. "Well, a little nervous, actually. It feels like a lot of responsibility. When I think about the reading I did for Hope—"

Carlotta drowned him out. "Nonsense! You're well prepared. And remember—Ivy's vet bill."

Carlotta leaned toward the little dog in the crook of Norbert's arm, and gently scratched her tiny chin. Ivy licked the apple blossom lotion on Carlotta's hands.

Margaret asked, "What are you nervous about?"

"Well, it's all fake, when you come right down to it. I'm about to become a—" as Norbert looked for the word, one of Aunt Pearl's terms popped into his mind "—a shyster. The readings that I've done for you and for Hope, there hasn't been any psychic ability involved. Not that I expected there to be. It's just Sherlock Holmes–style deductive reasoning, plus playing on people's credibility with generalizations."

"So what?" asked Margaret, a crease between her eyebrows.

"Well, I never thought I'd come to the point where I'd lie to people for money. It's the lowest thing I've ever done."

Carlotta sighed. "And they accuse women of being dramatic!"

"Oh, I intend to do it anyway," said Norbert. He really had no choice.

"Of course you intend to do it," said Carlotta. "What would have happened to Hope if you hadn't told her to get to a doctor?"

Birdie added, "That is an example of what you will do for people, just by paying close attention to them. Things like that will come up in your readings all the time, Norbert."

"Well, that's my intention. To stay focused on the querents and see how I can help them."

Norbert was surprised to hear himself drop the word "querent" into a conversation, as if that were a real word. As if any of this were real.

"That's right, Norbert," picked up Margaret. "And remember why you got into this in the first place. You'll be able to pay your bills and maybe even put a little money aside in case you or Ivy need it for a rainy day."

Norbert stopped smiling.

Birdie asked, "What is it, Norbert?"

"Oh, it's Ivy! Aunt Pearl was always with her, all ten years they were together. Since I've had her, I've hardly ever had to leave her home alone."

Margaret scoffed, "You can't bring a dog into a café, Norbert. We're not in Paris, France, you know."

Norbert looked out on to Main Street and the decidedly non-Parisian pedestrians. Baseball caps, sloppy T-shirts, athletic shoes in profusion, and bodies the opposite of svelte. No, no one, not even Norbert, who had never left the United States, would ever mistake the charming, but very American Gibbons Corner for Paris.

"I know that. I just don't know how I'll be able to leave her all alone. That's the only thing that's bothering me now." Norbert and Ivy looked at each other with doubt in their eyes.

Ivy was used to constant companionship; she had had that all her life. Norbert took her peace of mind seriously. And maybe there was another reason he hated to leave Ivy. She had become his little alter ego, everywhere he went. She was a comfort to him. He felt more confident next to her shivering four-pound body. He sighed to think that she and he would both have to deal with being separated, now that he had a job.

"She'll just have to manage, that's all."

The next day, the Club stopped by Norbert's house with a congratulatory gift from all of them.

Norbert hesitated before removing the red bow and masculine plaid wrapping paper and folding the paper in neat squares, "so it can be used again," he noted in his soft voice.

Norbert pulled from the box an item that seemed to puzzle him, and held it up, turning it this way and that. He hazarded a guess.

"Is this a man purse?"

Carlotta laughed, and the laugh for once sounded not scornful, but merry.

"That's what we want them all to think, Norbert!"

"It's a pet carrier!" cried Margaret. "Like the celebrities have!"

Birdie said, "Ivy will be snug as a bug in a rug while you do your readings, and no one needs to know!"

Carlotta added, "Least of all, Hope. She said, it's not a problem as long as no one ever knows—and by the way, she never said that." Carlotta winked.

Norbert said, "But isn't that breaking some kind of law?"

Carlotta, Birdie and Margaret all said at once: "Oh, Norbert!"

Each of his mystic teachers had imparted her own message to Norbert.

Birdie: "Give people your full attention for the twenty minutes. They'll give you credit for accuracy just out of gratitude that you focused on them. Above all, trust your intuition, Norbert. You are gifted with a strong, natural psychic ability. Tune in to it."

Carlotta: "Just observe people. They'll tell you all you need to know. Repeat back to people what they tell you—they'll think you're a genius. When in doubt, just fall back on the good old standards—'I see you having some car trouble in the next three months,' 'You're going to hear from someone you've been thinking about lately,' 'I see you at a social gathering having a wonderful time.'"

Margaret: "It's all just for fun. Make people happy. You are kind and encouraging, Norbert. Just be yourself. You will do them good. Let them believe in magic and enjoy themselves."

On the eve of his fortune-telling debut, Norbert was nervous. It was July first. The Club, in high spirits, had left his house reminding him of the reassurance he could provide people in the role of clairvoyant, and of his need to pay Ivy's vet bill.

Norbert, seated alone at his dining room table, with the

sun setting orange and red in the beveled glass window before him, cut the deck, drew a single card and turned it over. The Joker. He sat back and contemplated the clownish little man in tights and a silly hat. The words floated up easily, after days of intense memorization and practice: *"The Joker predicts personal transformation. A psychic awakening leads to a journey into another world."*

CHAPTER THIRTEEN

Ten of Clubs and Four of Spades:

How and why are you
blocking your own healing?
Take care.
You are on a path that leads into a dark void.

Summer Moon was a splintered, refracted ray of light.

She had the reputation of being a joyful young woman—
the happiest person anyone knew. Even though her parents
had died when she was a teenager, she was prone to quoting her "aunt" Birdie: "Gratitude is the secret to happiness."
What Gibbons Corner didn't see was the version of Summer
when she was alone.

The version of herself that she was at work was a role. Getting out of her Chevy Sonic in the teachers' parking lot and
slamming the door, it was as if there were an unseen director seated on the roof of the school, shouting, "And…*action!*"

Summer's life was a stopped clock. While outwardly, she
had moved forward since her parents' deaths, graduating high
school and college and embarking on her career, inwardly
she was still a frightened, vulnerable teenager. Entering the

teachers' lounge, she always expected some colleague to look up, frown and say, "You can't come in here without a pass."

Her grandmother frequently questioned her about her "beaux," but Summer had nothing to tell. There was no "relationship" for her, and there never would be. Each first date was followed by her refusal to answer any text or phone call from the confused man. She said to herself, *If he knew who I really was, he wouldn't even look at me.* She had no right to any attempt at "happily ever after."

To keep up her happy appearance with her grandmother and at work took every bit of energy she had. When she wasn't working or seeing Carlotta, she was at home, in her bed, trying to sleep. The thought that kept her awake was, "My parents shouldn't have died that night, and no one knows what I did."

In less than six months, it would be December 30: the ten-year anniversary of the worst thing she had ever done in her life. Grief should decrease with time. Time was supposed to heal all wounds. But did she deserve to heal? She decided long ago that she did not.

CHAPTER FOURTEEN

Nine of Diamonds:

A new beginning.
Financial reward beckons.
Go forward with confidence.

Margaret put up both her hands and exclaimed: "Oh, Norbert! You look *good* in black! You should wear it all the time! Why don't you?"

Birdie agreed, "It makes you stand out."

Norbert was not accustomed to receiving compliments from ladies. His face glowed pink above his black button-down shirt and black trousers. This was his *compromise* psychic outfit.

The Club had had something else in mind, altogether more flamboyant. They had arrived at his house the day of his first professional card readings with armloads of costume possibilities. They had had so much fun finding the stuff and trying to outdo one another's imaginations. It was vital that their protégé be appropriately dressed for his new role; the outfit would give him the confidence he lacked. Birdie had thought that Norbert should wear the theatrical black-and-gold cape. Carlotta had pushed for the white turban with a jewel in the center. Margaret had made a passionate argument for makeup—just a little—"to make your eyes look bigger and darker."

Norbert stood his ground. He emerged from his bedroom wearing his own idea of a "psychic outfit." Normal, everyday clothes, in black.

Carlotta appraised Norbert as if finding a facet of him she hadn't reckoned on. He wasn't going to be as easy to mold as she thought.

But she said, "You're right, Norbert. Simple is best. Black gives you mystery and authority."

Sometimes Carlotta had found that it was necessary to give a little on the smaller points, so that she could keep firm control on the bigger ones. Norbert didn't know it yet, but Carlotta and the Club were going to supervise him closely and maintain a strong grip on his fortune-telling business. As long as he remained grateful and subordinate in every other way, she would let him wear what he wanted.

Norbert, standing before the mirror by his front door, brushed white dog hair off his shirt and put his shoulders back, regarding himself from head to toe uncertainly.

Margaret said, "Well, at least you'll have the sign I made, to give you *some* razzamatazz."

Margaret had painted a garish sandwich sign board that she intended to set up on the sidewalk outside the café, to bring in the tourist trade. The message, on a purple-and-gold background, announced in curly yellow capital letters: NORBERT Z., AMAZING PSYCHIC, CARD READINGS TODAY.

Before his first professional psychic reading, Norbert was anxious in a way he hadn't been since elementary school on Sunday nights, when he had forgotten to do his homework.

What if he were exposed, as he deserved, for being a fraud? What if his mind went blank and he couldn't remember the meanings of the cards? Why was he doing such a crazy thing—he, who had never done crazy things before?

Ivy, unconcerned with ethical issues, slept in her carrier at his side. All was right in her world.

Today the café seemed brighter, making him feel there was nowhere to hide. He considered leaving, abandoning this wild idea. What was he doing here, pretending to be able to offer guidance to strangers by using a deck of cards? It was all wrong. He hesitated, though, thinking of his stack of unpaid bills.

Hope, working behind the counter, spied him before he could turn around, and came rushing forward to greet him.

"Welcome, Norbert Z!" she exclaimed, calling him by his new "professional name."

"Would you believe we already have a couple of appointments on the schedule for you? You're creating buzz. Did you know that?"

Norbert did not know that. He had never created "buzz" in his life.

"Now, you choose your own spot. You'll probably want a quiet corner. A booth, maybe?"

Norbert chose a booth in the back, one that adjoined the large window. He was sure that Ivy would like to poke her head out of the man purse and survey the street scene. As he settled her on the seat and slid in after her, he felt very nervous. The music seemed awfully loud today, and he thought he would never be able to concentrate in such a racket.

Norbert's first customer was a man who no longer loved his wife.

As he shuffled, the man said, "You use playing cards, eh?

I was expecting the ones with pictures. What do you call them? Tarot cards?"

"Uh, well, yes," stammered Norbert, hoping to sound as if he had been reading cards for years. "I find that ordinary playing cards are simple and, uh, more accurate."

The man didn't seem to notice Norbert's stammer, nor his inexperience, which Norbert feared must be obvious. Instead, the man watched the cards as Norbert laid them down, as if trying to puzzle out for himself what they might mean. He was taking a grave interest in his reading, and was more interested in it than in Norbert.

His cards revealed several things.

The man's unloved wife, sitting at a distant booth and eating a pastry she didn't seem to want, revealed much more. She was bulky and looked ill at ease in her own body, and a wave of heartbreak emanated from her.

The horseshoe spread presented three face cards. First, the Jack of Hearts: a pleasure-loving, partying, immature man; then the Queen of Hearts: a loving and supportive woman; and the Queen of Diamonds: a flirtatious woman. The surrounding cards foretold the likelihood of deep disappointment for the querent.

His name, the Jack said, was Jeremy.

"I just wanna know one thing," he said, lowering his forehead toward Norbert confidentially. "Should I leave her? I think it would be the fair thing to do. Because I don't love her anymore. I don't think I ever did."

"Why did you marry her?" murmured Norbert, automatically, not noticing what a personal question this was to be asking a stranger. But Jeremy did not object. On the contrary, he opened his life to Norbert.

"When I first met her, she made me feel…like a safe, homey kind of feeling—or something…"

"She reminded you of a loving woman who took care of you," guessed Norbert. He was surprised to hear himself make such an assertion. What did he know of this man's life? But it seemed he had guessed right.

Jeremy looked impressed.

"Right! My grandmother, actually." A soft look came into his eyes. "I adored my grandmother. And Kelly is like her—gentle and sweet. But she's not my type, you know? Let's face it—she's fat. I like thin, fit women."

Norbert did not point out that Jeremy could stand to lose quite a few pounds himself. Although Norbert had before him an unappreciative and shallow man, he also perceived Jeremy's conflict and pain, and his wish to have what he wanted without hurting anyone—too badly. Norbert also foresaw the regret that lay ahead of this Jack of Hearts if he joined his life with the fickle Queen of Diamonds.

Norbert's self-consciousness resurfaced. He was about to speak aloud the kind of observation he would normally keep to himself. He closed his eyes and took in several deep, slow breaths to master his anxiety.

When he opened his eyes, Jeremy was watching him, with respect and close attention. Apparently Jeremy took Norbert's self-calming breaths for some kind of psychic trance.

Norbert took in another deep breath, and when he exhaled, he spoke by pure inspiration.

"I see that your wife loves you deeply, more deeply than anyone else ever will."

"I know that's the truth," admitted Jeremy, stealing a glance toward Kelly, who was pushing her pastry around on the plate.

Norbert was relieved. He was guessing right. And Jeremy didn't seem to be aware of Norbert's anxiety, but was completely focused on the answers Norbert could give him. This gave Norbert a jolt of confidence to push through to the end of the reading. Norbert asked Jeremy to close his eyes, take in some slow breaths and listen to the message of the cards. Somewhat to Norbert's surprise, Jeremy obeyed easily, his head dropping and his shoulders rising slightly with each deep intake of air. He looked as if he were praying.

Norbert now found words pouring from him that did not sound like his own. He had never spoken this way before. He did not know where the words came from, but it seemed that they were coming up to him from the depths of Jeremy, somehow. And that was strange, because Jeremy didn't seem to have any depths.

"I see that you and Kelly have been together in many lifetimes, and that it is destiny that brings you together, for the good of each of you. And I see also, that in the coming days and weeks, you will find yourself falling deeply, deeply in love with your wife." Norbert's naturally soft voice sounded hypnotic, even to himself. "You will reach the understanding that you are twin flames joined together by Spirit, true soul mates, and when you look at Kelly, you will see her inner and outer beauty and be flooded with gratitude and desire. She will awaken a new passion in you that you have never known before. Now see, vividly, in your mind's eye—her heart...and your heart...and the strong cord that connects your two beating hearts. See how solid the connection is. See how happy you will make each other, through this unshakable bond, throughout your lives. Know that you are a lucky man, Jeremy. You have what so many others wish for. You have your soul mate."

Jeremy's eyes remained closed.

Norbert looked at him, and hoped that he would not walk away from the woman who loved him.

Norbert paused uncertainly, and then said, "You may open your eyes now."

★ ★ ★

After the reading, Norbert, twenty dollars richer, took a break to walk briskly to the beach, eight blocks north of the café. He was so galvanized that he had to move his body. Ivy rocked gently in the man purse/pot carrier as Norbert strode along; her nose worked in the cool summer breeze. The sky was the most exquisite shade of blue Norbert had ever seen. As he walked, he soaked in the fragrances of the coffee emanating from the Good Fortune Café, the flowers in the gardens behind the white picket fences, and the lake sparkling ahead. It was all so stimulating. The birdsong, always varied and intense in this little town between lake and woods, filled his ears. He was grateful to be alive in a world with birds.

When he reached the beach, he didn't stop, but walked out to the end of a pier, where he sat down, took off his shoes and socks, and dangled his feet in the spangled water of Lake Ontario. The gulls clamored and swooped overhead, and a swan glided, like a work of art, over the gentle waves before him. Norbert and Ivy breathed in the bouquet of this beautiful place: algae mixed with the gas and oil of the boats and the crisp scent of the lake itself. Norbert gazed past Black Bear Island, past the yachts and sailboats, to the blue horizon. He felt a part of this beautiful world. As he watched the gulls dipping and diving, his heart filled with joy, opening to a new path in his life. Norbert had a strong intuition for himself: that to go forward now meant that his life would never be the same. The reading for the man who did not love his wife played itself over again in his mind. He found himself repeating in his head: *That was the most thrilling experience of my life.*

When Norbert analyzed this first of many readings, he didn't understand it. He saw that Jeremy had a loving relationship and was foolish enough to throw it away, as if such things were so easy to replace. Norbert thought of Lois, and of how much he missed the love she gave him. This silly man might have been ready to make the worst mistake of his life. Perhaps Norbert had prevented that. Maybe Jeremy would wake up in time to keep what was good in his life.

Norbert didn't particularly believe in past lives, although his Professors of the Paranormal (that is to say, Carlotta's Club) had tutored him in such notions. However, face-to-face with Jeremy, Norbert found himself in a relaxed state of mind that led him to feel almost as if he were—and here, he really felt a jolt of surprise—walking around in Jeremy's brain. Had he hypnotized Jeremy? He hadn't ever hypnotized anyone before—although he'd once read an article on self-hypnosis and had practiced it, out of curiosity. It must have been about thirty years ago. "Change Yourself through Hypnosis" had been the title of the article, as he recalled. It had fascinated him. He had hypnotized himself a few times, giving himself the suggestion: "You are a confident person." He always wound up falling asleep, though, so he suspected he wasn't doing it right.

Everything that Norbert did in his first reading seemed to unfold naturally. All he said was what seemed clear and necessary at the time, nothing more and nothing less. When he reflected later that the reading seemed to consist of thoughts that were perhaps not entirely his own—past lives, soul mates and other fanciful notions—he decided that this was somehow no concern of his. The important thing was that the reading had seemed to make a world of sense to Jeremy.

A memory of his earliest ambition came back to him now. When Norbert was seven years old, his dream was to be a superhero, flying through the sky, known and seen by everyone, saving people and animals. He wanted to be like Superman, admired for always being on the side of truth and justice, and rescuing an appreciative citizenry. He would fly with his arms outstretched before him, and children, women and men would stop and point up at him with excitement. *Here he comes! Look! Up in the sky! It's Super Norbert!*

He would help the distressed and the lost. The frightened and the hopeless would count on him to solve their toughest problems. Certainly, as an accountant, he had done his best to give satisfaction, and he hoped that he often solved problems. But there was something in this first professional card reading that approached that exhilarating sense of flying and saving the day, which he had known in the world of his childhood imagination.

Norbert headed back to the café with a bounce in his step, Ivy's head bobbling in rhythm. He had another reading to do.

CHAPTER FIFTEEN

Ten of Hearts and
Four of Hearts:

Go ahead and have confidence in yourself.
If need be, "fake it 'til you make it."
You can do this!

Norbert's next client was a young woman in her early thirties. She wore a lanyard with an ID tag showing the photograph of a younger, smiling version of herself, and the words
"Eileen McCall, NURSE, Gibbons Corner Memorial Hospital." As she shuffled the cards, he had time to study the ID
and her weary, lined face. After she had handed him the last
card, she pressed her fingers firmly into the side of her neck,
as if to subdue a knot there.

Norbert naturally noticed things about people that others
missed. Although he was nearsighted and his glasses were thick,
he still saw more than most. It was because he himself was so
seldom noticed that he had the leisure to observe. And because
he was truly interested in people.

Norbert looked at the spread, feeling the young woman's
eyes on him. He felt a quickening of his heartbeat and was

aware that the palms of his hands were a little moist. He checked the last card he had laid down to reassure himself he hadn't left a damp fingerprint there. His readings for Hope and Jeremy had gone well. Could he keep up his courage and succeed again? He studied the cards, while thinking about the nurse lanyard that this woman wore, and he began to forget about himself.

He had read an article years ago that claimed that 83 percent of nurses are firstborn daughters of alcoholic fathers. He had retained this, because it seemed so implausible. However, he had seen this claim repeated in articles ever since. Perhaps it was one of those false "facts" that gets repeated until it becomes unquestioned. He wondered if Eileen had an alcoholic father. It would be interesting to know. But he did not want to say anything to make her sad.

"Well, I can see you need a vacation," said Norbert, indicating the Jack of Hearts and the Ten of Hearts adjoining each other. "You are a hard worker, and sometimes you don't give yourself a break."

Eileen's eyes welled, and she dabbed at her eyes with a tissue. "I don't really see how I can take a vacation…"

"But you've been thinking about it, and wishing you could," guessed Norbert. He felt Eileen's exhaustion, and he urgently wished for her to have a rest.

"Well, sure. I'd love to go to the mountains. Or the ocean. Or the desert." She laughed. "Anywhere that's different."

Again, his querent was accepting his authority to make guesses and assertions about her life. This encouraged him forward.

"That's it," affirmed Norbert. "You need a complete change."

He indicated the cards and said, "You've been taking care of other people for as long as you can remember." Norbert thought of his own childhood. While his aunt Pearl had taken custody of him and raised him, he had often been aware that he was the one taking care of her. He helped her pay her bills, clean her house, stock her kitchen and think things through. Although he loved her dearly, it was tiring.

Norbert continued. "You had to grow up early in life. You've been the responsible one, always, and now you're finally getting so tired of it."

Eileen put her hand to her chest.

"How did you know that?"

Norbert couldn't say, "Oh, just a lucky guess," or "I read a statistic in a magazine once." He was required by his role as fortune-teller to keep up the facade of knowing things through some mysterious source. It was a little frightening, to guess right, and to see Eileen regard him so gravely.

A new worry began to nag at him. What if he told Eileen— or anyone—something that caused harm? Hope, Jeremy and now Eileen all seemed so ready to believe that he knew things that he didn't truly know. The only way to proceed was to use what he had ascertained about her and then be as helpful as he could.

"Now, it seems the cards are suggesting that you make the time for a vacation. Go to the mountains—or the ocean—or the desert. Make the plans today." Surely suggesting that she take a vacation couldn't cause harm, hoped Norbert.

There was a bit more that he saw about this young woman. He might as well go ahead and say it.

"There is one thing you haven't been good at, even though you are a perfectionist."

The same articles that discussed the early responsibilities of nurses also suggested that perfectionism was part of their profile.

"You don't take care of *you*. That needs to change. In fact,"

Norbert said, looking back at the cards, "influences are at work, and it is already changing." Aunt Pearl's expression, "In for a penny, in for a pound," came back to mind. He would finish off this reading with a flourish of self-confidence.

"You will be on a plane in less than a month. It will be the best vacation of your life."

CHAPTER SIXTEEN

Two of Diamonds:

Others trust you
because you are sincere.

Norbert sat in his living room turning the pages of Carlotta's quaint old book. Its bottle-green cover was worn at the edges, and its pages were yellowed. He had memorized the card meanings, but still, from time to time, he liked to open the book at random and feel the company of the no doubt pseudonymous "H. M. King." It was such an obviously false and grandiose name. Suggestive of the British "His Majesty the King." Norbert wondered if the author had been poking fun at himself by it, and reminding his (or her?) future readers to not take themselves very earnestly, either.

Excerpt from *The Cards Don't Lie* by H. M. King:

The vast majority of people who get their fortunes told are women between the ages of eighteen and thirty-eight. There are querents who do not fit this profile, of course, but they are very much in the minority.

People approaching forty have become either more cynical with age, more confident in their own ability to see what's coming, or more frightened of the future.

Typical querents approach a psychic with either hope or fear predominating. The hopeful querent will face the reader seriously, and be very willing to ignore any false starts and give ample hints once the reader starts down the right trails.

Most people will respond strongly to: "You have a concern about finances." They will then feel gratitude toward the reader who follows up with "I want you to know that finances will improve in the very near future."

It would be accurate to tell any querent, "Someone is lying to you," "There is a great lie in your life," or "You are lying to yourself about something." Most young women will give their full attention to the reader who says any of these statements to them because chances are, while they believe no one could detect these facts about them, they are, in fact, all true.

People will feed the reader little bits of information so that he can create a better reading.

On Norbert's second day, there were another two appointment slots filled. People were signing up and setting aside time, willing to pay twenty dollars to consult him about their lives. With Ivy sleeping at his side, he read the cards, and his customers leaned forward to catch his words. It gave him a feeling of grateful happiness. He had become worthy of people's attention.

The next querent was a young woman with straight bangs, about twenty-six, named Jill.

"Here you have the Four of Clubs," said Norbert. "This is the popularity card."

"Me? Popular?"

Norbert's smile widened. This young lady was open to his influence, and he could help her to see herself in a new light.

"That's right. You don't realize how much people really do like you. You think you are all alone, but actually, there are many who would like to be your friend. Like this Jack of Clubs here."

"Oh!" said Jill. "Could that be Trevor?"

"Well," said Norbert, "let's see. This would be a fellow who seems unremarkable, maybe even boring, at first."

"Oh." Jill's voice went flat. "That would be Kyle."

"Yes, maybe that would be Kyle. But the thing is, he's not what he seems."

"He isn't?"

"Oh, no. He will surprise you. There's a lot more to him than meets the eye. The cards are saying you should give him a chance."

As Jill walked away, adjusting her shoulder-strap purse and straightening her skirt, Norbert felt a pang of responsibility and even alarm. That young woman was so susceptible. He had easily steered her away from an unknown (to him) Trevor to an equally unknown Kyle. What had he done? What if Kyle was a psychopath? He wanted to call Jill back, and tell her not to take his reading seriously, tell her to consider it "entertainment," a game. But she was already gone.

Natalie, in her early forties, sat down across from Norbert, smiling with her mouth but not with her eyes. In her seven-card horseshoe spread, there were no face cards at all.

Norbert paused, contemplating the spread, and at last he said gently, "Every card you've drawn is a Spade. This shows a long-lasting period of grief. It looks like you are—or feel you are—all alone."

Natalie's smile vanished as if she had been slapped.

Norbert reached inside his man purse, careful not to disturb Ivy, and pulled out the slender box of tissues he had begun to carry for such moments. Natalie took a choking breath as Norbert handed her a tissue.

"I've lost so many people that I've loved. Too many to name, by now. It feels like I'm left to watch everyone I love fade out, one after the other. And after so many losses, do you know what I've learned? It's this—when we go, we leave nothing lasting. So many times, after deaths in the family or the deaths of friends, I've cleaned out homes and apartments full of pictures of people that no one remembers, journals that no one will care to read, receipts that show that a life was lived and paid for. Nothing lasts. We leave only a few memories with a few people, and when those people go—what's left? Nothing. Poof. Like a bubble popping in the air. That's what a life amounts to. So what is the point to all the *striving*? What is the goddamn point of it all?" Natalie brushed a tear away and raised her voice. "Is it just about finding stuff to do...until we die?"

A man drinking coffee and working on his laptop at a nearby booth looked up with a frown at this outburst.

Norbert turned his smile in the man's direction, and tentatively patted Natalie's hand.

As Natalie balled up one tissue after the other in her fist and struggled to catch her breath, Norbert spoke in his soft voice, mesmerizing and reassuring, pointing to the cards and signaling where he saw hope, comfort, gifts that she possessed and direction for the future.

"I'm getting a strong impression of a woman a little older than you, a professional woman, who will help you."

Natalie looked blank.

"Have you been thinking of seeing a therapist to help you through this time?"

"Oh. Well, my doctor gave me the business card of a therapist who specializes in grief. She's in Edwards Cove. Do you think I should go?"

"The cards think you should go."

Natalie left the quiet man with these words: "You do have a gift, Norbert Z. A gift for comforting people and making people feel that their lives count for something. Thank you."

After Natalie had dried her eyes and left, Norbert felt his worry assuaged. He had sent the grieving woman to a grief therapist. She would be helped, and he was absolved of culpability in her case. He wondered for a moment if he should send all of his querents to therapists, just to relieve himself of the disturbing sense of responsibility he was beginning to feel, for lives all over town.

Carlotta stopped into the café that afternoon, to discuss Norbert's work with him.

"Well, tell me all about it!"

"What would you like to know?"

"Well—everything! Your doubts, your questions, the things you find challenging." Carlotta leaned forward, smiling widely.

"That's very nice of you." Norbert's eyes searched the wall above her head, appearing to look for a problem or question he might offer her. "You know, I seem to be finding my way."

"That's impossible!" she challenged. "You've barely gotten started. How can you not have any questions?"

Did he think she'd meant only to launch him, like a mother teaching a kid to ride a two-wheeler down a hill? That he would then be free to cycle all around town on his own? Because that was not her intention at all, and the sooner he understood that, the better.

Carlotta's plan was that Norbert would be an amusing and ongoing project for her and her Club. They would continue forming him, and he would continue entertaining them and being grateful for their help, every step of the way. He was a mild-mannered man. That had led her to assume he was a pushover. How could she ever have known he hid within his heart the ungrateful secret will to manage his own affairs? She wouldn't allow it.

"How can I not have any questions?" Norbert spoke wonderingly, as if figuring it out as he talked. Carlotta was struck by how compelling his quiet voice could be, here in his booth at the Good Fortune Café.

"It is strange, I guess, that I'm finding my way, reading by reading. It seems like I'm just relying on all those years of watching and listening—like you said I would. I guess I know more about people and their problems and hopes than I ever realized. Maybe that's what's propelling me forward through each reading. I'm not sure I understand it all myself." He looked with kindness into Carlotta's eyes. "But if I do have any questions, I promise you, I will ask."

That last remark sounded so condescending, as if he would be doing her a favor, and not the other way around. He wouldn't even be in this position if it weren't for her benevolence. Was he looking so kindly at her now out of a sense of familiarity? Because he had touched on her hidden grief in that practice reading, did he now assume that he had some personal connection to her—or even worse, an advantage over her? It was insolence, that's what it was. If she refused to visit that desolate place in her heart even with her dearest Summer, she certainly wouldn't allow Norbert to refer to it—even with a sympathetic glance.

She attempted to stare him down, and found herself sinking into his magnified brown irises. She shook herself free of his compassionate spell. She would not be bewitched. He was a fake, she had created him, and she must remember that.

CHAPTER SEVENTEEN

Ten of Diamonds:

Your project is gaining traction.

If there was one thing Norbert understood, it was the universal need to be seen, heard and, most of all, encouraged. It was what he had always wanted most, and it was what his customers wanted, as well. There was a world of magic for them in sitting opposite a sympathetic person who would pay close attention to their wishes and talk to them about themselves in the kindest terms. Norbert was learning that as he focused on his querents, his self-consciousness fell away.

The people who sat down across the table from Norbert at the Good Fortune Café all knew, on some level, that they were playing a game, and that it was not real. At the same time, on another level, they very much wanted to believe that there were answers to be plucked from the Universe for them, personally, and that this quiet man dressed in black had the power to do that plucking. And their desire to believe made the psychic reading no longer a game—but, in fact, real.

★ ★ ★

The summer advanced, and Norbert's business flourished. Tourists and residents alike were heard talking about him all over town.

Carlotta overheard a pair of patrons on the second floor of the library remarking in low voices:

"Have you seen him yet?"

"Oh, no! I'd be too scared! Have you?"

"Oh, yes! You really should go! He told me things he'd have no way of knowing. I don't know how he did it. I came out feeling like I had this new deep spiritual perspective on my life!"

Carlotta walked past with slow steps, running her finger along the call numbers as if searching for a certain volume.

"I know. You're not the first person to tell me about him. Isn't it kind of spooky, though?"

Walking down the stairs with her books, she thought, *Our Norbert Project is really picking up momentum. I'd better check in on him again. I will reel him in yet.* She smiled, and walked with a bit of a bounce to the circulation desk, where she checked out a novel by Gabriel García Márquez and two books on psychic development for Norbert.

Roseanne, who had sat at that post for years, scanned the books and said discreetly, "Carlotta, if you like psychic stuff, have you already seen the fortune-teller at your niece's café? I hear he's really good."

Margaret heard a couple of tourists in the Art League murmuring to one another.

"I'll go if you go."

"Do you want to?"

"Sure! I mean, I don't believe in it or anything. But just for fun! It's not like there's a ton of things to do in this town.

We've gone for the boat ride, and we've bought too many wind chimes already."

"Yeah, let's do it! People at the Alibi Bar last night were saying he's really accurate."

And the pair hurried out of the Art League and took a right, heading in the direction of the Good Fortune Café.

Huh, thought Margaret. *We've created a psychic!*

Carlotta stopped in at the café a second time to direct her protégé. He met her again with that same ugly self-determination that had surprised her the first time.

"Well, Norbert, I'm beginning to hear about you all around town! It looks like we've started you on the right second career!"

"Yes, thank you, Carlotta. I'll always be grateful."

Despite her warning that he was not ready to work independently of the Club, the exasperating man held his ground. He claimed to have no questions or concerns to share, and no need for guidance "at this time, thank you very much."

Carlotta was dumbfounded.

Norbert was changing. There was no denying it. His mealymouthed, soft voice was becoming an asset, endowing him with a hypnotic power. His understated, ignorable presence was beginning to look like a spiritual humility that touched people and added to his credibility. Norbert seemed to be casting a spell over the town. Carlotta thought Norbert had even cast a spell over himself: she wondered if he believed in Norbert Z, just like everyone else did.

Carlotta spoke in hushed tones before the students arrived at her oil-painting class. She had called Birdie and Margaret to come in early, for an emergency huddle on the Norbert Project.

Carlotta never was very good at whispering. She had been blessed with a voice that was meant to be heard. She could start out a sentence in a whisper, but by the middle, she was speaking at a normal volume. She couldn't help it.

"He thinks he's running the show," she hissed. "He's not checking in with us. He's not volunteering any information about the readings. This is not what we planned."

Margaret and Birdie inclined their heads toward her.

Margaret said, "Oh, dear."

"Yes," said Carlotta. "Oh, dear."

"Well," moderated Birdie, "everyone needs a *bit* of autonomy, don't they?"

"No," said Carlotta firmly. "Not on my watch. He cannot disregard our instructions."

"*Your* instructions," amended Birdie.

Carlotta continued, "He cannot just tell people whatever he pleases. He cannot be a free agent. He will have to be watched."

Norbert's readings were becoming more fluid. He began to read with confidence. At the same time, he was impressed with how quickly people bared their souls to him.

"Your first name, please?"

"Lindsay. Oh! Let me silence my phone. Just a sec."

Norbert glimpsed the screen saver on the young woman's phone: a photo of a black Pomeranian. He thought of an article he had read in *Dog Fancy Magazine*, quite a few years ago, claiming that dog breeds tended to align with their owners' personalities. Pomeranians, Yorkies and Chihuahuas were among the "agreeable breeds," and their owners cared about people's feelings, tried always to put others at ease, and most perplexing of all: appreciated art. But then, who, if asked, would say they didn't care about people's feelings and didn't appreciate art? Surely, very few.

As Lindsay handed Norbert the cards, and he laid them down one by one, he tested the theory.

"You appreciate art."

"Ha!" exclaimed Lindsay. "Well, that's pretty good! I'm an art teacher at the high school, so I guess I do."

Encouraged by this immediate success, Norbert went on.

"And you are gifted, Lindsay. Why are you not using your gifts?" He had discovered accidentally that this was a line that almost everyone identified with. And Norbert truly wanted to help people to use their gifts.

Lindsay sat back and gave Norbert her full attention.

"Well," she said, "I do feel guilty that I'm not doing my own art anymore. When you're a teacher, there's no time."

Norbert continued to look at her. Whenever he didn't know what to say next, he paused and simply looked at people. It was surprising how often that was enough to inspire them to dig deeper, or to tell him something more that he could use.

She went on, "You think I'm just making an excuse?" She seemed impressed with his shrewd ability to detect the truth. "Oh. Maybe I am."

"You need your own space," said Norbert. "Like a little studio. It could even be a closet that you clear out and remake into a workspace. If you have the space, and if you show up on a regular basis, and hold yourself accountable..."

"I have that, in my condo. But I never use it. I get distracted by friends, and errands, and TV, and then of course there's lesson planning... I just never get to my own work."

Norbert looked at Lindsay's cards.

"There's a big question on your mind?"

Almost everyone had a big question in mind.

"Well, as a matter of fact, there is. That's why I wanted the reading today. It's a real-estate purchase—on Black Bear Island. Should I do it, or not? That's my big question."

"Tell me about it," said Norbert. He wasn't "fishing." He really wanted to know.

"Well, there's a little cottage. I don't know why it caught my attention. I made an appointment with the Realtor, in fact, and I went to see it. I was just curious. But now that you're talking about my art—maybe there's a connection. It's semi-isolated over there, on the island. Right now I'm thinking that if I have a place like that to go where there are fewer distractions, and if I don't bring my laptop or my TV, if I just set it up as a simple living space and art studio, with all my supplies—oh, and my little dog, of course…well, it's a beautiful place, Black Bear Island. Have you been there?"

Norbert had.

"Yes. In my youth, I was very familiar with it. It was— *pristine*—then."

Norbert saw himself as a teenager, exploring the island numerous times with his Eagle Scouts troop. He had loved that place.

"It still is pristine!" said Lindsay with feeling. "It's peaceful. It's inspiring—it's everything an artist would want. And the cottage has north light, and it's just the right size. It's a good chunk of change, though. But I have it, in my savings. I *could* do it. I've thought maybe I could justify it by renting it out sometimes to other teachers, friends and family. But knowing how I am, I would probably wind up just lending it out. Or maybe not. Maybe I'd just keep it always available for me— since you say I need a studio."

"Where exactly is this property?" Norbert enjoyed hearing about Lindsay's dream cottage, and tried to see it in his mind's eye.

"It's one of the houses that hugs the shore."

Lindsay described to Norbert precisely where it was, how it looked and why she loved the very idea of it. Norbert caught her enthusiasm.

"I can see you there," said Norbert, honestly.

"Is that what the cards say?" asked Lindsay. "Do the cards say I should do it?"

The morning Norbert paid the last installment on Ivy's vet bill, he declared, "Ivy, I think this calls for a celebration."

Ivy put her ears back and wagged her whole body.

It was mid-August, and Norbert had been doing about twenty readings per week since he began in early July. He felt increased self-esteem as he thought of the encouragement and insight he had offered the unsure, and the enlightenment and comfort he had offered the self-deceived. He was doing good in the world, and to top it all off, he was able to support his Chihuahua.

Norbert attached Ivy's harness and leash, and they set off for the post office on Washington Street, where Norbert, with a bit of ceremony, dropped the payment in a blue mailbox on the sidewalk. From there, they continued down the street to the Happy Dog Boutique. Norbert was not only able to pay off Dr. Adams's bill, but he even had a bit extra for a little something special.

Norbert and Ivy walked, each one with a bouncing step, through the refreshing breeze that blew off the lake and through the decorative streets of their little town. They stopped and chatted—that is, Norbert chatted and Ivy wiggled—as they met familiar faces along their route. Tourists strolled hand in hand, pointing out curiosities in shop windows, and bicyclists rode past them, ringing bells.

The Happy Dog Boutique offered an overwhelming variety of options in treats, attire, dog beds and refrigerator magnets. Norbert began to feel a little silly. On the one hand, he thought, *Only in America could you find a dog shirt that reads, "I love bitches."* On the other hand, he felt an attachment to his constant companion and thought she deserved something nice. He also wanted a way to mark his financial achievement, however small it might seem to anyone else.

He spotted a display of "healthy" dog treats and inspected a variety that was soft to chew and cut into extra-small pieces. He read the ingredients and wondered if Ivy would like it.

The salesperson, a young violet-haired girl, offered, "How may I help you?"

"Oh, I was just wondering if she—my dog—would like these."

"Would you like one for her to sample?"

"Oh, yes, if it's allowed," said Norbert.

The violet-haired girl tore open the bag and extended a bit in her flattened palm to Ivy, who accepted it gratefully, licking the girl's palm clean.

"Aw, she's sweet. She seems to like it, all right."

"Thanks. We'll take those. And…we'll just look around a bit."

"Take your time."

Norbert's eye was caught by a display of bandannas. One pile was Ivy's size. Too bad the messages were wrong for Ivy: "Spoiled Rotten," "Drama Queen" and "Pugs Not Drugs." As he browsed, disappointed, the salesgirl's common, ordinary phrase came back to him: "How may I help you?" Actually, that would have been a perfect message for Ivy to wear. All she ever wanted was to be of service and comfort to everyone she met.

"Excuse me."

The violet-haired girl looked up from behind the counter.

"Is it possible to have a bandanna printed with a personalized message?"

"Why, sure!"

As the young lady noted down the sentiment for Ivy's new accessory, Norbert heard some stage whispering behind his back.

"Hey, that's Norbert Z—the one I was telling you about."

"You mean the psychic?"

"Shh."

CHAPTER EIGHTEEN

Four of Hearts:

You may trust yourself now.
A person in a power position may
feel threatened by your skill and confidence.
Beware.

"I'm thinking of a person that I love."

The young man's name was Dave, and he was a tourist. He approached his card reading with a gravity that still surprised Norbert.

The cards on the table indicated conflict.

"This person that I love, he's been good to me. He's been there for me when others weren't. There's a deep connection between us."

The young man paused, considering how to go on.

"That's what most people want, isn't it? A deep connection?" supplied Norbert.

"Yes, I think so. So I'm lucky. But I don't know if I can stay with him. You see, he also has this other side. Rampages, tantrums."

"He hits you?"

"Oh, no, of course not. Never. That's why I don't know if it's really a big deal. Maybe I should look past it. That's what I've been doing—looking past it. I always tell myself, maybe it will never happen again. But when he loses his temper, he crushes me. I mean, emotionally. Once he starts, nothing will stop him. Oh—unless someone stops by. Then he can pull himself together in the blink of an eye. You'd never know he'd been foaming at the mouth and berating me a minute before. Of course, he always apologizes. I know he's a good person. He doesn't mean to be that way."

Norbert felt this young man's sadness, and wished he had some wisdom to give him.

"And your question is—?"

"Will he change? Or, no, that's not what I mean. Okay—how can I help him to be the good version of himself more of the time? That's my question, I think."

Norbert sat back. Now was he going to become an amateur domestic-abuse counselor? What did he know that could help this querent? As he took a deep breath, something he had read in *Reader's Digest* just the night before came to him, like a gift.

"Dave, I'm going to tell you a fable. See if this helps at all.

"Once, there was a man who was about to cross a river, when a poisonous snake slithered up to him and said, 'Please pick me up and take me across the river with you.' The man said, 'You are a poisonous snake. I won't pick you up. You would bite me, and I would die.' The snake promised, 'I give you my word—I will not bite you. Trust me.' So the man picked up the snake and took him across the river. Once they got to the other side, the man laid the snake on the ground, and the snake bit his ankle. In pain and shock, the man cried, 'Why did you bite me? You gave me your word you wouldn't.' The snake answered, 'You knew what I was when you picked me up.'"

Dave looked disappointed.

"So, you're saying he's a poisonous snake? He can't be anything else?"

"I'm saying, there's a fable for you to think about. Whether it applies to your situation or not, that's for you to say."

Norbert watched Dave reluctantly accept his "light-bulb moment."

Norbert stole a glance at his own reflection in the metal napkin holder on the table. He liked what he saw there: a wise and skillful adviser. He was sorry for Dave's pain, but at the same time, he couldn't help but be just a little impressed with himself.

The more readings Norbert did, the better he understood the assertion in *The Cards Don't Lie* that it would be accurate to tell most people "There is a great lie in your life" or "You are lying to yourself about something." The lying, he noticed, had to do with what Birdie would call "life lessons." Each person had lessons to learn about self-respect, self-knowledge, self-realization, self-trust, or some untrue belief. The only thing standing between a querent and the life lesson—was the lie. Norbert saw himself shining a light of truth into people's lives through his card readings. He was grateful to be in this position to guide people. And his self-opinion had never been higher.

CHAPTER NINETEEN

Five of Clubs:

Disagreeable people present you with difficulties.
Someone is watching your movements
with displeasure.
Handle issues delicately, or they may explode.

Birdie hosted a dinner in her eclectic backyard one summer evening for the Club and Norbert. Norbert was invited for 6:00 p.m. The Club was invited for 5:00 p.m., so that they could talk about him before his arrival.

Carlotta and Margaret stepped through the wrought-iron gate, past the antique stone statue of a child painted celestial blue, and found themselves in Birdie's walled garden with climbing flowers, twinkling little white lights, bells, prisms and chimes hanging from the trees, half a dozen painted birdhouses and a Japanese rock garden. Most striking of all were the concrete planters in the shape of human heads: a Venus, a David, a Buddha and a Medusa. All emerged from the soil, with greenery sprouting from their scalps, looking serenely unconcerned about being buried up to their necks in Birdie's garden.

"You know, Birdie, what you need here are a few dozen

gargoyles. We'll have to remember that for your birthday," observed Carlotta as she sank into flowered cushions on a wicker couch.

Margaret started the conversation by chattering gaily about her daughter Vivian and the phone conversation they had had just that afternoon. "We talk every Sunday, you know," she said.

Everyone shared their happy Sunday occupations, a preamble to getting to whatever it was that Carlotta would want to get to.

As the before-dinner wine began to flow, Carlotta began to grumble.

"He's a loose cannon. We have no idea what he's telling people. He's not relying on us as he should. He could be saying anything. We need to rein him in."

Birdie tilted her red locks and looked over Carlotta's head. "Who?" she asked.

"Norbert, dear," explained Margaret. "Carlotta is saying she wants to run Norbert, and he's not letting her."

Carlotta opened her eyes wide at her old friend. "Margaret! What are you saying? Do you really think I try to 'run' people?"

"Of course not!" said Birdie innocently. "You just want to tell him what to do, for his own good, don't you?"

"If you're all going to gang up on me—" sputtered Carlotta.

"We're on *your* side," put in Margaret. "And it *would* be fun to know what he's saying, and to *whom*!"

"That is not the point!" said Carlotta. "This is not about fun."

"It isn't?" asked Margaret.

"Of course not."

There were a few moments of silence, and Birdie refilled the wineglasses.

"We have created this psychic and unleashed him on the public," began Margaret.

"So it is our responsibility to supervise him," concluded Carlotta.

"What do you have in mind?" asked Birdie.

"Well, I thought regular meetings would be appropriate. He would meet with all three of us a couple of times a week, to tell us what customers are asking him, and how he is answering them. And we could create some kind of evaluation form, a rubric, so to speak, and assess his work." Carlotta knew that her granddaughter, Summer, as a high school teacher, was regularly evaluated according to a rubric. Why should a fortune-teller be any less accountable?

"And would he give us his customers' names?" asked Margaret, smiling, with eyebrows raised.

"We can't evaluate his readings. We are not even there when he does them." This mild protest came from Birdie.

"A well-reasoned point, Birdie," said Carlotta. "So you are suggesting that I sit in on some readings with Norbert. Observations, we could call them. Well, I would have to clear some time in my schedule, but I do feel a responsibility to   "

"Knock, knock, knock!" called Norbert from the gate.

"Norbert!" called the Club, in chorus. "Come on in!"

"I thought I'd have to apologize for arriving a few minutes early," said Norbert, looking around at the ladies and the open wine, "but I see I'm actually late. Don't know how I muddled that!" He pulled Ivy from her carrier and she ran around the garden, greeting all her friends one by one. Everyone complimented her on her fuchsia-colored bandanna that read: "How may I help you?"

"Norbert!" exclaimed Margaret. "Are you getting taller?"

Norbert did, indeed, seem to be carrying himself a little bit taller.

Norbert chuckled. "I think I stopped growing a long time ago, Margaret. If anything, I'm shrinking slightly."

Birdie said, "Ah, but what about *inner* growth? I wonder if that's what you are perceiving, Margaret."

Birdie set out an assortment of summer salads: apples, agave and raisins; cucumber, vegan mayonnaise and dill; tabbouleh; pasta and olives; mixed melons. As the little group supped, drank and conversed, Birdie brought the talk around to Norbert's work.

"How do you find it?" she asked in her typical, vague way.

"I actually feel like I'm getting better at it all the time. It's not hard. Sometimes I wonder why it took me all my life to find fortune-telling and advising. It suits me so much better than accounting did. I remember you, Carlotta, saying it was like being a psychologist—"

"Except, you are not a psychologist."

"No, of course not."

"Because, as *you* said, Norbert, a psychologist has credentials." Carlotta popped an olive in her mouth and savored the salt. "And you have none."

"Oh, right. Exactly right."

"You see, Norbert, you are practicing fortune-telling without any credentials whatsoever."

"There is no credentialing for fortune-tellers, as *you* said, Carlotta."

"Correct. But there is supervision."

"What?" Norbert raised his voice slightly.

"Which we will provide, Norbert. Do not worry."

"What we want to know," Margaret rushed in, "is the names of the people you are seeing, and what their problems are!"

"Margaret!" corrected Carlotta. "Let me explain this to Norbert."

"Oh, Margaret," said Norbert. "I couldn't possibly tell you that. I mean, the readings are in a public place, and anyone can see who is coming to me, I suppose. But I would never divulge names—and certainly not what people are telling me. Oh, my. I couldn't. It would be against my ethics."

Carlotta placed her wineglass with care on the tile table and regarded Norbert.

"What ethics, Norbert?" she said, in an even tone.

"Well, professional ethics, I guess."

"There's no such thing," she challenged. "You are still a novice. You still need our direction and advice."

"Oh, well, that's very kind of you. I'm sure I do. I just can't gossip about anyone—not that you were asking me to, of course."

"Of course not!" said Margaret, with a frown. She raked her fork through the tabbouleh. "Birdie, where do you get this lemony stuff?"

"It's in the produce section of the Lucky Pig," said Birdie.

Birdie brought the attention back to Norbert with an open-ended prompt: "So, you were telling us what it's like."

"Well, people really do remember the hits and forget the misses, just like you all said they would. They often tell me what it is they want to know. I feel like if I just listen carefully, what I need to tell them becomes obvious. What's really puzzling is that people are giving me credit for things I never said. They come back and say, 'You were right—my business partner *was* stealing from me.' Stuff like that—and I'm sure I never said anything close to that, but in their memory, I did. People are recommending me to their friends, and customers are coming from faraway places because someone told them they got an accurate reading from me. My schedule is full every day. Everyone seems happy with my work. Honestly, sometimes it's overwhelming! In a *good* way!"

"How gratifying," said Carlotta, biding her time.

"Yes, it is. It really is. And I have the three of you to thank for it."

Birdie said, "Norbert, it's your own gift you have to thank. It's only because of your gift that you can do this work."

"Oh, yes," flattered Carlotta. "Your gift." She was quick to add: "And our guidance. Our training. Our knowledge and encouragement. And my niece's coffee shop."

"Yes, yes. I am grateful to you all. I'm catching up on my bills, and I'm enjoying helping people. So, thank you."

"And you can show your gratitude by accepting our direction, Norbert."

Norbert considered, rubbing Ivy's ears.

"Actually, Carlotta, let's do it this way. When I need help, I will let you all know. For now, I'm going to trust my own instincts."

Margaret and Birdie found a focal point to stare at for a moment. Margaret seemed especially interested in the cement Medusa head and the greenery that seemed to be exploding from its brains.

Carlotta pressed her lips together. Had she guessed how aggravating Norbert could be, she never would have rescued him from his financial distress.

"I have an idea!" she cried. "Let's play Literary Quotes!"

This was Carlotta's favorite game. She invented it herself many years ago, and was the uncontested champion. It was the perfect game to pull out just now, because Norbert surely wouldn't be able to join in. *Reader's Digest* subscribers were not, in Carlotta's estimation, capable of appreciating, let alone quoting, literature. This is the way it was played: The first person (that would be Carlotta) would recite a quote from literature. The quote was supposed to be verbatim, but in truth, the Club never checked. The person to Carlotta's right would come up with the next quote, and so on, around the circle. As people ran out of quotes, they dropped out, leaving Carlotta the winner. Years ago, she had given all members a notebook especially for collecting quotes as they read, so they would always have new ones for the game. (That was one reason so many had left the Club over the years, complaining, "You have to *study* to be in their Club.") Using the same quotations every time the game was played was frowned upon. Extra admiration was awarded if the quote was in any way apropos of anything the Club was attending to at the moment.

Carlotta, for form's sake, offered, "Shall I begin, then?" She cast her eyes to the leafy branches above them, as if searching in the recesses of her memory. "'Proud people breed sad sorrows for themselves.' Emily Brontë."

Margaret's turn. "Oh, dear. I never do well at this game." She slipped a tiny bit of bread to Ivy while Norbert wasn't looking. "Oh, I know! 'Christmas won't be Christmas without any presents!'—*Little Women*."

Carlotta objected, "Again? You always say that one, Margaret. The idea is to come up with different ones."

Birdie interrupted Margaret's humiliation with: "'The best and most beautiful things in the world cannot be seen or even touched. They must be felt in the heart.' Helen Keller, *The Story of My Life*."

"May I do one?" asked Norbert.

"*Can* you do one?" asked Carlotta.

Norbert, not perceiving the cut, said, "I think I can." He cleared his throat. "Here goes. 'I am the master of my fate; I am the captain of my soul.'—*Invictus*."

"That sounds familiar," said Margaret.

"They used to make us memorize poems in high school. I chose that one. I always liked it."

"Do you remember any more of it?" asked Birdie.

"Gee, I bet I do. I haven't thought about it in years, but let's see. It starts out…

Out of the night that covers me,
Black as the Pit from pole to pole,
I thank whatever gods may be
For my unconquerable soul."

"Is that Shakespeare?" asked Margaret.

"Oh, Margaret, don't be a ninny," Carlotta misdirected her wrath. "That's not even iambic pentameter. It's a nineteenth-century poem, certainly."

"Yes," answered Norbert, nodding as if he were giving useful information. "William Ernest Henley, 1875."

"Yes, a very minor poet. No one worth knowing," cut in Carlotta. "Hardly Shakespeare," she laughed.

And if a dinner party may be adjourned, Carlotta adjourned it.

CHAPTER TWENTY

Three of Diamonds:

Success. Good fortune is building.
Gratitude is the secret to happiness:
always remember this.
Enjoy this time, for nothing lasts.

By early August, tourists were streaming steadily into the Good Fortune Café, following the arrow on Margaret's gaudy sign like children following the charm of the pied piper. They approached the counter, asking to see the psychic. Appointments were made at twenty-minute intervals, and the cash-register drawer slid open and shut with a cheerful rhythm, as customers bought lattes, croissants, sandwiches and salads to have wrapped for later, or to enjoy there in the café while waiting for Norbert Z.

The stack of unpaid dentist and utility bills on Norbert's desk at home dwindled.

Norbert predicted and counseled with growing confidence. He encouraged people to move across the country or stay where they were; to accept or refuse job offers; to go or not go on trips. He might advise one person to forgive offenses others had committed, while conversely cautioning the next person to practice self-protection from toxic influences. In both cases, Norbert would feel guided by evidence, the desire to be helpful and some lucky guessing. He would be reassured of his accuracy by the quick acceptance of the querents themselves, that this was what they knew deep inside all along.

There was a line Norbert began to insert into at least one reading per day, because he found out by accident that it seemed to work wonders with most people. The line was—and it was important to say it quietly and with tenderness—"No one would ever *dream* how *sensitive* you are." The first time he said this to a querent, a thirtysomething woman, he said it because he saw it; he felt it. When he said it, her eyes met his, and he saw the tears there, and something else: gratitude for being seen and understood. Norbert knew now how affirming it was, how healing it was, for *him* to be seen and understood.

And so he began trying the line on others—the young, the old, men and women—and each time he experienced that eye-to-eye connection, that release of the shoulders, that deep exhalation: *You see me. Thank you.* These customers would then feed him bits of information. They wanted this man who was so special that he could see their secret sensitivity to be able to deliver a special reading.

Norbert's voice, which had been so soft as to be a liability all his life, now, in this new role, became mesmerizing, and an important part of his mystery. People leaned forward to catch every word that fell from his lips.

He found himself in the role of confessor, counselor and comforter. He knew how to make each person feel unique and important. Every customer went forth after a reading to recommend the psychic "Norbert Z" to everyone they met:

to fellow lodgers at the Harbor Home Bed and Breakfast, to customers in Butler's Book Store, and to friends back home in Pennsylvania and New Jersey.

When Norbert thought about his life up to this moment, it seemed that all along he was being prepared to meet with people across a table at the Good Fortune Cafe in quiet, focused conversations, and guide each person forward into a better destiny.

If only he could have known, during the dark hours of his earlier life, that one day, all his loneliness and silent observation would count for something.

Margaret stopped by Norbert's house with mangoes in a brown paper bag from the Lucky Pig Grocery. Both Margaret and Birdie were stopping by briefly from time to time now. Norbert was surprised to think that he now had friends.

"They're so good this time of year!" She set the bag on his kitchen table.

Norbert invited her to stay and drink some lemonade, and Ivy seconded the invitation by running excitedly around her feet.

"Just for a moment, thank you, Norbert."

As he brought the glasses to the table, Margaret said, "I've been wanting to tell you—your advice about my daughter? *So* helpful!"

Norbert felt a sense of wonder and at the same time, doubt. "Really?" he asked.

Margaret's blue eyes were shining with joy. "Really! After your reading, I was able to see things from her eyes. We talked, Vivian and I, a real conversation for the first time in ages. I remembered what you said, and even though it was hard, I let her empty her heart to me, and when she was done, I told her I was sorry. And I really am. Even though I don't remember things the way she does. But for once, I didn't say that. And I didn't try to explain that all of that is in the past now—because *she* said it. It seemed like she was only waiting for me to listen to her and honestly say I was sorry, and then she was able to let it go. And now we're talking. It still gets rocky sometimes, but when that happens, I try to listen more. Such a little thing. And now I have my daughter back! I can't thank you enough. You've done something so remarkable for me. I don't know how to repay you."

Norbert arranged the green fruit in a wooden bowl, absorbed in pleasant sensations, reflecting on how his life had changed. He had friends who visited him and brought him thoughtful gifts of fruit. People liked his company. A week didn't go by now that someone didn't express gratitude to him for something he had said. It was good to be Norbert. He sighed happily.

"Norbert," said Margaret, leaning forward, "you know something about my earlier life, but I don't know anything at all about yours. Did you grow up in New York?"

"Yes, I did. In Buffalo. My aunt Pearl took charge of me when my mother died. I was four. My father had left us two years before that."

"What was she like, your aunt Pearl?"

"To me, as a child? She was lovely and loving." He laughed softly. "But I do think she forgot all about me for long stretches. She was—unusual. The kids in town used to make fun of her. Guess she was the town eccentric." He felt a pang of disloyalty saying this, but it was true.

His memory traveled back to his childhood home, crowded with piles of useless items, to the tenderness and safety that he felt there despite the chaos, and to the fear and inferiority he felt on the porch, where kids would sometimes gather to tease Norbert about his mismatched clothes and his weird aunt. With shame, he recalled joining in the laughter against her, hoping that this would make him one of them, and he would cease to be their target.

"And did you like school when you were a child?" asked Margaret. Of course, she would not be comfortable getting into the details of childhood pain. She would steer him to something neutral, like school. And that was fine with him.

"I did! I was never what you would call an intellectual, of course. But I read whatever was put in front of me. Reading was always my escape. It was easier for me to read than to be social. And when I discovered the beauty of math!"

"Did you say, 'the beauty of math'?" asked Margaret, wrinkling her brow.

"Oh, yes! There *is* a sort of calm beauty to numbers, you know."

Margaret didn't know.

"Math is a system for organizing things. It's a system which, if followed, will make everything come out right." He beamed at Margaret.

"I never thought of it that way."

"Oh, yes! I could have studied math forever. But I needed to study for a career, and from math, I was directed into accounting—which is not the same thing as math at all, but still, it suited me. I liked accounting. I worked at it for forty years."

"Ah," said Margaret. "And were you ever married?"

Norbert met Margaret's gaze, and he watched her bright eyes become solemn as she realized she had said something that caused him sadness.

"Oh, I'm sorry, Norbert. I shouldn't pry. That's me, all the time, talking too much. You don't have to answer that."

"That's all right. Yes. I was married for five years. It was a long time ago. My wife died," he said simply.

"I'm so sorry."

"As I said, it was a very long time ago."

It was 1981. Norbert was thirty-eight years old. Lois Barnes, a secretary in his office, swept him off his feet, so to speak. Lois was a glowing, black-haired, bright-eyed beauty who smiled so charmingly at him and drew him out of his cubicle to eat lunch with her.

Norbert had been a retiring bachelor. He felt that he lived almost completely unperceived by others. He often thought that he wouldn't be surprised if one day he disappeared into thin air, and no one even noticed.

But Lois did notice him. She took every opportunity to approach him and ask him questions about himself. He wondered why she was doing it. At times he was afraid she must be making fun of him. How could such an intelligent and vivacious girl find *him* worth her time?

Everything about her was new to him. He had never had a girlfriend before; he had never had the courage even to ask a girl out. Lois made it easy: she pursued *him*. After so many years alone, he couldn't believe his luck. Lois got him to talk and seemed to find him fascinating.

He loved everything about her: he loved her straight black eyebrows, and he loved the way she searched his eyes when she talked. He loved how she respected his thoughts and asked him questions. She encouraged him to try to tell jokes, even though he wasn't any good at it. He'd usually get the punch line wrong, which only made Lois laugh all the harder—more than she would have if he'd gotten it right. He loved watching her laugh. They never ran out of things to say. She said they were "soul mates."

At last, Norbert was emboldened to propose, and Lois accepted with tears in her eyes. Their marriage began happily, with joyful holidays and happy hours of nest-building. But it all ended in grief when Lois contracted an aggressive cancer. The prognosis was very poor. They were both in shock. They had so many plans for their future. They determined to beat it. They felt sure that they would.

Norbert spent all of his savings on traditional and then alternative treatments—in short, anything that offered a glimmer of hope.

Within five years of their wedding, though, Lois was gone, and Norbert was alone again.

CHAPTER TWENTY-ONE

Three of Clubs:

Your business is highlighted.
Success is growing faster
than you realize.

After Margaret had gone, Norbert took down an old wooden box from his bookcase while Ivy watched attentively. In the box were a packet of notes from Lois, and her heart locket on its gold chain. The locket had been a gift from him, and she had worn it every day. He opened it and studied the small photograph of his young face on one side, and her lovely face on the other. These items always brought him feelings of pain mixed with pleasure. He was so grateful to have had her, even for the short time they were given to be together. Putting Lois's things gently to the side, he looked at the rest of the contents of the box. He turned over postcards, notes and printouts of emails that had been sent to him from around the region and around the country, care of the Good Fortune Café. Many wrote to say that they took his advice and were glad that they did. Others wrote to tell him that although they had told him he was wrong, they were now writing to tell him he was right, after all.

Dear Norbert Z,
In your reading, you said I would have car trouble. I told you that wasn't likely because my car is new. Just wanted you to know I had a flat tire on my way back to Ohio, so you were right. Now I am waiting to see what else will come true. I hope what you said about love & marriage will be just as accurate.
Sincerely,
Megan Curtis

Norbert now told fortunes with authority. He no longer hesitated or stammered. He had grown to understand that his querents, by paying their twenty dollars, had already expressed confidence and hope, and that his duty was to focus on them, and not on himself.

Norbert marveled at the respect and interest he was drawing to himself. His quiet hours of studying people were paying off now.

He had noticed years before, for example, two coworkers in his office who both had a certain gesture. They would take one hand and pull the other wrist toward the center of their body, especially in meetings where they might be feeling some stress. He learned, just from listening, that there was another thing both these people had in common. Both had had a parent—in the woman's case, it was her mother; in the man's case, his father—who had had a stroke, paralyzing one side of their body. Both had been very involved in the care of the disabled parent. Norbert had concluded that hours of sitting with the parent, helping him or her get hold of the dead limb instead of letting it dangle, and the distressed emotions that they felt in that situation, had left each of them with this very characteristic gesture of unconsciously mimicking the parent. Unaware themselves that they were doing so, they used it when they wanted to soothe themselves. Norbert was able to try out this theory when a customer came into the Good Fortune Café for a reading.

A middle-aged tourist called Martha sat down before him, and after handing Norbert the seventh card, she wrapped her left hand around her right wrist, which she then subtly pulled to her lap.

Norbert said, "Has one of your parents had a stroke, paralyzing one arm?"

Martha looked from her cards to Norbert, her eyes wide. "How could you possibly know that?"

Bypassing the question, Norbert continued to try his luck. "You would have an especially strong identification with this parent or be very involved in this parent's care?"

Right again.

Martha, it turned out, had come to town to stay and study at the nationally famous Center for Deeper Understanding, a white-pillared institute of yoga and alternative thought on five wooded acres just outside of town. Was Norbert familiar with it, she wanted to know.

Of course, Norbert knew about it. All of Gibbons Corner thought of this odd retreat center as an important source of tourist revenue, even if it was a little unorthodox. Some of the biggest names in New Age thought lectured there. It was a place that, a few months ago, stood for everything Norbert had wanted to shut out of his life: astrology, divination, numerology, crystal-ball gazing. Everything that had so enthralled his aunt Pearl. But now, as Martha told him of how her "eyes were being opened to new ways of seeing" at the Center, he politely indicated interest. Martha assured him that she would be talking about him and his incredible psychic ability to Edith Butler, the director at the Center for Deeper Understanding.

When Martha left, Norbert sat back, listening to the gurgling and sputtering of the latte machine. He looked around at the new positive thought messages all around the café on posters and chalkboards: "Life is a gift" and "Honor yourself and others." Hope herself was revitalized, energetic and positive, joking with customers, and adding new and trendy options to a menu that hadn't been altered in years.

Just yesterday, Norbert had seen his first client, Jeremy, the man who had said he no longer loved his wife, walking arm in arm with her down the street, the two of them absorbed in one another like newlyweds.

Norbert, who had never been listened to before, was now being intently listened to every day. People actually made *appointments* to listen to him now. He thought back to his Dale Carnegie–reading days. "Talk to someone about themselves and they'll listen for hours," wrote that expert on making friends and influencing people. He had always wanted to talk to people about themselves and ask them questions. Since the Club had taken an interest in him and taught him how, his lifelong desire was realized.

Norbert couldn't help but see that in his own small way, he was now influencing lives all over town—all over the country, really. People were making different choices in their lives because of his readings, because of him.

CHAPTER TWENTY-TWO

Five of Hearts:

Beware of the envy of another person.
Not everyone is happy about your success.

As word came back to Carlotta about the amazing accuracy of Norbert Z's card readings, she began to feel a grudging admiration for him. To give credit where credit was due, she had to recognize her own genius at work in the inception of his career. However, what he had made of it since she and the Club had launched him was impressive, and his business and reputation had grown much more quickly than she ever would have thought possible. As Roseanne from the library and Gloria from the bakery recounted to her the astonishing "hits" in the mysterious man's readings, Carlotta found herself wondering uncomfortably if Norbert Z really did possess psychic abilities. And then she admonished herself, remembering that she herself had invented Norbert Z.

Carlotta's admiration of Norbert's ascent was mixed with increasing displeasure. He was off and running after just a push from the Club, and he was not looking back. This was not what Carlotta had had in mind when she invented the Norbert Project, nor when she and the Club had staged the Intervention at his house less than three months before. The Project she had created in her own prolific mind had grown legs and walked away from her. A Project was not supposed to do that. It was not serving its purpose as a tool to keep the Club in her everlasting thrall. On the contrary, Margaret and Birdie now seemed to be in Norbert's thrall. Perverse creatures, both of them.

The essential thing about a Project was that it kept one's mind from wandering where it had no business wandering. Dwelling on the past, missing those who had left this life, wishing that things were otherwise: these were the states of mind that Carlotta abhorred. Projects, new ideas and courses of study were the necessary distractions that lifted Carlotta's heart and gave her a reason to push forward. Summer could have been a worthy Project, but she had slipped from Carlotta's control when she had gone to college, and was no longer allowing herself to be directed. Carlotta knew that was normal. Still, she would have been gratified to make a love match for her granddaughter. If only arranged marriages were not so frowned upon in Gibbons Corner. She knew she could have chosen well for Summer.

One day, Carlotta, with a sigh, mentioned her granddaughter, Summer, to the Club, wondering when she would find a nice young man to give her direction in life.

Margaret objected, "Oh, I don't know. Having husbands didn't give *us* very much fulfillment. You didn't like being married any more than I did, from what I recall. And Birdie never bothered with marriage at all. I think she made the best choice. Don't you?" As if sensing she was venturing where Carlotta would not allow her to go, Margaret returned to the topic of Summer. "She's a career woman! What does she need with a young man? She's doing fine on her own, isn't she?"

Carlotta said, "Well, then, not a young man, perhaps. But there's something she's lacking. She seems just a little confused. I feel she needs help finding her place in the world, somehow."

"I think it's just 'being in your twenties.' *I* remember. Don't you? It takes time," said Margaret.

Birdie, with a sharp intake of breath, suggested, "Have Norbert read Summer's cards, Carlotta! He'll be able to help her find her way!"

That was the last straw—*"le coup de grâce"*—as Carlotta told the Club, with ice in her voice.

"Are you both forgetting that Norbert Z is not real? That we invented him? That he has no answers for anyone? That he's making it all up? What is *wrong* with the two of you?"

Margaret and Birdie gave Carlotta a moment to calm down. They knew how she was, and had stopped taking her outbursts personally a very long time ago.

Not cowed, Birdie continued, "People are saying he's very accurate in his readings. Do you know Norbert Z now has six reviews—all positive—on Yelp? That will put Gibbons Corner on the map!"

Margaret was confused. "Yelp? Is that something to do with Ivy?"

"No, Margaret," clarified Birdie. "It's an internet thing. It means that people will be coming to town just for the purpose of seeing Norbert."

Margaret whistled in appreciation.

She has so many annoying tics like this, Carlotta thought.

Carlotta, to show she was not disturbed by Norbert's success, laughed lightly and said, "Our very own Frankenstein is putting Gibbons Corner on the map. Who would ever have expected it?"

Norbert's influence was spreading with alarming speed, like an uncontrolled fire. If Carlotta had been capable of the ridiculous fault of envy, she would have been unhappy indeed.

Carlotta invited Norbert, and Norbert alone, to her house for lunch. She told herself it would be her final attempt to pull him back into her sphere of control, and this was best done without the distraction of the rest of the Club—especially the distraction of Margaret. Carlotta would need all her powers of concentration.

Norbert arrived with blue hydrangeas in hand at Carlotta's redbrick Georgian-style house on Clarence Avenue.

Carlotta took the lovely pom-pom-shaped flowers in her left hand and welcomed Norbert in, putting her right hand on his upper back, and shutting the door behind him with a resounding clack.

Come into my parlor, said the spider to the fly.

The random line of juvenile poetry ran through Carlotta's busy mind, but she said instead, "Come into my—humble abode, Norbert!"

Norbert looked around at the impeccable neutral interior, with original paintings hung and propped tastefully every-where. The paintings were Carlotta's own and those of her friends. All the Club members supported one another's art, and all had similar collections of paintings in their homes. Norbert couldn't fail to recognize a landscape of his own that Carlotta had bought just a week ago.

Toutou, Carlotta's black miniature French poodle, came to greet Norbert. Carlotta enjoyed telling people that "toutou" is French for "doggie," and she reminded Norbert of that now. Toutou displayed faultless manners, as any dog of Carlotta's must do: no barking, no jumping and no whining, but decorously welcoming the visitor, and then lying down in her fluffy personalized bed under an end table.

Carlotta exclaimed, "Norbert! You didn't need to bring flowers! Oh, but I love blue hydrangeas! Did you know the flower meaning?" Carlotta felt uplifted to be able to start off the visit by telling Norbert something he surely didn't know. She had memorized all the meanings of flowers and pulled out this knowledge at every opportunity.

"Actually, I do," said Norbert. "I brought blue hydrangeas on purpose, because they symbolize gratitude. 'Gratitude for the recipient's understanding.'"

Carlotta glowered at Norbert over the puffy blue bouquet.

"Yes, but every flower has more than one meaning, Norbert. Hydrangeas can also stand for vanity, you know. Not in this case, I'm sure! You are not a vain person at all!" Carlotta laughed her tinkling laugh, and quickly plunged the flowers into a deep yellow-painted ceramic vase, not wanting to lose a moment of this opportunity to rework Norbert into a more satisfying image.

At Carlotta's white French-provincial dining room table, over green salad, eggplant pasta salad and lemonade, Carlotta pulled, and Norbert stood firm.

"I wanted to have a serious talk with you, Norbert, about the fortunes."

"Ah, yes? The readings?"

"Is that what you call them? Readings?" asked Carlotta, indulgent.

"That is what they are called," agreed Norbert, smiling.

"Be that as it may. You are still a beginner, as you know. Remember, in the '70s, we studied this stuff in the Club for many months—or maybe a year or two. I honestly don't remember. I don't think you realize how much you still have to learn."

"I am always open to learning, Carlotta, thank you. And I also find that I learn from the readings themselves. I keep refining my art with each reading I do."

"Art?" Carlotta considered that she would have to choose her battles, and not fight Norbert on his word choices if she wanted to get to the crux of the issue. Better to use some flattery whenever possible, to grease the wheel. "Yes, you *are* an artist, of sorts, aren't you, Norbert. I mean, besides being a visual artist, a talented painter—you did see that superb prairie-thing of yours that I bought and propped right in my entryway?—you are also an artist of, well…an artist of advice, shall we say?"

Norbert seemed to be enjoying the eggplant pasta salad to no end. He was heaping more onto his plate.

Good.

"I've been hearing—well, one *does* hear, Norbert—it's a small town, after all—that some of the advice you are giving is quite specific, isn't it?"

"What do you mean?" Norbert's cheeks were stuffed like a squirrel's, and there was a bit of pasta sauce on his chin.

Not attractive.

"I've heard that you've told one person, for example, to leave a career where she was making a good living and find something that would make her happy, another person to not marry his fiancée, and a third person to go back to school to study veterinary medicine. I would say that these are illustrations of specific advice. Wouldn't you?" Carlotta smiled her best charming smile, the one that most people felt compelled to return.

Norbert, however, regarded her soberly. His own sempiternal smile straightened out. He dabbed at his chin with the cloth napkin.

"Carlotta, what are you saying? People come for readings, and I tell them what I see."

"Yes, Norbert, as we taught you to do, remember? But you must keep in mind that the readings are to be vague and ambiguous. You will get yourself into trouble by telling people exact things like this. Instead, say, 'You are at a fork in the road and have much to consider in the area of career,' and 'Be sure that the people you trust are worthy of your esteem,' and 'You may be feeling negative influences and will need to decide how you will handle them.' Things that could be true for anyone. That way, you won't have disgruntled customers coming back and accusing you of steering them wrong."

Carlotta smiled again, this time hoping to project kindness and altruism at Norbert.

Norbert rested his fork on the flowered china plate and considered Carlotta.

At last he said, "I'm not sure what you don't understand, Carlotta. The people shuffle and hand me the seven cards. I read for them."

Carlotta put on a shocked expression. "Norbert! Stop pretending! Don't forget, the Club and I—we're the ones that taught you how to tell fortunes! You know very well you are not 'reading' a gosh darn thing!"

Norbert continued to look at her steadily, and for a moment Carlotta feared he was right now "reading" something about *her*. She shook herself free of his spell. What nonsense.

"Norbert, I will have to remind you of your ethics," said Carlotta. It was time to get severe. "I am sorry to say this, but you are lying to people."

"Carlotta, may I remind *you* that *you* said there is no such thing as professional ethics for a psychic? And may I ask you to try to understand—I am not lying to anyone."

"Oh! So you actually *believe* that random cards drawn from a playing deck have specific messages for you to give to an individual?"

"As I recall, it was you who first said that it doesn't matter what *I* believe. It's true. Honestly, Carlotta, at times, I don't know anymore what I do believe. But that doesn't trouble me, because somehow, what I do or don't believe doesn't seem to be a part of this. All that matters is that I am helping people!"

"Very slippery reasoning, Norbert Z," said Carlotta, her eyes flashing. "Spoken like a true *shyster*!" Carlotta regretted the words even as they fell from her lips.

CHAPTER TWENTY-THREE

Five of Diamonds:

Wounds to your self-esteem
caused by ingratitude of others,
a personality clash, and possibly even a power struggle.
Great annoyance and unpleasantness.

Norbert left without trying the dessert. Carlotta had also felt this was for the best. Like two wooden soldiers, they marched to the door, and Norbert was gone, for all the world acting as if *he* were the injured one. Never would she have believed he could be so self-absorbed.

Licking her wounds, Carlotta pulled two volumes from their hiding place in the drawer of an end table. Reading had always been her greatest solace when the world became intractable.

These two volumes were secreted away, unlike the classics in hardcover with gold writing on the spines that adorned the floor-to-ceiling bookcases. These were two books that Carlotta protected from prying eyes.

The first was: *How to Discuss Classics You Haven't Read*, by Dr. Harvey Phigg, PhD. It was an excellent resource that saved Carlotta a great deal of time.

The second was: *French to Impress*, by Ursula Renard. This was another gem. The blurb on the back began thus:

Whether you want to renew familiarity with French studied in high school, or simply learn a few useful phrases to sprinkle into conversation in order to make a more sophisticated impression in your social circle...

A New Idea was taking form in Carlotta's teeming mind. Let Norbert spin off like a lost satellite into the unsuspecting universe. All she needed to get the Club back on track—*her* track—was another good idea, and, of course, she had it already.

French.

They had followed her into astrology, collage, crochet, genealogy, poetry writing, flower arranging and oil painting, to name only a few of the passions she had taken up and foisted upon them. They would follow her into the language of Victor Hugo. They had never resisted her yet. Yes. French would be the next Big Thing. Carlotta would begin by dropping a few phrases of French into conversation. She would let it be understood that she had been studying French and had been becoming fluent, without mentioning it to anyone, out of modesty. In no time, Margaret and Birdie would be asking for French lessons with Carlotta and begging to accompany her to foreign ports, so to speak. Norbert would be lost in the dust, as far as the Club was concerned.

The Club, always faithful, had never yet failed to ignite passionately with every idea she had ever presented. She knew them so well—better than they knew themselves. That was one comfort, anyway.

After the unpleasantness with Norbert, Carlotta was glad to get her mind off recent aggravations. Carlotta was having her annual show at the gallery. Margaret, in solidarity, had painted a sandwich board sign: *Carlotta Moon, Featured Artist, Come on in!* and had it placed on the sidewalk. Carlotta herself had put an ad in the *Gibbons Corner Gazette* and had left flyers at the picturesque Harbor Home Bed and Breakfast, as well as at the low-end chain hotels on the outskirts of town.

She had dressed with even more than her usual care, in black slacks and a flowing button-down white artist-y-looking shirt, silver sandals and a bit of silver jewelry. Dressing well was one of the pleasures of being alive, she reflected, as she rounded the corner of Clarence Avenue and Main Street.

She stopped in her tracks. There was a small crowd of about twelve or fifteen people waiting on the sidewalk before the gallery. None of the artists had ever before attracted such attention at a show. After seven years of oil painting, Carlotta was exalted. The public was discovering her at last. Carlotta walked more quickly, mentally practicing witty things she could say to them.

As she approached, she did pick up an odor of alcohol from the little group. No matter. Fans were fans.

"Here's somebody!" announced one of the band at Carlotta's approach.

Carlotta gave a little wave. "Hello!" She projected her charm toward them all. "I am Carlotta Moon," she added modestly.

"Yeah," said a woman in a dress that was too tight for her. "So maybe you know—does Norbert Z really work here?"

Carlotta's spark blew out on the spot.

"They told us at the Alibi Bar that he works here. Because the Good Fortune Café is closed at night, and we all want readings now."

"I have no idea what you're talking about," enunciated Carlotta, with surgical precision. "This is an art establishment." She flounced past the drunken mob, into the air-conditioned stillness of the gallery.

Quel ennui!

How annoying.

★ ★ ★

Norbert was just settling down for the night with a cup of Peaceful Dreams Herbal Tea. He enjoyed his evening of solitude with Ivy after a day of readings. In the quiet of his home, he reviewed his day, and the faces of his customers appeared in his mind's eye: encouraged, reassured, hopeful. That was how they looked when they left him, and that was what helped him to feel that he was doing good. At least he hoped so. He was still not entirely used to the power he seemed to exert over people, and he was a little afraid of it.

Whenever he felt unsure of himself, he thought of Carlotta. After working to make him tell fortunes, she was now working to undermine his confidence in himself. Stroking Ivy's oversized ears, he smiled. He held no grudge against Carlotta for using the term "shyster" the day of that awkward lunch at her place. He saw that she was desperate to find the words that would control him, and there was nothing he needed to take personally. She was simply a gifted, natural leader. Like all natural leaders, she felt secure with a pack, an army or a club following her, and had developed with precision the skills needed to keep herself always clearly in the lead. The deepest fear of the natural leader was of being deposed, because this leads to a crisis of identity, and to a sense of not being necessary at all. Norbert had come to understand Carlotta very well.

Norbert's phone rang. The caller ID showed that it was his cousin's nephew, Zack. Not the person Norbert wanted to talk to before going to sleep. Zack was the unluckiest young man Norbert knew, and his infinite chain of misfortunes had been a drain on Norbert's savings—back in the days when Norbert had any savings. After Norbert began to have hard times of his own, Zack's calls had dwindled mercifully to none at all. It had been years since he'd heard the unfortunate fellow's voice.

"Uncle Norbert?"

"Why, Zack. Hello. How have you been?"

"Hey, Uncle Norbert! I'm glad you're still— Hey! It's been a long time. Sorry I haven't called for a while."

"That's all right, Zack." (It really was.)

"Well, how are *you*?"

All requests for money began with exactly that inflection. Norbert knew it was not a real question, but rather a required phrase to open a conversation in which Zack would go on to explain that someone stole all of his tools out of his van so now he couldn't work, or that he was mugged and was knocked unconscious and was out of the hospital but now he had a lot of bills to pay, or that all three of his roommates had suddenly moved out on him and now how was he supposed to pay the rent?

"I'm in a mess, Uncle Norbert." Zack's voice went weak, as if he were in pain. "I injured myself and I haven't been able to work in a while."

Earlier in Norbert's life, people had assumed he was wealthy because he gave away money so freely. He could not say no. He did not want to say no. He enjoyed the look of gratitude, the sense of being seen, even if only for a brief moment. He came alive when he was perceived as the person who could solve the problem—the person with the answer. And now he had no money to give. He and Ivy were getting by, but there was no extra in his checking account for philanthropy.

"Uncle Norbert? You still there, man?"

Norbert, the psychic adviser, had been helping his customers to draw boundaries in their personal relationships, and now it was time for him to draw one of his own. He'd never done such a thing before, and didn't know if he was up to the task. He was temperamentally incapable of being unkind.

"Zachary," said Norbert, calling his nephew by the name he used when he was a little boy, "do you remember when you and I used to take electronics apart and put them back together?"

"What? Well, I don't remember too much about that. What I really wanted to talk about was—"

Norbert interrupted.

"It was your favorite thing to do." Norbert saw, in his mind's eye, the young and enthusiastic Zachary, and felt love in his heart for that child. "Those were good times, eh? After a while, I didn't even help you. I'd just watch. You could take anything apart and reassemble it. That shows a lot of intelligence, I always said. You were the smartest thing. And now you are a grown man. You are very capable of figuring out this problem on your own. I have every confidence in you."

"So…?"

"So give me a call back when you work it all out. I'd love to hear how you managed it. You always do find the way. You are remarkable, Zack. You were born remarkable."

Norbert, smiling gently, hung up.

CHAPTER TWENTY-FOUR

Four of Spades:

The past must be released,
to allow space for the present and future.

Summer's parents came to her in her dreams. Sometimes they were disappointed and silent, and sometimes they beckoned her to follow them. Sometimes they were furious and frightening, and the dream was filled with a static noise. Today, as the birds sang beyond her darkened windows, her dreams of her parents were lovely.

It was that night again. But this time, it all played out differently, as it so easily might have done. This time, she didn't go running out the door when Rory honked his horn in the driveway. This time, she stayed in the house, drinking tea and looking at astrology magazines with her mom. Her dad sang Bob Dylan impressions, and they all laughed, and the love sparkled in the air of the room.

She awoke feeling something like happiness. It was the memory of what happiness used to feel like. Was it Saturday?

Gramma had coerced her into agreeing to walk Toutou for her every Saturday morning. Summer knew very well that Gramma was as strong and energetic as ever, and she could walk her own poodle. This was only a clever ruse to get Summer out of her apartment and into the daylight and fresh air.

After that night, the night that it happened, Gramma had taken her into her home on Clarence Avenue, and had finished raising her and had guided her into college. How old had Gramma been then? She must have been seventy, assuming the care of a fifteen-year-old girl. Not every seventy-year-old would have felt equal to the task. How had she managed it? She was a tough old bird, and the best person Summer knew.

Gramma had been attentive and affectionate and actually seemed grateful to have the responsibility of raising Summer. She had always been one to keep her mind and hands busy. They had been close before "it" happened, but afterward they had forged a strong bond that endured to this day.

Toutou would be waiting for that walk. Summer hated walking around town. She feared that when people looked at her, they must see right through her, to her guilt.

She swung her legs over the side of her bed.

No one knows. It was ten years ago, and still no one has figured it out. Even Gramma doesn't know what I did. If she knew, she wouldn't love me the way she does. Everyone in town knows how Charlie and Barbara Moon died. But no one knows I killed them.

CHAPTER TWENTY-FIVE

Two of Clubs:

There is yet time for you to take a different path.

It was the end of August, still summer, yet with a hint in the breeze of the autumn to come, and the fortune-telling trade was going well. Norbert had been doing readings for two months, and already felt strangely at ease in the role.

A scruffy-looking youth looked up at him gravely when Norbert, pointing to the Two of Clubs, told him, "There is yet time for you to take a different path."

A young woman with a nose ring became pensive when he signaled the Eight of Diamonds and told her, "You have something good in your life. Do not let it go."

Norbert had the satisfaction of helping people to think about the direction of their lives and to discover their own power to change it. Norbert also had the satisfaction of buying himself a decent pair of shoes.

As Margaret and Birdie had begun to visit him, he had begun to return their visits, just briefly passing by, bringing avocados from the Lucky Pig, or flowers from his garden. Norbert, holding a bunch of tiger lilies, stood on Birdie's doorstep feeling a mixture of curiosity and trepidation. He'd been in Birdie's garden when he came to the garden party, but he had never entered her house. If there were a haunted house anywhere in Gibbons Corner, Norbert supposed this would be it. Norbert, however, did not believe in haunted houses, or in spirit visitations of any kind. But he did believe in Birdie. He saw in her a genuineness that he did not see in many people.

Birdie swung open the door and welcomed him into a home that was airy and full of sunlight. There were green plants everywhere, and there was a comfortable cross breeze flowing throughout the space, making it feel like part of the great outdoors. He had expected enclosed dark spaces and Victorian antiques, but there was none of that. If spirits lived here, he thought, they must be nature spirits.

Tetley, Birdie's ancient parrot, sat on his perch and sharply regarded Ivy, who peeped around with interest from her carrier.

Birdie took the lilies happily, and put them in water in a clear vase right away. "Lilies are for purity. That's what Carlotta always says."

Norbert's attention was arrested by the large parrot perched near the window, peering at Norbert first through his right eye, and then through his left.

"Norbert," said Birdie, "meet Tetley. Tetley, this is Norbert."

"Hey there, woo-hoo! How ya doing?" rasped Tetley.

Norbert turned to Birdie. "How did you train him to do that?"

Birdie, smiling, said, "First you'd better answer him, or he'll keep asking."

"Oh!" said Norbert, feeling silly. "I'm fine, thank you, Tetley. Uh. How are you?"

Tetley responded with a perfect imitation of a phone ringing.

Birdie signaled for Norbert to have a seat near a large window, and she seated herself across from him. Ivy was out of the carrier and on Birdie's lap in a flash.

"I'm so glad you could stop by," said Birdie. "I could have dropped it off at the café."

Birdie produced a hand-crocheted cream-colored collar with a large crimson flower, and fastened it around Ivy's neck. She had estimated the size perfectly. Ivy accepted the present with good grace, and appreciated the extra attention it brought her.

"And so, Norbert," said Birdie, as if continuing a conversation that had never started, "you are using your gift. You have come to understand that there are unseen hands at work in all our lives. You have opened the door to your spiritual side."

"I don't know about that, Birdie. If you mean the card reading, well, I just pretty much go with the odds, and it seems to work out. What I do focus on is helping people."

Birdie seemed to be listening to something that made her smile gently.

"You are still resisting it."

"Not at all! I'm not resisting anything. I just understand... I don't know...randomness."

"Randomness?"

"Yes. Like statistics, you know?"

"No, I don't know."

"Well," said Norbert, glad to inform Birdie on a subject he had been good at in school, "the card readings, they 'work' by way of randomness."

"Hmm?" asked Birdie.

"It's like this—say I get the idea before I start my readings on a given day that I'm going to say a certain thing to three different customers today. We can just pick anything at all, like—" Norbert scratched his head "—well, 'The pressure at your job has been building steadily and they keep putting more on your plate.' Let's say that's the statement. Now, that is a very common experience these days. Chances are, if I say that to three people, it's going to be true for at least two of them. And the third person will probably try to make it fit somehow. The third person might say, 'Oh, you're seeing the job I just left, or, oh, I think you're seeing my spouse's job,' or something like that."

Birdie, untroubled, said, "And what would give you the inspiration to give that particular message to three people that day?"

Norbert wondered why Birdie couldn't keep up.

"It's not an inspiration. It's a decision."

"You think it's a decision."

"No. I *know* it's a decision. I decide it, in my head."

"You decide it because it's been given to you."

"*Given* to me? By whom?"

"Given to you by Spirit. Because Spirit knows that three people are going to come in who need to hear that message."

Norbert sighed. Birdie was a lovely and interesting person, but she didn't understand how rational his psychic readings were.

"Well, if you're bad at statistics—and I'm not saying you are, of course—well, then, you believe in the paranormal because you don't understand randomness. Do you see?"

"I see," said Birdie, "that you are a good man, Norbert. And I have it on good authority that you will continue to get opportunities to grow into your spirituality."

Regardless of his disagreement with Birdie's perspective,

there was no denying that her focused and personal attention made him feel good.

On leaving, Norbert had to resist the odd impulse to pay Birdie twenty dollars for her reflections.

CHAPTER TWENTY-SIX

Four of Clubs and
Ten of Hearts:

You have people who love you unconditionally,
although you may not realize it.

Summer stopped by Carlotta's house on the way home from
school one afternoon.

She longed to get home and shut her apartment door on the
world. She wanted to get to her couch and wrap herself up
like a cocoon in a blanket of silence. In three months it would
be December 30. Why, this year, did she need to keep track
of the days leading up to the awful anniversary? She couldn't
help it. At home and at school, she watched with dread as the
calendar pages turned, turned so quickly, as if that date were
hurtling toward her through space like an asteroid. She feared
the approach of winter like never before. Her need to isolate
herself had intensified, if that were possible. But she couldn't
let many days go by without touching base with her grandmother. She parked in the driveway and put a bright smile on
her face before getting out of her car.

Her grandmother's eyes lit up with joy at the sight of her. They sat on Gramma's patio, soaking in the glory of a warm, early fall day.

She thought she'd point the conversation in the direction of her grandmother's new Project again. That should get her going, so she wouldn't ask too many questions about Summer's nonexistent social life.

"Gramma, I'm thinking of seeing your psychic for a reading—you know, just for fun."

"I wouldn't bother, dear. It would be a complete and total waste of your time. And he's not *my* psychic. He's just a gimmick to boost business in Hope's café."

"So you're saying he's bogus? You mean you have a charlatan working at Hope's place? Does she know he's a fake?"

"Oh, Summer, how you put things. I didn't say he was a fake. I *said*…" Gramma took a long drink of water. "Have you been seeing much of your friends lately? How is Marisol?"

Marisol was Summer's former Spanish teacher and her *only* friend, really. Summer didn't have much time or energy for socializing. Marisol was just the right kind of friend: a mentor with a very busy life, too busy to need anything that Summer couldn't give: anything like frequent contact, answers to texts, or consistent, personal connection.

Miss Fernandez had looked straight at Summer and remarked, "You have a very good accent."

It was seventh grade. Summer looked up with surprise from the columns of Spanish words she and her classmates were repeating in turn after the teacher.

Summer was an unremarkable student, and had never been singled out this way. The result of this unexpected compliment was that she immediately fell in love with Spanish and with Miss Fernandez. The other kids didn't try at all to imitate the teacher's accent. This was middle school. It was not worth the risk of being mocked by their classmates, so they repeated the vocabulary words with inflections as exaggeratedly American as possible.

After that one bit of praise, Summer focused on Spanish single-mindedly, as if it were the only thing in life that mattered. She wrote out all the homework exercises from *Hablamos Español*, and did the extra credit, striving to get Miss Fernandez to point out her talent again.

From middle school on, Summer's career aspiration was to be a Spanish teacher—like Miss Fernandez. Fortune smiled on her after she graduated from college, and she was hired in the foreign language program at Gibbons Corner Senior High School—just next door to the middle school where she had fallen in love with Spanish and Miss Fernandez only nine years before.

Summer enjoyed her work, but she also had the persistent feeling that she was an impostor. She was playing the part of Miss Fernandez. Like Miss Fernandez, she wore the latest styles and she owned cute shoes in every color. She organized her class much the way Miss Fernandez organized hers. Her teaching style came straight from her role model, and not a day went by when that early encourager was not in the back of her mind. She wondered if others could see that she was faking it. How could they not?

From time to time, Summer had lunch at the Green Buddha Diner with Marisol Fernandez, now that they were colleagues. In the sun-drenched and plant-filled vegan eatery, Marisol had been moved to a tearful smile when Summer told her how much that lightly offered compliment (long forgotten by Marisol) had influenced the trajectory of Summer's life.

"You never know," said Marisol, raking her fork through her Indian curry bowl, "how your words or your attention are affecting another person. It's scary to be a teacher sometimes. I think, what if I'm having a bad day? I could say something that a kid will never forget. I could change a future, or break a spirit."

Summer opened her eyes in mock horror.

They both laughed, and Marisol amended, "I guess that's an exaggeration, huh?"

Summer shuddered, secretly thinking that it might not be an exaggeration.

"The fact is, you influenced *me* for the *better*. I have no idea what I would have done if I hadn't fallen in love with Spanish." (Summer did not mention that she had also fallen in love with Marisol. That schoolgirl crush had passed, but not the admiration or the gratitude.) "I might not have gone to college. I wouldn't have the confidence that I could do anything especially well. I'd be a different person. I'll never know." Summer took a bite of her Mediterranean falafel wrap, as they contemplated how the small things in life affect the big things.

"Speaking of influencing lives," said Marisol, "how is your Girls' Group going?"

Summer and the know-it-all school social worker co-facilitated a "mentoring group" for girls.

"It's okay. It's no big deal."

Summer knew her ulterior motive in taking on this responsibility was to get a window into the bewildering minds of fifteen-year-old girls—to understand her own mind at that age.

"Well, *I* think it's a big deal. You give up your plan period once a week to listen to high school sophomores talk about their feelings and their home problems? I wouldn't do it. I need my plan time. I'm not selfless like you. You're a really good person."

"I am *not* a good person," said Summer, bristling.

Marisol laughed easily. "Okay. You're not. Whatever. Is something bothering you?"

Summer hesitated. Could she talk to Marisol? They were the only ones in the restaurant.

"Do you remember when my parents died?"

"Of course I do. How could I ever forget that?" Marisol's big brown eyes were warm and caring.

"Well." Summer considered what she could say next. Could she say, *I killed my parents, actually. Did you ever suspect that, Marisol?* No, she could not. As she searched for words, Marisol scanned her face, and must have seen the hopelessness there.

"Oh, Summer. Summer, what's wrong?"

"Never mind," said Summer, pulling back. She had no right to cause anyone else pain by unburdening herself. "Don't mind me."

"You're not okay, are you? Something's not right. Do you want to talk about it?"

Summer said, "Oh, I'll be okay. It was ten years ago, you know. A very long time ago now."

"I'm sure a person never gets over a thing like that. It was so senseless."

You have no idea, thought Summer.

In a rally worthy of her grandmother, Summer managed a convincing smile. She told Marisol a funny anecdote from her classroom. They laughed.

They ordered the cashew vanilla fudge, one order, two plates.

CHAPTER TWENTY-SEVEN

Ace of Clubs and
Eight of Clubs:

When these two cards appear together,
you receive a business offer that carries with it
enormous power to change the trajectory of the future.
You must consider carefully, staying true to yourself.

Norbert's fortune-telling extended beyond the tourist season.

It was a Tuesday afternoon in October. Norbert's readings were now intuitive—not in the ESP sense, but in the easy-to-do sense. One reading had built upon the other until he had come to feel very professional and competent in his new, late-life career.

The querent was a short, brown-haired woman with furry eyebrows and a bulbous nose. She was wearing an odd combination of old brown-and-yellow clothes. With her quick movements and her furtive glance, she put Norbert in mind of a small, watchful, active animal. She seemed to be full of good humor, and her little brown eyes were bright.

"Well, Norbert Z," she began, "what do the cards have to say about *me* today?"

Norbert received the seventh card from her little paw and placed it at the end of the horseshoe spread.

"May I have your first name, please?"

"Edith," she said, watching him. "And if it helps, my birth day is February 11, 1938. I'm an Aquarius."

"Very well, Edith," said Norbert, surveying the cards. He knew nothing about astrology, one of the subjects he had avoided his whole life, so made no comment on the little woman's Aquarian birthday. However, the cards gave him a message quite out of the ordinary. Of the seven cards, four were aces.

"I see a lot of power here," began Norbert, and he wondered if he were mistaken. This woman looked eccentric and destitute, not powerful. "The cards speak of immense resources and even of magic. A great deal of mental and spiritual force. The power must always be harnessed and challenged so that it is used for good purposes. It is the power to build and heal, but also the power to destroy. You can do so much good with it, if you use it with proper intentions." Norbert glanced at Edith to check if this were a "hit" or a "miss."

"And?" she encouraged.

Norbert saw that she was not surprised. It was as if she said, *Tell me something I don't know.*

"And..." he continued. "You have the Four of Hearts, here. This is a very good card. The Four tells of an important gift— it could be a material gift, or it could be a great service, or a special favor. Next to the Four, there's the Seven of Clubs, which tells of a business partnership. And on the other side of the Seven, you have the Jack of Clubs, which can represent an unremarkable or dark-eyed man, one who seems unexceptional at first, but has the potential to be interesting and beneficial to you..."

Norbert's voice trailed off, as he recalled that in a reading a few months ago, when he was receiving psychic lessons, the Jack of Clubs represented Norbert himself.

He looked up at Edith, who was observing him as if she expected him to react to the punch line of an obvious and very funny joke.

"I've been hearing a lot about you, Norbert Z," she said, "from all and sundry, for a few moons now, and I've come to see for myself the wonders that you work. You're very good. Now—" she clasped her clawed fingers together and leaned forward "—how would you like to come out to the Center for Deeper Understanding?"

"How would I—?"

"You've heard of it," asserted Edith.

"Uh. It's that New Age place on Highway Four, just outside of town?"

Of course, Norbert had seen it many times, a two-story, white-pillared mansion set back off the road, with fruit orchards behind it.

"Hmph. Is that what the townies call it? 'That New Age place.' Listen, Norbert Z, come and see for yourself what we do there. We can use someone with your talent."

Norbert was speechless. Was this a job offer?

"What are you doing tomorrow evening at five o'clock?"

A few hours after Edith Butler's reading, Norbert, with Ivy rocking along in her carrier, walked with quick steps to Oil Painting with Carlotta.

Norbert and all the Club members continued working and studying at the Art League. His painting had undergone a great deal of change in recent months. He had moved on from Native-American-derivative-style paintings based in brown, black and red, into a more Peruvian-derivative style. Now he painted his canvases black to begin with, and then used bright colors to paint pipe-smoking shamans, mountain village scenes teeming with people and llamas, and celestial entities sweeping white ectoplasm across starry skies.

Since the eggplant salad incident, Carlotta had cooled no ticeably toward Norbert. She now made a point of asking nothing at all about his readings, and instead spoke violent French to the Club whenever he appeared.

As Norbert entered, Carlotta was studying the painting of the adolescent Liam: a weeping skull. Glancing from Norbert to Liam, she uttered the first French phrase that occurred to her.

"*Oh, mais c'est trop beau!*"

Liam said, "Uh, Mrs. Moon? I don't understand French."

"Oh!" laughed Carlotta. "Was I speaking French? Sometimes I don't even realize it! *C'est trop beau* means— How would you say? 'It's very beautiful.'"

Liam looked again at the black-and-white skull. He shrugged his shoulders.

"Bone Joor," attempted Norbert, setting up his canvas on an easel.

"Oh, Norbert, how funny you are, trying to speak French. *Bon soir*—that is 'Good evening.'"

"Bone Swar," replied Norbert. He set Ivy's basket next to the wall, as far as possible from the turpentine fumes, and she jumped in, turning in circles before curling into her sleeping position.

Margaret complained, "I don't know why you want to speak French, Carlotta. It's too hard."

"*Chère Marguerite,*" responded Carlotta. She gave Margaret a warning look.

Birdie and the young mother were setting up their work. That joyful feeling of quiet industry was beginning to hum through the studio when Norbert said, "I received an interesting invitation today."

"Oh, no!" exclaimed the new mother. She had painted the fairy-tale princess's eyes two different sizes. *"Now what?"*

Carlotta was on the spot, instructing, "A painting is a series of corrections. Always remember that. Oil paints, unlike life, are forgiving. Every mistake can be corrected, or else turned into something else that improves the painting even more." She indicated with a few simple words and gestures how to remedy the mistake.

Norbert used to experience this type of thing all the time. He would make a remark, and others would carry on as if they hadn't heard him. However, since he had begun his career as a fortune-teller, he had gotten used to being heard.

He tried again, louder this time.

"I've been invited to the Center for Deeper Understanding."

Carlotta, Margaret and Birdie stopped their work and looked at him.

"By the Reverend Edith Butler," added Norbert, lifting his chin. "I believe she is the director of the place?"

Carlotta choked. *"The Reverend?"* She shook her head. "Be warned, dear Norbert. Be very careful indeed. We can tell you all about that woman. Edith is an ordained-by-mail kind of reverend." Carlotta laughed her tinkling laugh. "Oh, yes! You just send away for it! Just respond to an ad that says 'Become ordained today!—It's legal!—Perform marriage ceremonies for cash!'"

Norbert asked, "You know her?"

"In a town like this—how could we not know her?" asked Margaret. "A long time ago, she was even in our Club." She stole a glance at Carlotta. "I always liked her."

"And," asked Norbert, "she performs marriage ceremonies

for cash?" He thought the marriage business must be slow, to judge from Edith's raggedy clothes.

Margaret chortled, "Edith's an heiress. She has no need for 'cash.' She's as rich as Croesus. She runs that Center for Deeper Understanding—and Butler's Books on Main Street—at her own expense, just for fun. Her nephew manages the bookstore for her. But she likes collecting titles for herself. And every time she gets a new one, she writes a press release, and we read all about it in the *Gazette*."

Birdie intoned, "Edith Butler. Yes, she was in our Club in the '70s, when we were studying astrology and palmistry. She left, though, when we switched to psychology. There was some kind of unpleasantness, wasn't there?" Birdie looked at Carlotta.

"Forty years is a long time back, Birdie. *Mon dieu!* I haven't spoken to the woman in ages. But she can be seen scurrying all around town with her can't-be-bothered kind of appearance—"

Birdie suggested, "We can always choose to be *kind*, Carlotta. Appearances are not so important, are they?"

Carlotta insisted, "I *am* kind. But come on. Brown-and-yellow cardigans and long skirts and saris and whatnot—she's always been an odd bird."

Birdie said, "*I* always thought she looked like a skylark."

Everyone looked at Birdie.

Birdie added, "Or something."

Carlotta brought the conversation back to Norbert's invitation. "Anyway. *Attention*, Norbert. *Fais très attention.* That means 'Be very careful.' One's reputation is very important. Unlike an oil painting, once your reputation is besmirched, it is very difficult indeed to repair it. It is unwise in the extreme to be involved with disreputable people."

"Of course, that's true," agreed Norbert. "But is Edith Butler disreputable? I understand that people come from all over the country to study at the Center for Deeper Understanding. It's famous nationwide for yoga retreats and courses on astrology, numerology and stuff like that."

"I rest my case!" Carlotta declared. *"C'est ridicule!"* Carlotta tossed her head, looking to Margaret for support.

"Reedeekyool," repeated Margaret, obedient. "But *why* should I say 'reedeekyool'?"

Birdie came to Margaret's assistance. "Oh, 'say' is how you pronounce *'c'est,'* or 'it is,' in French. So *c'est ridicule* means 'it's ridiculous.'"

"It certainly is," affirmed Margaret. "French is too hard. Speak English, Carlotta."

When Norbert telephoned Edith to say that, on further reflection, he could not consider telling fortunes at the Center because he had a business arrangement with Hope Delaney at the café, Edith said, "Oh, Norbert Z, I don't want you to read fortunes here! I want you to be our new past-life regressionist!"

Norbert objected, "I don't even know what that is."

Edith chuckled and said she would explain all about it in person. When Norbert hesitated, Edith said, "Bring your entourage, Norbert! Bring what's-her-name and her Club. We'll do a group past-life regression for all of you—free of charge— a two-hundred-dollar per person value."

Edith sounded so excited about doing it, Norbert didn't want to repeat that he had no idea what "it" was. When he presented this bargain to the Club at the Art League on Wednesday afternoon, they met the offer with enthusiasm.

"I'm in!" exclaimed Margaret.

"I'm willing," said Birdie.

"I'm shocked!" said Carlotta. "Shocked! This is the twenty-first century. How can you all be so silly? Past lives! A bunch of self-indulgent nonsense, that's what that is."

"Oh, Carlotta," said Margaret, "it doesn't matter if it's really true. It's just for fun!"

"So now we waste our time on things that are not even true?" fumed Carlotta.

Birdie quoted "'Whatever satisfies the soul is truth.'—Walt Whitman."

Margaret challenged, "If you don't want to go, Carlotta, don't."

Carlotta did not expect that bit of treachery.

"Do not worry, Margaret. I will not only go—*I will drive.*"

CHAPTER TWENTY-EIGHT

Four Jacks:

You will attend a strange gathering
and experience amazement.

Carlotta's sedan coasted smoothly down Highway Four toward the Center for Deeper Understanding. Her passengers—Margaret, Birdie and Norbert—were appreciating the beauty of Gibbons Corner in the fall. The leaves had begun to change color. As the sunlight filtered through them, their town was even more charming than in summer. The whole world all around was gold and red, and there was a faint aroma of wood burning in fireplaces in nearby homes and cottages.

As they rolled along, Carlotta said, "How about a round of literary quotes?"

"Sure!" the group agreed.

"I'll begin, shall I?" said Carlotta. Without waiting for assent, she began:

Alice laughed: "There's no use trying" she said; "one can't believe impossible things."

"I daresay you haven't had much practice," said the Queen. "When I was younger, I always did it for half an hour a day. Why, sometimes I've believed as many as six impossible things before breakfast."

Norbert was impressed that Carlotta could recite such a long prose quotation. He thought that he could never manage it. But then, she'd been practicing for years.

"Oh, Carlotta," said Margaret. "I think you picked that quote on purpose to ruin our fun. You just enjoy being cynical."

Showing off, Carlotta took another turn. "'A cynic is a man who knows the price of everything, and the value of nothing.'—Oscar Wilde."

Margaret, looking at the woods on both sides of the highway, quoted, "'I think that I shall never see a poem lovely as a tree.'—that World War I soldier. What was his name? I forget."

There was a pause as everyone tried to remember. He died on a battlefield in Europe, they did remember that. No, the name didn't come.

"I'll remember it later when I'm not trying, I know I will," muttered Margaret.

"Or when we can look on the internet, we'll Google it," said Carlotta, proud of her technological savvy.

Birdie, going on with the game, contributed, "'There are more things in Heaven and Earth, Horatio, than are dreamt of in your philosophy.'—Shakespeare, in *Hamlet*."

Norbert, who had been troubled about finding a literary quote somewhere in his brain, brightened up. "*I* know a Shakespeare quote: 'Lord what fools these dreamers be.'—*Midsummer Night's Dream*."

Carlotta clicked her tongue. "Oh, Norbert, I'm afraid you've got it wrong. It's not 'dreamers.' It's 'mortals.' 'Lord what fools these mortals be.'"

The Club usually didn't challenge misquotes. But then, Norbert was not a member of the Club.

"Oh," said Norbert, disappointed. "But the quote is about those people all sleeping in the woods. I thought it was 'dreamers.'"

"Nope," said Carlotta, with special emphasis on the 'p.' *"Mortals."*

Norbert understood Carlotta's mood. He saw from his first mention of Edith that there was an old rivalry between the two women. He also knew that Carlotta, from the beginning, had intended to control him and his fortune-telling work, and had been disappointed when he didn't let her. He could almost read her mind today: *If I don't get to run Norbert, I'm certainly not going to allow Edith Butler to do it.*

Carlotta turned right into the long ginkgo tree–lined driveway of the palatial Center for Deeper Understanding. Yellow leaves trimmed the road and garnished the lawns.

"'Vanity of vanities, all is vanity'—Ecclesiastes I," she concluded the game, as was the custom.

As the little band in her car craned their necks at the elegant white-pillared mansion surrounded by gardens and orchards, Carlotta pulled around to the parking lot off to the side.

They walked along a path laid with wide flat stones that were inscribed with sentiments such as "Love is all" and "Be here now."

Norbert observed that Margaret was in a joyful hurry, and that Carlotta was rushing along, determined to get in front of everyone.

Walking behind them all, Norbert reflected: both Carlotta and Edith were managers. But Edith was a manager with a staff and a veritable castle. How would Carlotta fare on the territory of her opposite number?

Moved by the natural prettiness of the place, in spite of herself, Carlotta stopped. Margaret, who had been looking down at her orthotic shoes to avoid a mishap, ran into her.

"Oh! Pardon, Marguerite," exclaimed Carlotta. *"Je m'excuse."*

The whole gang stopped together for a moment and soaked in the breathtaking charm of this spot. Ivy poked her head over the top of Norbert's man purse, to twitch her nose and inhale all the new information in the vicinity. The birds sang, chanted and whistled, seeming to sing of the gratitude in their hearts to be living here, in Heaven. The lake shimmered and rippled in the distance behind the Center. Across the harbor, on tree-covered Black Bear Island, threads of smoke arose from the cottages of wealthy tourists. All around the Center, there were marigold borders, apple and pear orchards, and vegetable gardens exuberant with tomatoes, cucumbers, lettuce and peppers. The bursting fall color, combined with the aesthetic design of the Center, bewitched them all. For Norbert, the perfection here was so touching that he felt tears rising to his eyes, touched to behold so much concentrated loveliness.

"What a place to come with our paints and easels, huh?" breathed Margaret.

"It's like a place of enchantment!" assented Birdie.

They had arrived at the bottom of the staircase when the door burst open.

"Carlotta Moon!" crowed Edith as she ushered Norbert and the Club into the entryway of the Center. "I thought you were dead!"

"Edith Butler," answered Carlotta. "How *gracious* of you!"

The little group laughed.

"I see," said Edith, "that your Evil Cabal has gotten smaller over the years."

The little group laughed again, this time less gaily.

Norbert said, "So you all know each other? Then I don't have to introduce anyone?"

"We go *way* back," affirmed Edith. "Several lifetimes, in fact."

"Funny, Edith, I only recall *this* lifetime," protested Carlotta.

"And at *your* age, I bet you can't even do *that* very well!" Edith looked like a merry little otter.

Carlotta recoiled from the insult. For once, it seemed that she could think of nothing clever, and only repeated, "Edith! How *gracious* of you!"

The Club sensed trouble. Carlotta was at a disadvantage. She never repeated a sarcastic reprisal. Her comedy was always fresh.

Margaret, ever-supportive, said, "Carlotta, hahaha! *'How gracious of you'*—that is so *funny!*"

"I *know!*" chortled Edith. "And she's said it *twice!*"

For a moment, no one moved. This visit was off to an awkward start.

Edith amended, "I'm just goofing around, you know. I'm only two years younger than Carlotta myself. Seventy-eight and proud of it! Anyway, we *revere* age here at the Center for Deeper Understanding."

Edith turned to the other ladies. "Margaret Birch! Hello, my dear! Birdie Walsh! How are you, you dear soul?" Edith embraced each in a bear hug. "I've been waiting for the day you all would come to my Center, and see what we've built here. I often think back to our early experiments in our living rooms with oracle decks and astrology charts. That's where this all started, really! We were all such good friends, too!" Edith stopped and contemplated Carlotta. "Well, whatever may have happened in the past, chalk it up to our lower level of development at the time. I'm sure we are all of us much closer to our higher selves by now!"

Birdie looked at her dreamily, and Margaret seemed to be falling under Edith's spell, too. Carlotta looked annoyed, and glanced back toward her car as if she were thinking of leaving already.

Edith turned her full attention to Norbert. "Norbert Z, you are a vibrational match for the Center for Deeper Understanding. You belong here at this time. Now, before we get to the group past-life regression, I'll show you all around the Center."

Moving faster than any of them, Edith ran them around the rooms of the mansion.

On the right of the entryway was the Crystals Shop. Edith sped through the aisles and around the tables, pointing out necklaces and earrings made of jade ("to increase love and nurturing"), iolite ("to promote psychic healing") and kyanite ("excellent for protection while channeling and visualizing"). She waved toward the tarot cards, and let Norbert and the Club sniff the incense and essential oils. There were elephants and Buddhas and blue-skinned Hindu goddesses—or were those gods? Norbert really didn't know what he was looking at, but he liked the colors.

On the left of the entryway was the Great Room of Compassion and Loving Kindness. Indeed, each room had a name, which was announced by a ceramic plaque just outside its door: Acceptance, Peace, Wisdom, Healing, One Hand Clapping, The Third Eye, and Synchronicity, among others. Each room had its own character expressed through decor that harmonized with the name it had been assigned.

Edith showed Norbert and his guests the vegetable gardens and orchards behind the Center. She spoke as if only Norbert was there, and the Club was invisible to her. Striding down the paths in the streaming rays of twilight, she talked on and on, allowing no interruption.

"Ah!" cried Edith. "I hear one of you sighing! Because it's so beautiful here, or because you're out of shape and can't walk as fast as I can? Ha ha! Yes, Norbert, I knew if you just saw it, the magic of this place would reel you in. Look at those sweet peppers!

"Everyone who works here is welcome to share in the bounty, Norbert Z. It's all organic."

Rushing forward, Edith recited a list of the classes and services that the Center provided. Norbert did not understand what some of them were: gong meditations, spiritual retreats, soul retrievals, séances, reiki healing, belly dancing, seeing and clearing auras, and connecting with angels.

"We also offer Laughing Yoga. Laughter is a life-extender, Norbert Z. You should try it. Everybody in a room for an hour, just going *'ha-ha-ha-ha-ha-ha-ha.'* It's so healthy."

She laughed a full belly laugh that filled the air with merriment. Edith had a contagious kind of joy about her, and Norbert liked that. When she kept on laughing, Norbert finally couldn't resist, and the two of them laughed together, although for the life of him, he didn't see what was so funny. Margaret and Birdie joined in, too, because they liked to laugh. Carlotta observed them all as if they'd gone mad.

Edith's mirthful face abruptly composed itself into a businesslike one.

"There's still one thing we do need, Norbert Z. And that's why I've invited you here today. What we need is a past-life regressionist. I know you could do the job. There is a huge demand for past-life readings now. People want to understand themselves, and understand their own behavior patterns, or why certain things keep happening to them. A past-life reading can help a person to make sense of things, to heal, to move an emotional block out of the way and go forward."

Norbert asked, "Are you saying you don't personally believe in—uh—*past lives*?" This topic was very strange to him.

"No, I am not. I actually *remember* all my past lives, Norbert Z. Being able to remember them is very helpful to me in this life."

Norbert was curious, in spite of himself. "Can you give an example?"

"I could give thousands. That's how many past lives I've had."

Norbert could feel the Club shifting behind him.

"Just one would be good, thank you."

Edith's furry brows jumped up and down over her eyes, as they did when she spoke of anything that really delighted her.

"Well, whenever I have any kind of a battle to fight in this life, I just remember my life as an Aztec warrior."

"You were an Aztec warrior?" Norbert tried not to let his eyes travel the roundness of Edith's body.

Carlotta made a sound that started out as a guffaw but turned into a cough. Margaret and Birdie were listening in rapt attention.

Edith, deaf to Carlotta, said, "Yes, indeed, Norbert Z. Of course, when I was an Aztec warrior, I was in much better shape than I am now." Edith put her hands on her plump hips, as if remembering her warrior stance.

Norbert asked, "And thinking about being an Aztec warrior helps you somehow in this life?"

"Absolutely. I know that I am brave and strong inside, no matter what people see on the outside. So I have no fear. Do you see?"

Norbert answered, "Honestly, Edith, I have to admit, I don't see. I don't understand any of this."

Edith asked, "You *do* know what reincarnation is, I assume?"

Norbert put both hands up to his glasses to adjust them. "Sort of. It's the belief that when you die, your soul is born again in the body of a baby somewhere?"

"That's as good an explanation as any," encouraged Edith.

"*If* you call that an explanation," sniped Carlotta.

"Well, of course, Carl Jung, Jack London, Henry Ford and many other great minds could explain it with more words," said Edith, easily scoring off Carlotta once again. "They were all proponents of reincarnation. But we'll go with Norbert's understanding of the process for now."

"But I *don't* understand it," protested Norbert. "Why wouldn't we remember if we'd had a previous life as another person? And what is the point of being reborn?"

Edith seemed glad that Norbert was asking questions. "We come back again and again, because we are here to learn, for the purpose of advancing our souls.

"As to why we don't remember," Edith went on, "a few lucky people, like myself, do remember. The Buddha remembered all his lives, including one as a goldfish, I think.

"Now, I myself remember lives both human and animal. For example, when I was a brown bear, I wasn't the vegetarian I am today, you know. Oh, no. I used to love to eat fish! Yes! I used to catch them with my claws in the icy river. How they wriggled when I bit their heads off!" Edith said this with a nostalgic sigh. "There are things you can enjoy as a brown bear that just wouldn't give you the same kick in your life as a human. This time around, I'd no more eat a fish than dig a den to hibernate in."

Carlotta smiled brightly for the first time today, as if entertained by the images this narrative created in her mind.

"Now, Norbert Z, you ask why people don't remember their past lives, and of course, you are right—most people don't. They might have had some memories as little children, but if these are not encouraged, the pictures fade away. However, when I was a little girl, I used to say to my mother, 'Remember when *I* was the mommy, and *you* were the little girl?' Most mothers would just laugh and think that was silly, and the memory would not be caught, you see. But *my* mother was very forward thinking and knew all about reincarnation, and so she asked me to tell her more. There I was, only four years old, and telling her about the lifetime when she was my daughter and I was her mother, and I always gave her candy and let her stay up late at night. My mother wrote all these memories down for me, and as I grew, we added to them. That's how I came to have so many.

"However, my situation was exceptional. Most people who want to know about their past lives need to be hypnotized as adults in order to retrieve those memories. And that's where you come in, Norbert Z. As a past-life regressionist, you just hypnotize people and help them go back to a buried memory of a previous life."

Norbert protested, "I couldn't possibly—"

"Norbert, we need your talent here. You can't refuse to at least consider my offer."

"And yet," put in Carlotta with her brilliant smile, "he has."

Margaret giggled supportively. They all knew how hard this was for Carlotta, to now be a captive audience of her old rival. Here she was, forced to take a tour of Edith's impressive institution of education—just the sort of "Center" that Carlotta herself would have loved to found and dominate.

Edith went on as if Carlotta had not spoken. "I'll teach you everything I know about past-life regression, Norbert, but you are the one who has the gift. And as for hypnotism, that is easily learned. There's nothing to it."

Norbert had a strange sensation of what a past-life regressionist might call *déjà vu*. Not too long ago, he had been urged into trying something he didn't believe in, with the words "there's nothing to it." That time, it had been Carlotta urging him to tell fortunes with cards.

"What gift are you talking about, Edith?" asked Norbert.

"You have the gift of clairvoyance. I saw that when you read my cards. That's your qualification, right there."

Norbert had given up arguing with people about his so-called "gift." He did not know what to make of Edith's ideas and her offer. Her enthusiasm was overpowering. He would need time alone to think about it.

"As a faculty member, you will be listed in our catalog with your photo and a bio. That catalog goes all over the country. Your fame will spread. You will also have access to our orchards and vegetable gardens for your personal use. You will have the privilege of taking any classes here for free. I like my faculty to be well-informed of all aspects of our work, and to cross-promote classes.

"As I said, I will provide you with training, books and all resources, and I will, of course, pay you for your time. Would ninety dollars per hour be in your fee range? Just for the training hours, of course. Once you begin working with our clients, I will pay you 50 percent of clients' registration fees for our services and courses. Fifty percent would work out to a professional fee of $110 for a private, past-life reading session for one person. And then, of course, for group regressions—those are two hours each—we would require five to seven people to make a group—I would pay you $1,000 to $1,400 per two-hour session."

There was a collective sharp intake of breath from the Club.

Norbert's reflexive smile straightened. He was shocked.

Edith amended quickly, "Of course, the percentages are somewhat negotiable, Norbert Z. I want you to be happy here."

Norbert wondered if he was at yet another turning point in his life—he, who just five months ago would have thought all his turning points were behind him. He was about to speak, but Edith stopped him.

"Just try the group past-life regression as a participant tonight, Norbert Z. Then take a little time to think about it, and you can let me know. No obligation!"

Norbert was dazzled and befuddled all at the same time, and he sensed a similar brew of sensations in the Club who stood behind him. On the one hand, the amounts of money Edith had mentioned were staggering. Could she be serious? Norbert was living simply and getting by; still, the thought that he could rebuild security for future years by earning such sums—well, he had no choice but to consider it, at least. His obstacle was that he didn't have the foggiest idea about reincarnation. But if he could learn about it, as he had learned about card reading, well, this would be something like taking a job promotion and getting a raise, wouldn't it?

CHAPTER TWENTY-NINE

Two of Hearts:

An adventure.
Open your mind.
Loosen up.
Prepare to have some fun.

Edith led the little band back into the mansion with the promise that they were "going to love the past-life regression class." It was in the One Hand Clapping Room.

A man who looked like an unhappy professional wrestler stepped into the doorway after Edith ran through. He stood with his legs spread, taking up as much space as possible. He extended his hand and grasped Norbert's. His grip hurt the fine bones in Norbert's hand.

"Stanley Oppenheimer," asserted the bald-headed, barefoot man, making severe eye contact with Norbert. "Astrologer," he added, in a tone that said, *Top that, if you can.*

Norbert, smarting, answered, "Norbert Zelenka."

He realized that this man was claiming the room as his own territory by blocking the entrance and forcing everyone to submit to his aggression as price of entry. Norbert wondered if he would go easier on the gentler sex.

"Ow!" wailed Margaret. "You hurt my hand!"

Stanley paused; apparently people did not usually call him on this maneuver of his. "I apologize," he managed, before stretching his pincer toward Carlotta.

"Let's just wave," said Carlotta, passing so close to him he was forced to step aside. Carlotta extended a protective arm in front of Birdie.

"My name is Carlotta Moon, this is my friend Birdie Walsh, and the woman you just injured is our dear friend Margaret Birch."

Stanley cracked his knuckles and apologized again.

Carlotta murmured with sympathy to Margaret, *"Oh, Marguerite, quelle dommage!"*

To which Margaret couldn't help whispering back, "Pass me the *frommage*," on cue. So, Norbert thought, she couldn't be *too* badly hurt.

Within the large, cool, darkened room, a woman walked around swirling a burning stick in counterclockwise circles.

"This is white sage," she sang out to them, trailing the smoke around the room.

She was a middle-aged woman wearing a white dress that looked oddly like a nightgown, and she twirled as she swirled. "I am Hermione Duckworth," she sang, looking steadily at Norbert.

"I'm sure you are," said Norbert, unnerved.

These were odd people, and it was odd for Norbert to think of others as being odd.

"Burning a white sage smudge stick," Hermione sang on, "is how we clear all negative vibrations from this space. I am cleaning, cleaning, *all* the negative vibrations. I allow only harmonious energies to remain."

Stanley supported her efforts. "Got to get the bad juju outta here before we begin our spiritual work today, you know?"

Norbert nodded, "Of course." He didn't know what bad juju was, but was confident he'd be better off without it.

"Stanley, stop playing the Lion at the Gate and come help us out here." Edith was organizing a circle of armchairs upholstered in red velvet, and was assisted by another woman. "Daphne Cook, meet Norbert Z and his guests," said Edith. "Daphne has had many interesting lives as well, haven't you, Daphne?"

Norbert observed a small, humorless-looking woman with her steel-gray hair cropped close to her head. She looked like a former nun.

Edith said, "You'd never guess this, but Daphne is a former nun. And so our spiritual journeys lead us far and wide!" Edith opened her arms to emphasize the width of Daphne's journey.

Daphne, unsmiling, looked from one member of the Club to the other, like a child being forced to meet new children at nursery school.

Birdie prompted, "You've had many interesting lives, Daphne?"

"Oh, yes," answered Daphne. "I was in Pompeii in 79 AD when the volcano erupted, sending lava and ash over the whole city, obliterating it in just a few moments."

Carlotta murmured, "Such unfortunate timing for you."

Daphne blinked.

Edith rang a little bell.

"Let us gather in our circle, all seekers." Edith waved toward the red chairs and set an example by sitting herself down and settling the brown-and-yellow layers of her clothing about her.

Norbert and the Club followed suit. Stanley cracked his knuckles a final time before sitting. He tilted his head toward Norbert, as if to a comrade, and quipped, "There's a seeker born every minute, eh, bud?"

Norbert felt an overwhelming dislike of Stanley.

Daphne, formerly of Pompeii, sat on the other side of Stanley, looking at her feet, which were clad in beige loafers. Hermione, holding her long dress between thumb and forefinger like a fairy-tale princess, glided to the center of the circle.

Edith introduced her: "Hermione is our visiting past-life regressionist. She has been here for two days, and her classes have had full enrollment each time. But, unfortunately, she will be going back to Arizona tomorrow. Hermione will be hypnotizing us and leading each of us to our own buried past-life memories. Let's all turn our attention to Hermione."

Hermione made contact with each expectant pair of eyes, turning herself in the circle. "Thank you, thank you, truth seekers, for bringing your energy here today. Let's just take a moment to *feel* our energy, shall we?" She put her hands together over her heart and closed her eyes. "It's *goooood* to be here!" Hermione breathed deeply to show everyone how to do it. "I am the author of many books on reincarnation, including my latest, *Who Do You Think You Were?*"

Hermione allowed a few moments for the title to register. She interpreted its meaning: "You see, even before you do a hypnotic past-life regression, something in you already knows about your past lives. Each life leaves an energy imprint on your soul. And science tells us that energy cannot be created nor destroyed. A trauma from a past life can still be affecting you in this life."

Hermione's movements were graceful and her voice was calming.

"For example, a year ago, a woman I worked with remembered a life as a prisoner." Hermione's voice dropped, allowing her audience to imagine the awfulness of the memory. "She said she related to this because she felt like a prisoner in this life, as if something was preventing her from making free choices and moving forward. After she understood where this emotional block was coming from—from her awful life as a prisoner—she was free to shed the impression that she was not free." Hermione raised her arms as she spoke, illustrating the concept of freedom. "She was able to choose goals and act on them. My friends, it *changed her life!*

"In my writing, over and over, I say: 'Recall it and resolve it.'

"So today, we're going to use hypnosis to bypass all the conscious, left-brain, critical judgments. Through hypnosis and imagination you will reach a memory of a past life. Do you have any questions before we begin?"

Hermione smiled encouragement.

Norbert was observing Hermione's performance, and trying to imagine himself in such a role. It seemed beyond his reach, for he still considered himself a practical person in spite of the fact that if he were filling out a form he would now have to list his profession as "fortune-teller." He tried to see himself standing before a group of people instructing and hypnotizing them. It seemed impossible. But then, so did reading cards, before he began to do it. Before him lay another twist in his path, and if he took this way, once again, his life would never be the same.

Birdie raised her hand. "What *is* hypnosis, exactly?"

"What a wonderful question!" beamed Hermione. "Hypnosis is nothing more than focused attention! You are in and out of hypnotic trances all the time, without even realizing it. When you're driving and listening to the radio, and then you arrive at your destination and don't remember the trip—you've been in hypnosis. It's simply the very natural state of focused attention. Next?"

"I hope you won't have us quacking like ducks?" asked Margaret, laughing lightly and looking around at the group for approval of her witticism.

"No, not at all! That's stage hypnosis. No quacking, and no barking, either. Well, not unless you were a duck or a dog in your past life." She smiled reassuringly. "Other questions?"

"What if we don't 'go under'?" asked Carlotta. "I'm sure *I'm* not hypnotizable." Norbert thought that Carlotta had no intention of submitting to this exercise.

"Well, then, you'll miss the experience, won't you?" said Hermione, untroubled.

Carlotta looked irritated.

Birdie asked, "And we will remember everything when we wake up?"

"Yes, you will," answered Hermione. "The whole point is to retrieve memories. And you'll find, besides, that hypnosis is a very pleasant and relaxing state. You will enjoy it. With that said, is everyone ready to begin?"

Norbert was certainly ready to have a pleasant and relaxing experience. Touring this place, receiving the strange job offer from Edith, meeting these odd people, and being aware of the Club following behind and what they might be thinking of it all, had worn him out. The thought that he would soon have to make a decision that might once again change the direction of his life was overwhelming him with the desire to escape into sleep. He was very, very tired.

"And so we begin," said Hermione, and her voice became very sweet and fluid. She spoke on and on, in a calming rhythm. "Make yourself as comfortable as possible in your comfy chairs. That's right. Close your eyes, if you will, please, and just be sure you have nothing crossed—no crossed arms or crossed legs, because that crosses your meridians."

Norbert couldn't guess what meridians might be, but he was too tired to ask. Closing his eyes felt fine.

"Plant your feet flat on the floor, grounding yourself with the earth. And now, just begin to take some nice deep cleansing breaths, in through the nose, and out through the nose, just really bringing your attention to your breath…just noticing. Nice, deep breaths… Notice how the air feels going *in* through your nostrils, and how it feels going *out*… *And…follow…the sound…of my…voice*. Now, throughout this exercise, you may find your mind wanders from my voice at times. That's okay. Just gently bring your attention back to the sound of my voice."

The room was perfectly still, except for the sound of breathing all around the circle. Even Ivy, in her carrier, was snoring ever so softly, so that only Norbert could hear.

"There may be sounds around us, and you may not even hear them…or if you do, they will serve only to send you deeper into relaxation."

"Let's begin now by relaxing each and every part of the body. Bring your attention to your feet. Relax your toes and your feet, and let them just…*melt*. Now bring your attention to your ankle joints, let them relax and…*melt*." Hermione continued directing the group to relax and melt every body part, bit by bit, all the way up to the scalp. Norbert felt very happy.

"And now," said Hermione, her vowels becoming longer and her voice even more soothing, "the body is totally relaxed. Let's go now to the mind, where we will begin to gently and peacefully go down through the levels of consciousness until we reach the unconscious, and it will be *so* pleasant and relaxing to do this.

"See yourself going down a long flight of stairs. Down, down, down. When you finally get to the bottom, you will be in a former life, with all the sights, sounds and smells of that time surrounding you once again. Keep going down the stairs, deeper and deeper, deeper on down, down, down and down. As you reach the bottom step, look around. I will count from three to one, and when I get to one, you will be in your former life. Three…two…*one*."

Hermione paused here for what seemed to Norbert like a long time.

"Walk along. Notice—what are you wearing on your feet and body? Describe to yourself—where you are…what you are doing…what are your thoughts and your feelings."

If Hermione said any more, Norbert did not hear her.

CHAPTER THIRTY

Four of Diamonds:

Be open-minded,
and allow yourself to explore new ideas. Why not?

He was walking along in a vivid world. He was in a forest, much like the forest they had driven through to come to the Center for Deeper Understanding. He walked until he saw someone.

The person Norbert beheld in his trance was a sleeping man who looked very much like Norbert—or how Norbert would look if he allowed himself to grow a beard. The sleeper was propped against a tree, and his beard was long and flowing—flowing the length of the man's body and on past his boots. Such an odd, long beard. It didn't seem a very interesting life; for as long as Norbert observed him, the man just kept on sleeping.

As Hermione's voice directed him to get ready "to return to the here and now," the name "Rip Van Winkle" came to Norbert. "Ridiculous!" he thought, drowsily.

Everyone in the group was blinking and looking around at everyone else. Some were stretching and yawning.

Norbert wondered what the others had experienced. Certainly he had done the hypnosis wrong. He couldn't have been a fictional character in his previous life.

Edith was handing around a big bowl of "homegrown, organic apples! So crunchy and juicy!"

"Before we take a break, let's debrief on our experiences, while they are still fresh!" Hermione turned about the circle, looking for a volunteer.

Carlotta was looking refreshed and pleased. She grabbed the biggest, reddest apple from the bowl before passing it on. Norbert thought, *So she didn't "miss the experience." No, she never would. And she's happy about who she was.*

Carlotta began to raise her hand, but Hermione saw Margaret's hand first.

Hermione said, "Yes? What was that like for you?"

"I saw myself as a man, a soldier dying on a battlefield, and I knew I was in France. And my full name came to me!" Margaret stopped for full dramatic effect. "Joyce Kilmer!"

Birdie drew in her breath. "Margaret! *I think that I shall never see a poem lovely as a tree.* Joyce Kilmer is the poet whose name you were trying to think of in the car!"

Hermione said, "That is exceedingly rare, to remember one's name. Very often we get a scene of some sort, but to have a name! Well, that's lucky, isn't it?"

Margaret was glowing, like a child who has done well.

Norbert saw Carlotta ready to take her down a peg or two.

"Yes?" asked Hermione in Carlotta's direction.

"I remembered my name, as well! I saw myself writing, writing, and I was wearing eighteenth-century feminine clothing. At last I saw the title of the book I was working on. The title was—" Carlotta could stop for dramatic effect as well as anybody "—*Pride and Prejudice.*"

As Carlotta prepared for this impression to sink in around the group, Daphne spoke up. "You must be mistaken."

All eyes turned to Daphne, the former nun.

Daphne said, "We can't *both* have been Jane Austen, can we?"

Carlotta's satisfied smile faded. "Are you saying that you think *you* were Jane Austen?"

"I'm saying that I *was* Jane Austen. I clearly remembered, just now, a long chat with Cassandra."

Carlotta tossed her head. "Cassandra *who?*"

It did not take a Jane Austen fan to sense that Carlotta had just made a fatal mistake.

Daphne crowed, "Cassandra Who! Cassandra was only Jane Austen's—I mean *my*—sister and lifelong confidante!"

"Friends, friends!" interjected Hermione soothingly. "There is no need to argue! Clearly, you both remember being Jane Austen. Clearly, you were both Jane Austen."

Both Jane Austens looked nastily at one another.

"Let me explain the concept of soul groups. This is important knowledge for all of us. Between lives, you see, our souls return to something like a big pool, or a big soup, you could say. When it's time to reincarnate into an entity on the earth plane, a scoop is taken out of that pool. That scoop may contain essences of more than one soul. It all gets mixed up together, you see. We are all one, you know. So what we have here is two sister souls—what are your names, please?"

Daphne said, "Daphne," and tilted her head, as if ready to wrap her mind around the concept that Hermione was offering.

Carlotta said, "Carlotta," and folded her arms, as if to say she knew this was all silly to begin with.

"Yes, Carlotta and Daphne. Two sister souls who inhabited the same body once as Jane Austen, and then got ladled back into the soup, to come back again as two separate individuals, to meet here, today, at this hour! Now, isn't *that* synchronicity?" Hermione could not have looked happier.

Norbert felt a pang of compassion for Carlotta. This whole day had taken her off her own turf and onto her rival's. Instead of enjoying her carefully tended certainty of her own superiority, she had been feeling sharply inferior to Edith. The past life as Jane Austen was her one chance to show her own exceptional status. And now she was being asked to share it. It was all just too much for poor Carlotta. Norbert gave her a smile of encouragement, but she frowned irritably in return.

Hermione called on "the lady with the lovely red hair."

Norbert had been wondering what Birdie was making of all of this. Did reincarnation conflict with a belief in spirits lingering around Earth, or did the two beliefs work together, he wondered.

Birdie, swallowing a bite of her apple, said, "I'm not sure if I was really hypnotized, but I was very relaxed."

Hermione was reassuring. "Relaxation is all it is. Nothing more."

Birdie continued, "Well, whether it was a dream or a memory of a past life, I don't know—"

Hermione again encouraged, "Yes, these memories will tend to feel like dreams—or as if you are just making it all up. Go on."

"It seems I was a famous painter."

Carlotta, as if she had been holding herself back for as long as she could, burst out, "It really does strain credulity, doesn't it? So many world-famous people here today?"

Hermione agreed. "It *is* unusual. People typically remember very quiet lives, in deserts and on farms, in villages or on islands. But we do not doubt the unconscious. If you remember it, then it is so."

Carlotta tapped her foot.

"Which famous painter in particular, Birdie?" asked Norbert.

"One of my favorites. Frida Kahlo." Birdie explained to the nonartists in the group, "She was a Mexican painter of the early twentieth century who used surrealism and vivid colors."

Margaret enthused, "That makes sense! That's why you love painting in *this* life!"

Carlotta said, "Oh, for Pete's sake. Wait just a minute, please. What year were you born in, Birdie?"

"1943."

"When did Frida Kahlo die?"

Birdie didn't know. No one knew.

Carlotta pulled out her iPhone. "Google will know!" she proclaimed.

"'Frida Kahlo,'" read Carlotta. "'Died 1954.'"

Carlotta turned to Hermione. "Explain that one, if you can. Birdie was eleven years old when Frida Kahlo died. They were both living at the same time. So how can Birdie be her reincarnation?"

"There is no problem here," answered Hermione, serene. "There is a concept called 'parallel lives.' Imagine, if you will, the soul as a beam of light that can be split in two directions. Those two directions can represent the two different bodies that are animated by the same soul. So, yes, strange to say, there can be two or more people living at the same time, who share the same soul."

Norbert and the Club looked at one another.

Hermione smiled and stated, "It's a *miracle-fact*."

Carlotta's eyes opened wide at this inventive use of language. Edith said, "I'll share my memory! I was living on a planet with a beautiful green light. I had fingers with suction cups at the ends of them. It was a happy life!" She folded her hands over her belly in satisfaction.

"Yes, some of our lives were on other planets. Lovely, Edith! Stanley?" prompted Hermione. "Would you like to share?"

"I was an astrologer in ancient Rome," he said. He tossed his apple from one hand to the other, back and forth.

"And you're an astrologer *now!*" exclaimed Margaret, apparently forgiving and forgetting how he had crushed her hand an hour before.

Stanley nodded. "Yeah."

Norbert perceived that Stanley was a cynic. He also saw that Stanley wished to gain control of Edith and the Center for Deeper Understanding. Hermione, on the other hand, was a sincere person, who believed her own spiritual message. Edith, also, was genuine; Norbert could see that. But Stanley was a con man.

"Yes!" beamed Hermione. "Very often we carry the same profession with us from one life to another." She was having a good time. She had the air of a woman doing what she was meant to do in life. Nodding toward Norbert, she asked, "Norbert? You're the last one. Would you like to tell us what you saw of *your* past life?"

Norbert cleared his throat. Feeling silly, he shared his past-life regression experience with the group.

After everyone stopped laughing, Norbert realized they had all been laughing in different ways. Norbert himself, in embarrassment; Hermione, in delight; Carlotta, in scorn; Birdie and Margaret, in amusement; Stanley, in relief from boredom; and Daphne, because everyone else was laughing.

Edith was untroubled. Full of good humor, she sank her teeth into an apple and turned it round and round as she gnawed it, considering Norbert's experience.

"So you were Rip Van Winkle!" she said in a congratulatory tone.

"But, Edith, Rip Van Winkle is a fictional character!" said Norbert, wondering if Edith knew that.

"Norbert Z, you should know that this whole world is an illusion anyway. So you were a fictional character. What does it matter? Don't you know—there is a lot of truth in fiction."

Carlotta and her Club were strolling down the lantern-lit stone path away from the Center for Deeper Understanding toward Carlotta's car. The stars overhead were bright, and the group stopped every few feet to admire the night sky, and argue about which planets were in view.

As Norbert prepared to follow the trio, Edith took him aside on the doorstep and whispered, "It will do such good for Daphne's self-esteem, to know that she used to be Jane Austen. It will give her something to talk about at parties." She smiled and sighed. She went on, "Here's the thing—everyone wants to feel special, Norbert Z, and don't you think that's very touching?"

"I do, Edith," said Norbert. And he did. "And I do see how people might be helped by this work you do. Maybe, in the end, it's all about what helps people to cope with life and be happy." Norbert looked toward his friends who were walking slowly to the parking lot. "Thank you, really, for showing me around and giving me this experience. And thank you for inviting Carlotta and her Club, too. That was very kind."

"It wasn't kind, Norbert Z, and you know it. Don't pretend with me. You see everything. I wasn't being kind to Carlotta. I wanted her to stick it in her ear. She didn't want me in her Club forty years ago, so I went and built a whole Center which has become nationally famous, and she's not in it. Ah, my friend, maybe I'm not as aligned with my Higher

Self as I thought." She looked pensively after the retreating figures of the Club.

Norbert paused at this confession. Yes, Edith had, in fact, wanted Carlotta to stick it in her ear.

"Be that as it may, Edith, I appreciate your offer to come and work with you, but I don't need time to think about it. I won't be the past-life regressionist you're looking for. This isn't my...uh...well, it isn't my spiritual path, I guess we could say."

"I respect that, Norbert Z." Edith tapped Norbert's shoulder in a gesture of esteem. "You are an honest man."

Norbert hesitated.

"Edith, there's something I need to tell you about Stanley. I'm not sure you are aware—"

There was a glint of understanding in Edith's bright eyes.

"Is it about his obsession with getting control over me and the Center for Deeper Understanding? Ah, yes!" She laughed. "I *saw* you connecting the dots, Norbert Z. Yes, Stanley thinks he will one day direct me the way Carlotta thinks she will one day direct you! Ha! And isn't *that* great fun? That's why I keep Stanley around. He's not much of an astrologer, really. He's a big blustery fake. But he does make me laugh."

Norbert considered this with some relief. He said goodnight and turned to go.

Before closing the door, Edith twinkled her eyes at him and said, "I like you, Norbert Z. You're the genuine article."

In the car on the way back to town, the conversation was spirited.

"Reincarnation!" fumed Carlotta, disappointed that she couldn't believe herself to be the re-embodiment of her favorite author. "Of all the silly ideas!"

"Not so silly," protested Margaret. "It's a spiritual belief, isn't it? You can't call it silly, then, if it's someone's spiritual belief."

Carlotta philosophized, "Oh, for that matter, any religious doctrine, once explained, is revealed to be absurd. That's how you know it's a religious doctrine." She laughed. "People trying to make meaning of things. It's all absurd."

Margaret added, "It's people's faith that makes the absurdity go away. We all need to have faith in something, don't we?"

Birdie said, dreamily, "People *do* need to believe in something. Even if what they believe in is the hopelessness of belief."

The Club and Norbert thought about this for a moment.

Birdie added, "What did the French philosopher say? 'The heart has its reasons of which reason knows nothing.'"

"All right, that's enough of not being reasonable for one night," said Carlotta, irritably.

Birdie said, "May I see that catalog, though? I'm curious."

Birdie read aloud from the course catalog of the Center for Deeper Understanding. While Carlotta mocked, Margaret and Birdie exclaimed. Finally, Margaret's interest was piqued by a class that reminded her of their enthusiasms in the '60s, when astrology was rediscovered by the masses. This was a course that would not conflict with their classes at the Art League: "Astrology: Beyond the Basics," on Thursday nights.

"Oh, what nonsense!" exclaimed Carlotta.

Margaret said, "Why are you always the one who gets to say if something is nonsense? Can't there be different opinions?"

Before Carlotta could recover from this rebellion, her other friend joined in.

"Why should it be nonsense?" Birdie challenged. "We always found a lot of truth in it, as I recall."

Norbert felt protective of Carlotta. She had already suffered enough. He came to her rescue.

"Oh, but aren't you forgetting that the Fine Arts Film Society shows its movies on Thursday nights? Just the other day, in the watercolor class, you were all so excited about seeing those foreign films and participating in the discussions afterward. Looks like if you take the astrology, you'll be missing out on all those intellectual meetings."

By the time Margaret and Birdie were dropped at their respective doors, they had reconsidered, and they were convinced that as interesting as astrology was, it would be even more fun to see the foreign films with Carlotta instead.

CHAPTER THIRTY-ONE

Five of Spades:

A crisis. Seek help.

Summer forced herself out of her lair and into her car. She didn't like walking in town, but she didn't like driving, either.

Sometimes, driving home from work, a horrifying thought would strike her: What if she had run someone over? How could she be sure she *hadn't* run someone over? She had been listening to the radio. Her mind had wandered. Should she retrace her path, and see if there was a body on the road? Or no, it would make more sense to park her car, and check for fabric or blood on the front bumper, wouldn't it? Or was she crazy to be thinking such thoughts? That she could have killed someone without knowing she had done it.

The inside of her head echoed like a can. She wanted to shake the thoughts out of her head. She was sick to death of her own thoughts.

The impression that she might have run someone over was

horrible, but at least it made her feel something. She longed now to feel something—anything. Any feeling would be better than this numbness.

She got in her car and drove out to Route 4, just outside of town, and began to cruise through the countryside. It was beautiful, she knew. Her eyes saw the winding roads, gentle hills and fall colors, but her heart felt nothing at all. *Feel something. Feel something.* Her foot pressed the accelerator by small, barely noticeable increments, but always downward, downward. *Feel something. Even fear.*

She was flying over the speed bumps.

Wake up! Wake up!

She went sixty, seventy, eighty, ninety miles per hour. Something kept her foot from pushing even farther. What was it? Anxiety? Fear? Yes, she was feeling something.

The green countryside was blurring into a streak. She told herself to close her eyes and keep pushing, but her eyes and her foot did not obey. Far up ahead, she saw a coyote loping along the road. What if she hit it? She couldn't hit it. In terror, she brought her foot to the brake and coasted to a gradual stop. She pulled onto the shoulder. She put her hands to her face and felt tears that she did not even know she had been crying. She was still alive.

But she could have killed someone. Again.

CHAPTER THIRTY-TWO

Three of Hearts:

You are challenged to defend yourself.

Norbert at last had the reckoning Carlotta had predicted for him over that eggplant lunch at her house. It was destined to happen sooner or later.

It happened just when Norbert had begun to feel a sense of exhilaration in his readings. It came just when he had been thinking that what had begun as an emergency solution to Ivy's veterinary bill had now become a path of life purpose that he could never abandon. That is when his suppressed but lurking fear jumped out at him.

He was a man about forty years old, and his black hair was slicked back with some kind of oil, it seemed. He said his name was Mark. He handed over his twenty dollars and shuffled the cards, as all querents before him had done. When Norbert received the seventh card from him and took back the deck, Mark sat back and folded his arms.

"Maybe you could help me with a decision. I have to decide between a job in Philadelphia and another one in Chicago. Which one should I take? My wife says Chicago."

Norbert studied the cards for a few seconds in silence. He didn't see a fork-in-the-road decision there. There was no card indicating a move or a job offer, either. He would begin with what he did see.

"This Jack of Hearts is you, I feel, a fun-loving person. The Queen of Hearts is a kind woman who is always at your side…your wife? I see you making a big purchase, something for enjoyment, and I feel it will be something like…a boat?"

The picture of a boat came clearly into Norbert's mind. Pictures had been coming into his mind during readings, and he always shared those with the querents. Usually, these impressions turned out to be meaningful to them, to Norbert's unending surprise.

"Now here is the deception card. Someone is lying."

"What do you mean?" demanded the oily-haired man, leaning in. "Who is lying?"

"Well, let's see." Norbert felt blocked. This had never happened in any reading yet. He thought aloud, "Someone is lying to someone, for sure."

"Oh, for sure," agreed the man. He nodded. "No doubt. Someone, somewhere in the universe, is lying to someone. *That's* useful."

Norbert looked up at the oily-haired man. Norbert opened his mouth and closed it again.

"How do you *do* it, *Norbert Z*?"

As Mark raised his voice, a hush fell over the café. Norbert felt the eyes of customers who were putting aside their phones and tablets, and resting their forks on their plates.

"You fraud," sneered the man. "Yeah, someone is lying to someone, all right. Every day, right here." The man's laugh was more like a spitting sound. "How do you types sleep at night? What bullshit!"

Hope came around from behind the counter, wiping her hands on her white apron.

"May I help you?" she asked.

"You may help me understand why you have this *bullshitter* in here collecting money fraudulently," exclaimed the man.

Hope said in a near whisper, "Give him his money back, Norbert."

Norbert, snapping out of his state of shock, pushed the twenty dollars across the table toward the oily-haired man.

"Damn right. Give the money back to *everyone* you've cheated, *Norbert Z.*" He was shouting now. "I might buy a boat, huh? In a town on a huge friggin' lake? No way! You *are* amazing!" His laughter was harsh and attacking. "You can't bullshit a bullshitter, Norbert Z. Didn't you know that?"

"I'm sorry, but I'll have to ask you to leave now, sir," said Hope.

"You're not half as sorry as you will be when you hear from the Better Business Bureau." He stood. *"A kind woman who is always at my side!* You're so full of shit! I don't have any woman at all at my side—kind or otherwise!"

"How is that possible?" Hope murmured, as she accompanied Oily Hair to the door.

The customers, who had been watching the entertainment with a mixture of discomfort and pleasure, looked away from Norbert and Hope, and went back to busying themselves on their phones and tablets.

Norbert was focusing his eyes on the natural design of whorls in the wood on the table. He was flushed and flooded with shame. Something within him condemned him. The oily-haired man was right. While he sat here, day after day, feeling exhilarated with the sense that he was important in people's lives, the naked truth was that he was nothing more than a—just as the man had said—bullshitter. He was bullshitting all day, just making things up to everyone, and telling himself grandiose lies while he did it. The humiliation was crushing.

Hope came back to his booth. He could not even look at her.

"Hey," she said. "Don't worry about it. Every once in a while you get a loony. What can you do, you know? Have a slice of lemon cake. On the house."

That night, Norbert did not sleep well. He lay awake in his little white bedroom, mentally replaying the oily-haired man's accusations. That man had said all of Norbert's customers should be refunded their money, that Norbert was essentially a crook, a liar, a scammer. He didn't feel like a scammer. With most of his customers, he felt like an appreciated adviser. But was he only fooling himself? He felt anxious and frightened, like a child about to be discovered doing something wrong. Perhaps this disagreeable man was his warning to stop telling fortunes, before it would be too late.

Carlotta and the Club were having tea at the Good Fortune Café one early November afternoon. Their booth was near the door, and they received little blasts of cold air every time it opened. They could see Norbert at his booth, in the depths of the café.

Margaret was watching in undisguised fascination as a customer approached Norbert and sat down. She was dipping her chamomile tea bag up and down in her mug as she gazed in rapt attention.

Carlotta distracted her: *"Marguerite, tu ne trouves pas que le thé à la camomille c'est*—how do you say—*trop soporifique?"*

"What are you saying, Carlotta? You know I don't understand French."

"*Soporifique*—it just means 'soporific' in English. I'm asking if chamomile tea has a soporific effect on you."

"Oh, no, not at all. It just makes me a little sleepy."

Carlotta arched her eyebrows. Poor Margaret never could keep up.

"*Regarde notre protégé, Carlotte,*" said Birdie, protective of Margaret. "Norbert looks like he's been reading fortunes all his life, doesn't he?"

"*Mais oui, c'est vrai!*" answered Carlotta. "We taught him well!" Carlotta was softening ever so slightly in her attitude toward Norbert. He was still working at the trade she and her Club had taught him. So Edith could just put *that* in her ear.

"And Edith," observed Carlotta aloud, with satisfaction, "in spite of the money she offered him, didn't manage to pull him into *her* racket. So we see—not everyone can be bought." She enjoyed the sense of winning a victory over the Aztec warrior.

Birdie said, "But that was such a fun experience at Edith's Center, wasn't it?"

"Oh, *Edith.*" Carlotta waved a smooth, dismissive hand. "*C'est la folle du village.* She is— Oh! How do you say it in English? I'm so immersed in French, I'm actually forgetting English! Oh, now I remember—the village crazy lady."

"Really?" asked Margaret, with an edge of challenge in her voice. "You're forgetting your native tongue, Carlotta, which you've been speaking for eighty years. Really?"

How tiresome. Now Carlotta would have to spout a stream of French to prove to her friends that she was not a liar. She searched her teeming mind for some bit of memorized French.

"*Oui, vraiment, Marguerite. Des fois, pour trouver le mot juste—*"

Suddenly, a shadow loomed over the table, and Carlotta, Birdie and Margaret all looked up at once.

It was a tall woman with a sharp nose, her dark hair sticking down straight under her hat, brandishing a paperback book displaying the title: *Guide Touristique de New York*. With startling speed, the woman launched into a French monologue:

"*Bonjour. Pardonnez-moi, mesdames. Je vous ai écouté parler français, et je me suis demandée si vous voudriez bien me donner des conseils. Je suis ici en visite du Québec, vous voyez, et comme ce n'est pas vraiment la saison touristique, je voudrais savoir...*"

The little group listened to the Quebecois tourist going on in French. Of the Club, only Carlotta had the vaguest idea what the woman was saying, and in Carlotta's case, it truly was the vaguest idea.

What she could gather was this. It seemed the dreadful woman had overheard Carlotta speaking French—in a private conversation that was meant for her friends only, and that was not meant to be spied on by francophone tourists. This exceedingly tall Canadian traveler, not content with a perfectly good guide book on New York State, written in her own language, had felt it necessary to publicly inflict herself upon Carlotta to demand advice on what a traveler to Gibbons Corner might do in the off-season. The ghastly giant thought it always best to ask natives about the attractions of their own land. Carlotta's excellent French accent and impressive French grammar had led her to believe that Carlotta would not mind the intrusion so very much. Actually, Carlotta was not sure if the tourist had said admiring things about her accent and grammar, but she might have said something that sounded like it. It was impossible to understand the woman.

As the inscrutable speech went on, Margaret smiled annoyingly at Carlotta. Birdie smiled at Carlotta also, but with faith, and played with her rings. (*She had so many! She looked so kitsch.*) Birdie had never voiced a doubt about Carlotta's French, touchingly convinced that Carlotta spoke the language better than any Parisian.

Carlotta tried to call to mind French phrases to have on hand when the beastly woman would stop talking (if she ever would). All that came to her were English phrases. Phrases such as "chickens coming home to roost," and "day of reckoning," and "pride goeth before a fall."

Watching Carlotta struggle and sink, Margaret, who was never given credit for her intelligence, seemed to grasp the situation perfectly well. She came to Carlotta's rescue, tearing out a page of her sketchbook. And although Marie-Claire (as the Canadian was called) spoke no English and Margaret spoke no French, the two communicated by drawing and gestures, and they understood each other like fast friends. Smiling, Marie-Claire went on her way with an artistic map of nearby Edwards Cove drawn by Margaret.

Carlotta, looking on, thought that Margaret was just as beautiful now as she ever was in her long-ago youth.

No one would ever, at any time in the future, refer to Carlotta's French humiliation, least of all Margaret.

A couple of weeks into November, Norbert checked in with Hope about the oily-haired man's threat to report the Good Fortune Café to the Better Business Bureau.

Hope laughed. "Don't tell me you've been worried about that, Norbert!" She was looking ever younger, lighter and more radiant in the last few months.

"I wouldn't want you to be closed down because of me," said Norbert.

"Ha! That'll be the day. No worries there! I'm all paid up with the Better Business Bureau—that's the main thing. And there is nothing shady or illegal going on here."

"There isn't?" asked Norbert. Sometimes he had his doubts.

"Of course not. People come in to have their cards read, and you help them intuit their own solutions. It's harmless. That guy was just looking to give someone a hard time, and it was your lucky day, that's all."

Hope laughed, suddenly remembering something. "I guess I never told you this. It's been so busy around here lately. But I did see that guy—and guess where he was!"

Norbert couldn't guess.

"On a boat. You said he'd buy a boat? He was on a jet boat—with a lady. They looked like they were 'together.' So, I think your prediction was right. About the boat and the woman in his life."

"Well, if so, I hope he's happy now." And Norbert meant it. He paused, troubled. "Sometimes I still hear him, calling me a—" Norbert looked around and lowered his voice "—a *bullshitter*. No one has ever called me that in my life. I don't think I'll ever forget it. It made me doubt myself. *Am* I just making it all up? I wonder. And I do worry, at times, that I might steer someone wrong, or that a querent might base a decision on what I said, or what they think I said, and then some kind of tragedy would be my fault. I've been waking up in the middle of the night, as if a siren has gone off, feeling this panic that I'm about to cause something truly awful to happen to someone. That's when I think, I should stop the fortunes, stop while I still have the chance to avoid doing something bad."

"Norbert, no." Hope patted Norbert's arm and winked at Ivy, who peeped at her from the comfort of the man purse. "You do nothing but good. You were the one who made me see the truth about Rudy—"

"Hope, I've told you before—you remember it wrong. You already knew the truth about Rudy. I had no idea about any of it."

"The point is, it was only when I was sitting across from you and my cards that it all became clear to me. I knew what I had to do to unblock my life. Before your reading, I was blind to everything that was wrong."

Norbert only shook his head.

"It's true. I thought I was in love, and I was miserable. After I talked with you, I dumped that sucker's ass, and look at me now!"

Norbert did look at her. He saw a happy, energetic, confident woman. It was a dramatic change. But, he was sure, none of that was his doing.

"And what about my heart? You warned me I should get it checked out."

"That was just because of a *Reader's Digest* article I read about bluish fingernails."

"Does it matter? The point is, there was a problem I didn't know about, and you kind of saved my life, I think."

Norbert said, "I do get letters and emails from people thanking me, and I'm glad they are happier than they were. But at the same time, I still have this nagging feeling that fortune-telling is just not on the up-and-up."

"Oh, the up-and-up, eh? Let me tell you what kind of fortune-telling is not on the up-and-up. So listen to this—my friend goes to a fortune-teller in Buffalo who tells her that the reason so many bad things are happening in her life is that she's been cursed by her husband's ex-wife."

Norbert started.

"Yes! Cursed! Can you imagine?"

Norbert could not.

"It gets worse. This fortune-teller, it just so happens, is able to *remove* the curse. But only if my friend gives her one thousand dollars in cash. Which she does."

"Oh, no!"

"Oh, yes! One thousand dollars to light special candles. But my friend doesn't feel any better about all the bad stuff that's happened."

"Of course not," said Norbert, aghast.

"So the fortune-teller says, this must be a very powerful curse. This woman must hate you a lot. This curse will keep doing you harm until it is completely removed. I will need three thousand dollars to light candles that are even more special."

Norbert shook his head.

"So my friend keeps giving her money, and the fortune-teller keeps texting her they're almost done, it's going to require just a little more money. And then do you know what happens?"

"What?" asked Norbert, hoping for the best.

"The fortune-teller vanishes. Disposable cell phone untraceable. Storefront empty. No one in the vicinity knows anything. My friend—who, by the way, is smart—is out thirty-three thousand dollars. All the money she'd been putting by for her retirement! That crook took the last of it and disappeared. The police don't even want to touch the case."

"But that's awful!" said Norbert.

"Right. So if you wanna talk about shady, or not on the up-and-up, there you go. But you, Norbert, you charge very little and you really help people. Honestly, you are like a light in this place. Every time I look over and see you there at your booth, consulting with a 'querent,' as you say, I feel safer. You remind me of my dad, God rest his soul. He was kind and honest, too."

Norbert was deeply touched. *Is that what I am? Kind and honest?*

"Please stay, Norbert. Never think about stopping the fortunes. I want you to stay, and not just because you are good for business. You are good for me."

Norbert was deeply touched. Hope saw him as a light in her café. She bore witness to the truth—that he was helping people every day. He was doing good in his little corner of the world. She wanted him to continue telling fortunes.

Of course, he would.

CHAPTER THIRTY-THREE

Three of Hearts and
Ace of Spades:

Your own recklessness throws you into danger.
You will need to be heroic if you are to avoid
the consequences. Try to learn from this.

It was the last Saturday in November, and Summer was walking Gramma's black miniature poodle, Toutou, by the lake as was their routine.

Toutou was a sprightly little dog, weighing only sixteen pounds. Gramma kept her immaculately groomed, and "in diamonds," so to speak, as her collar and leash were decorated with a bit of bling—tastefully done, of course.

Like Gramma, Toutou adored Summer. Summer wondered why. Acquainted with her own shortcomings as she was, Summer didn't find much in herself to adore.

Well, perhaps Toutou loved Summer because she, against Gramma's orders, would always let the dog off lead when they got to the beach. Gramma insisted that any dog, given enough temptation or fright, will bolt, and it simply was not worth the risk to unhook that leash. Summer, with the recklessness of her youth, felt—and did—otherwise.

She considered that Toutou, despite her frilly name and ridiculous haircut, was still basically a descendant of the noble wolf, and yearned with all her being to run free. Summer herself felt happier watching the little dog run and be her true self, racing the wind and at one with nature. Toutou loved to meet other dogs and wander where she willed. So when they hit the sand, Toutou would stand still while Summer unclipped her. Away the little bundle of black curls would frolic, ears blown back in the breeze, mouth open in what surely was a wide smile.

Summer, the wind whipping her face and making a loud ruffling sound in her ears, ran along after Toutou, and Toutou, good sport that she was, continually looped back for Summer.

As she ran, Summer thought back to the therapist her grandmother had taken her to when she was fifteen.

That poor therapist—what was her name? Summer didn't remember. But she tried every trick in her book to get Summer to open up. Conversation cards, art therapy, letting the silence hang in the air. Summer would have felt sorry for the woman, if she could have felt something.

"This is a handout on the stages of grief," the therapist had said.

Summer had taken it and laid it next to her on the sofa without looking at it.

Words came from the therapist toward Summer, but she did not hear them all. "Not your fault" was one phrase that did emerge from that orange lipsticked mouth, to bounce around the room. "Not your fault." The phrase echoed in the air like inscrutable words in a foreign language that Summer did not know.

"Guilt is a part of grief," tried the therapist.

Summer had thought, *Does she know about my guilt? Does she know what I've done?*

Summer had turned off the voice of the woman and watched her mouth move.

She never went back.

From the corner of her eye, Summer saw a dark streak, dashing down the beach.

As if an alarm bell had suddenly begun to clang in Summer's head, she sensed danger.

Where was Toutou?

Suddenly, as if in a slow-motion movie sequence, Summer turned and threw herself on top of Toutou, who had just looped joyfully behind her feet. Summer hit the sand, landing in a protective shell around the little dog. She left no light between the sand and her body, with her knees drawn as close as possible to her shoulders and her head facedown. There had been no thought on Summer's part, just the sudden impulse to protect Toutou from harm.

"Thunder! Thunder! Heel! Come back! Come! Come! Thunder!"

The large shepherd mix was upon them, circling Summer's turtle-shell form and snarling. Summer could hear the big dog moving around her, snuffling and growling, and she felt him try to push his muzzle under her armpit. He began to dig with energy into the sand around Summer's waist. She had been prepared for the big dog to sink his teeth into her back, side or scalp, but now it was clear he was not interested in her, but only in the little dog sheltered under her heart. She knew that if he could get to Toutou, he would murder her. There was nothing she could do but stay firmly rooted into the sand. Toutou lay meekly between Summer's chest and the ground, waiting.

An eternity later, the voice shouting useless commands approached, out of breath. "I'm sorry, I'm sorry, oh, I'm so sorry!"

When Summer heard the click of the leash on the collar, she stood up, with a trembling Toutou in her arms.

It was a teenage boy, his chest heaving with the effort of catching up with his dog.

"It's a good thing you did that. Thunder never attacks people. But he hates little dogs. I don't know why. But he's really a good dog. It's my fault. I shouldn't have let him off leash. I'm really sorry."

Thunder continued to lunge, whine and bark at Toutou, who was now shaking in Summer's arms. The boy pulled Thunder back, and the dog complied more under the influence of his prong collar than his young owner. The boy gave Summer an appraising look.

"Hey—where do you go to school?" The kid smiled wide and took a shot at his luck. His dog continued to lunge and snarl.

Summer shook her head and frowned her teacher-frown. The teenager's smile faded. He shrugged and turned back in the direction from which he and his dog had come. The boy and dog struggled off back down the beach, in a push-me, pull-you fashion.

Summer, watching them scramble off, was aware she would later think of all the things she should have said to that kid who let an aggressive dog run loose at the beach. But for now, she stood in the frigid wind, shivering along with the little dog in her arms.

"I will never let anyone else die," she said into the black curls covering Toutou's head.

Sometimes at night, Norbert lay awake in his bed with Ivy curled under his arm and wondered, *How many years of this happiness and fulfillment still lie ahead of me?*

Norbert's card readings were back on track now, after the unpleasant confrontation with the oily-haired man. He continued to see new people and repeat customers day after day, people who expressed gratitude and validated his accurate assessments of their situations and solutions.

Of the many effective phrases Norbert was learning in fortune-telling, one of the most useful was "Don't be surprised if you—" He used this phrase whenever he wanted to suggest that someone do something. "Don't be surprised if you find yourself enjoying your home more than ever, and spending happy hours there."

"Don't be surprised if you take up a new hobby that you never expected to try."

"Don't be surprised if you notice that your self-confidence is growing, and you reach out more to others."

This phrase came in handy for Gigi, a woman in her thirties who came into the café wrapped in excessive layers. It was a wet, dark day, and the wind off the lake had turned bracing. People walking by on the sidewalk were wearing jackets now. But Gigi was wearing a hat, scarf and gloves, and when she sat down opposite Norbert, she kept all of her insulation on. Her face was tight with resistance to the cold.

"Don't be surprised," said Norbert, "if you find yourself moving—very soon—to Nashville. Or Santa Fe. Have you ever thought of moving to either of those places?"

Norbert had always wanted to visit both of them.

Gigi smiled briefly at the thought.

"I've *thought* of a lot of things. But no way could I ever move." She looked out into the bleak day.

"There's an obstacle," said Norbert.

"There's an obstacle called my mom. She is very protective. I can't travel anywhere without her. But she doesn't want to go anywhere. I feel like I'm still waiting to live my life."

"There is an older woman in your life represented by this

Queen of Spades. She is perceptive and knows how to manage people."

"Yep!" said Gigi. "That's Mom, all right!"

"Yes, I think it could be your mother, as you say. You see, right next to her is the Ten of Clubs, representing a wall, a block or a boundary."

"Boundary! Ha! My mother never heard of a boundary."

"Especially not where you're concerned, right?"

"Especially not where anyone's concerned. She's all up inside everyone's business. But, no, you're right—she's especially nosy and bossy with me. She's got something to say about everything—from my dating to my dress to my decor. All of it critical. And yet she depends on me for everything."

Norbert had been an assiduous student of the Dear Abby column. He knew something about this kind of situation.

"Yes, you see, right here in the cards, you are being asked to set a boundary with her. Now, she may not like it, and she may not respect it, but you will need to be firm. Or you could just spend the rest of your life complaining about her. It's up to you. See, part of the problem is that you have allowed her to push across your boundaries."

"Easy for you to say. Have you *met* my mother?"

"No, I haven't had the pleasure." Norbert looked at Gigi over the tops of his lenses to communicate his sense of humor to her, even though he couldn't see a thing when he did that.

He resumed, "I do know from your cards that she won't make it easy, Gigi, but this is a life lesson for you. You need to take responsibility for your part in this. It's not all her. You have been allowing it."

"But—"

"When you are ready to truly grow up, you will set a boundary and not allow it to be crossed."

"Ouch."

"I'm sorry. The cards don't lie." Norbert pointed to the Jack of Clubs and the Three of Spades. "The message in your cards today is this—you will only grow into who you are when you get far away from your early influences."

Gigi looked glumly at the Jack of Clubs. He held his club tight in his fist and frowned at the little hills of dirty snow beyond the window of the Good Fortune Café.

Gigi left annoyed, yet pensive.

Norbert felt the weight of his own influence. He felt that familiar fear of the power he had so recently attained to alter destinies. But even more, he felt gratified. People listened to him intently. He helped them. It was what he always wanted.

CHAPTER THIRTY-FOUR

Eight of Spades:

You are challenged to withstand criticism.

One afternoon in early December, there was a great snow-fall. The stuff was piling up in crystalline hills, and the snow-plow with flashing yellow lights was rumbling down Harrison Street, splattering slush to the left and the right.

Norbert, arriving home at four o'clock in the near dark-ness, had tucked Ivy up in her cozy basket and come out to shovel the sidewalk. It was glorious. Norbert loved to shovel snow. It was the best winter workout, and he loved to do hard, physical work.

Father Jim from St. Edmund's called across the street to him, "Be careful there, young fella! Wet snow is heavy, you know!"

Norbert waved and smiled. "Don't worry about me! Doctor says he wishes he was as fit as I am!" Then Norbert regretted saying it. Was this pride? He never thought he had anything to boast about. His young, plump physician really had looked at Norbert's labs with what seemed like envy mixed with admiration, and had said those very words. Norbert was lean and strong, and the young doctor had given him an enthusiastic "clean bill of health."

The pastor, far from correcting Norbert on his commission of one of the seven deadly sins, only laughed and said, "In that case, come shovel at the rectory when you're done at your house! Only kidding, Mr. Zelenka. Only kidding! The parish takes care of that for us!" And the pastor plodded off through the snow toward the rectory.

Father Jim Donohue was a man known in Gibbons Corner for his taste for golden candlesticks, daily fresh flowers for his altar, and costly millefiori paperweights for his enormous mahogany desk.

Norbert had defended him and St. Edmund's to the Club: "Yes, but remember the food pantry."

"Yes, but remember that's all volunteer work and donated food from merchants," Carlotta had countered. "The church just allows the volunteers to use the space. The churches like to appear to be helping people, while really they are just self-serving."

If there was one thing Carlotta could not stand, it was hypocrisy.

Norbert judged no one but himself.

He paused on the sidewalk and caught a snowflake on his gloveless finger. He admired how the light glinted off it so delicately, and he watched it melt into a drop of water on his fingertip. He thought once again of Mrs. Applegate, his fifth-grade teacher: *No two snowflakes are alike. Each one is beautiful. And each one of you must discover your snowflake nature.*

And what was it Birdie had said, back in May at the art gallery? *We are here to grow into who we are.*

He had had a good day telling fortunes, he reflected, as,

exhilarated, he continued shoveling the sidewalk in front of two neighbors' houses, and their walks, as well. He had assured a worried woman that "something lost will soon turn up," and he had informed a lonely man that "one who admires you greatly is hidden in plain view." Everyone seemed to be happy with him.

Perhaps he had discovered his snowflake nature. Perhaps he was growing into himself.

The reluctant fortune-teller had become an increasingly self-assured one, as he saw the benevolent influence he was exercising through the power of his soft voice and kind heart. And so the readings went on, day after day.

A woman of about fifty slid into the booth across from Norbert. She was not scheduled for a reading.

"Hello," said Norbert, smiling as ever. "If you would like a reading, the procedure is that you sign up for a time slot at the counter."

"I most certainly would not like a *reading*," hissed the woman. "I won't take up much of your time, *Norbert Z*," she said, and she pronounced his professional psychic name with contempt. "Who *are* you? What are you *doing* here?"

Her rage blasted Norbert like a hot sandstorm. Norbert felt her blinding fury and knew there was nothing to do but brace for the onslaught.

"You gave my daughter a so-called *reading*. She was coming just for fun. You told her to have boundaries with her *mother*. *What the hell?* We used to have a beautiful relationship. She never made a move I didn't know about. Now she's withholding information from me! And I've done *nothing wrong*! What *right* do you have to do what you are doing here? There oughta be a law to stop unscrupulous people like you."

The unhappy mother hesitated a moment between crying

and continuing her attack. She went on. "Does it make you happy to ruin families' relationships? To play on people's vulnerability? Who, exactly, do you think you are? What kind of a person *are* you?"

Her voice trembled as she pronounced these last words. She slid out of the booth and rushed out of the Good Fortune Café.

Norbert was deeply troubled by this woman's visit. He had become used to the image he saw reflected in his customers' eyes, and that image was of a man appreciated, validated and even respected. As the words "What kind of a person *are* you?" echoed in his mind, Norbert was shaken. To be the target of such a burst of anger made him feel vaguely guilty.

Who, indeed, did he think he was, advising people on issues he really knew nothing about? The angry woman left him with a feeling of apprehension that was difficult to shake.

CHAPTER THIRTY-FIVE

Three Queens:

Strong personalities
make for stimulating company.

Carlotta decided at the first-year anniversary of her son's death that Christmas would still be Christmas. Charlie and his wife had died together on December 30, ten years ago. It was the most soul-wrenching loss of her life.

However, to give in to her feelings by refusing to participate in Christmas would be to draw attention to her private grief. Carlotta was not a woman to be pitied. Many things could she accept from people: admiration, allegiance, jealousy and even resentment—but never sympathy. To indulge her own buried grief and sadness would be to "make a big scene," and to encourage people to talk about it. It was too private to discuss. With anyone.

Therefore, Carlotta prepared to run the Club's Christmas party, just as she did every year. She was needed to run things. It was her *raison d'être*. The preparations leading up to the

Club's Christmas gathering involved three preliminary dis-agreements.

The first argument centered on the mutual antipathy be-tween Carlotta and Myrtle, Margaret's enormous black-and-white cat. Margaret wanted to host their *soirée intime*, as Carlotta called it. (The unpleasant encounter with the French-speaking tourist behind them, Carlotta was back to sprinkling French into everyday conversation.) Margaret loved Christmas more than anything in the world, and decorated her condo lavishly every year. It was the perfect place for their little party, and yet somehow every year, it was never her turn.

"It *has* to be my turn *sometime*, Carlotta."

"But, Margaret, my allergies," Carlotta said in a singsongy voice that implied Margaret should know all about her aller-gies.

"Oh, allergies, my eye," said Margaret. "You don't have any allergies, and you know it. What you have is a phobia, pure and simple. You're afraid of cats."

Carlotta laughed. "Really!"

"Really! And the way you get over a fear is to face it. Not to avoid it."

Carlotta said, "It's not a fear. It's a dislike. Yes, I'll be hon-est with you, Margaret. I don't like Myrtle. She is the worst kind of narcissist. She's always slinking around and trying to get her own way."

Birdie, with her odd way of looking through a person, put in, "*Who* tries to get her own way?"

Margaret hooted.

Carlotta shot a glare at Margaret and gave in on this first argument. "Fine. Margaret's place, then. I'll put my aversion to Myrtle aside, for your sake, Margaret." Let no one say that Carlotta had to have *her* own way.

Margaret beamed. "Now as for presents!" she exclaimed.

Carlotta then began the second argument: "I thought we could dispense with presents this year. After all, we all certainly have everything we need or want."

Margaret stood up. She was so excited to be able to give her favorite literary quote, apropos of the conversation, for once: "'Christmas won't be Christmas without any presents!'—*Little Women!*"

Birdie smiled beatifically at Carlotta. Yes, Carlotta had set Margaret up to be able to deliver her *bon mot*. That was Carlotta's generosity of spirit.

"All right, then," said magnanimous Carlotta. "What shall our theme be for presents this year?"

The three friends pondered.

Birdie reviewed, "Well, we've done Art Supply Presents, Dollar Store Presents, Winter Hats, Miniature Things, Theater Tickets, New Biographies, White Elephants…"

Carlotta sat back and let her friends continue remembering themes from Christmases past and move on to suggesting themes they might use this year. She'd give them about four minutes.

Carlotta's theme, Creature Comforts, was taken up immediately by the Club. Their own ideas paled in comparison. They all agreed that Christmas had become stressful for all of society, and that it didn't have to be that way. Comfort items, like fluffy socks, fragrant lotions and herbal teas, would be perfect for this year. Simple, easy items, no fuss.

"And finally, for the guest list!" enthused Margaret, thus initiating the third argument.

Carlotta bristled. "What are you talking about? There is no guest list for the Club's Christmas Gathering. It's just the Club."

Margaret looked to Birdie for support. "I thought—well, the Club has become so small—I thought, just for this year—I mean, he's not in the Club, of course, but he's become a good friend to each of us—well, I thought we could invite Norbert."

The night of the party, it was too cold to snow. The air was clear, and the stars were bright and splashed in profusion across the deep dark sky. Norbert was standing outside Margaret's condo on Washington Street, craning his neck back to observe the planets, when Carlotta came driving up with Birdie and parked on the street.

Carlotta had not wanted Norbert to be included in their little after-dinner party, but since she'd had to concede defeat on that score, at least she would have the satisfaction of being in charge of him for the evening.

"Norbert! *Joyeux Noël*, dear!" she said, as she hooked her arm around his, obligating him to be the gentleman who would guide her safely across the salt and ice.

Norbert pointed above them, and asked her if she knew which one of those stars might be Venus.

"I read that Venus and Mars should be visible now," he said. "Mars is the red planet, of course. I think it's that one over there." He swung his arm toward the west. "But that one there—?"

Carlotta was not about to tolerate questions to which her answer would have to be "I don't know." That was her policy.

"Norbert, that's so interesting, but I'm just freezing. Aren't you? And Margaret is bound to be nervous until we all arrive, so…"

Carlotta watched Norbert cast a last regretful glance at the heavens and then commandeered him and Birdie to Margaret's condo on the third floor.

Due to Myrtle the cat, Carlotta had not spent much time at Margaret's place. The decor in Margaret's home was not tasteful, and reflected Margaret herself. Rather than classic, neutral colors, Margaret chose what she liked: juvenile colors like rose pink and mint green. Rather than sleek empty space, Margaret chose clutter: figurines, too many cushions and walls covered with paintings created by herself and her friends. Margaret's own paintings alternated between two subjects: flattering self-portraits and floral still lifes. The overall effect of the space was too sweet. It cloyed. It was overwhelming to refined senses. It took some adjustment, aesthetically.

As they took off their coats, the Club and Norbert exclaimed complimentary things about Margaret's Christmas decorations. On her front door, she had hung a sign she had painted herself: "All is calm, all is bright." There was a small tabletop tree in ghastly pink, hung with silver tinsel. There were little electric candles everywhere.

Outer wraps disposed of, Carlotta was pleased to see that they were all dressed to the nines. She felt quite proud of her friends. Everyone looked very put together. Carlotta and her friends wore midlength dresses with flattering cuts. Carlotta herself was dressed in black, with silver shoes and jewelry. Birdie wore a fluttery forest-green dress that was divine against her red hair. Margaret wore purple, but one learned not to expect perfection; at least the style was becoming. Norbert was also more than acceptable, she had to admit, in his gray sport coat with a white button-down shirt, argyle sweater-vest, chinos and red tie. Margaret pulled a red rose from a vase and stuck it in Norbert's lapel, and the ladies admired the effect. Christmas, realized Carlotta, was all about beautiful clothes.

Breathlessly, Margaret ushered her guests into the living room. The "simple" Christmas had once again taken on its own force. Margaret, it was plain to see, had knocked herself out. She had made a "simple" gingerbread house from scratch; designed a "simple" cloth sack for the grab-bag gifts;

and somehow, despite her petite stature, had hung "simple" garlands everywhere. She was pink with pleasure.

The guests took time to notice and praise everything, while Margaret had her moment in the limelight. Carlotta cast a wary eye at the cat, nasty thing, as it lay stretched out upon a floral footstool, watching with its vile eyes and thinking its hellish thoughts.

Ivy poked her head out of her carrier and took one look at Myrtle. Whatever it was that passed between them caused dear Ivy to duck back into hiding and not show her face again for the rest of the evening.

"Oh!" shrieked Carlotta, as Myrtle pulled herself up to sitting. Myrtle steadily regarded Carlotta.

"Is something wrong, Carlotta?" asked Norbert.

Birdie explained, "Carlotta and Myrtle don't get along."

Carlotta objected, "When you put it that way, you make it sound like we're equals!"

Myrtle shot Carlotta a death stare. Carlotta refused to engage and looked about the room—at the Christmas decorations and her dear friends. And also at Norbert.

Birdie tried to get Myrtle's attention by jiggling a red ribbon along the carpet. She made kissy noises toward the feline.

Norbert raised his quiet voice to an odd falsetto, most unbecoming for a man, and still the beast stared, unblinking, exclusively at Carlotta.

"We're all dying to pet you, Myrtle," implored Birdie. "Why do you only have eyes for Carlotta?"

That's when the monster, still leveling her malevolent gaze at Carlotta, rose, arched her back in a yoga stretch, and then, to Carlotta's terror, began to march deliberately toward her. Carlotta had the distinct impression that the weasel-like creature could read her thoughts. She refused to look directly at Myrtle. She would not give her access. Eyes are the mirrors to the soul—someone wrote that, didn't they? Where had she read that some people credit cats with psychic abilities? Nonsense, certainly. But the vixen did look at Carlotta as if she knew something unfavorable about her. Could a cat be a vixen? She had already associated Myrtle with a weasel, but that was all right; weren't cats descended from a kind of weasel? But a vixen was a female fox, wasn't it? Carlotta's thoughts raced and tumbled over each other in the most disorderly way as she fought the panic rising up inside her chest with each inexorable step Myrtle took toward her, glassy green eyes never wavering. Carlotta looked down at the pointed tip of her Christmassy silver shoe and back at the approaching animal. But, no, Carlotta would never hurt an animal. Unless it attacked her first. At last, Myrtle reached Carlotta's feet and sat down, continuing to contemplate Carlotta from up close. When Myrtle leaped, there was a sharp intake of air from Birdie, Margaret and Norbert. Myrtle landed with the grace of a ballet diva on the couch. Carlotta jumped and gave a little exclamation.

"Merciful Heavens!" She quickly regained her composure and commented in a calmer tone, "It startled me."

Myrtle sat herself down beside Carlotta and faced the room, looking for all the world as though she had come over to gossip with the only sane person here about all the other bizarre characters before them.

Up went simpering cries of "Oh, aw, Carlotta, she wants you to pet her!"

Carlotta focused on slowing her breathing. In through the nose. Out through the nose.

Margaret said, "She *never* sits with me like that, and I'm the one who feeds her!"

Myrtle shot Margaret a withering look and closed her eyes,

like a teenager who has had all she can take from her irritating mother.

Birdie said, "She senses something about you, Carlotta. Cats are intuitive."

Carlotta answered, "Don't be ridiculous."

Myrtle rubbed her head and neck along Carlotta's skirt, trilling.

Birdie exclaimed, "Aw! She's *singing!*"

Carlotta, continuing to focus on her breath, felt her heart rate slowing down. She glanced sideways at the vermin. It was just a domestic cat, after all, she told herself. She could tolerate this. She looked quickly away again.

Norbert said, "You know why she avoided everyone else and went to you, Carlotta? It's because we were all trying so hard. Cats avoid people who stare and gesture at them. They find those things threatening. You didn't take any notice of her, so she felt safe going to you. I read an interesting article about this in *Reader's Digest*."

"Oh," said Carlotta, smiling and looking sideways at Margaret. *"Reader's Digest."*

Norbert was such a lowbrow. It was a pleasant distraction to be reminded of her own intellectual superiority.

Myrtle rolled on the couch and squinted at Carlotta. Carlotta could almost hear her say, "I've got your number, sister."

Birdie, as every year, was in charge of the mulled wine. Warm and sweet. Carlotta found it went down especially easily this year, and she felt Myrtle willing her to drink to excess. But she would not. She never did.

Carlotta had brought her lime sheet cake, always a crowd-pleaser, and she cut and passed that around. Christmas, reflected Carlotta, was all about delectable food.

The conversation began with the weather, as it must. The fluctuations in temperature from unseasonably warm to record-breaking cold. You had to be ready for anything in this climate. Polite and nonintrusive inquiries about family members near and far.

"And Summer?" asked Margaret. "Has she found her young man yet?"

Carlotta thought of Summer, who insisted on spending Christmas Eve and Christmas Day alone. It was odd behavior. Carlotta did not approve of odd things. But she mentioned none of this to her friends.

"Oh, Margaret! Young women today don't pine after marriage like Jane Austen characters, you know. Summer is a modern, independent young woman! She's quite happy." Mentally, Carlotta added, *I hope*.

Margaret took the hint and did not pursue that line of questioning. Carlotta reflected that the truth was, Summer did not confide in her about matters of the heart. *If* Summer had any matters of the heart to confide. She hoped that Summer was finding her way, although she had an odd sense that all was not well with her granddaughter. Best not to think about things one could not control. Much better to turn one's thoughts to Norbert and his fortune-telling. After all the work she and the Club had put into him, it was bitter indeed that he was denying them the pleasure that was their right.

Never admit defeat.

"Norbert! How is business at the Good Fortune Café?" asked Carlotta. She would love to get him to admit some problem he might be having in his new "career." If he would open the door just a crack for her to jam her foot in…

Norbert's fixed smile flickered.

"Anything we can help you with? Any…difficulties lately?"

"I seem to be managing, Carlotta, thank you."

"Ah. The apprentice thinks he has outgrown his wizard, so to speak?"

"Carlotta," interfered Birdie, "I think it's already settled that Norbert is a professional now."

If Carlotta blanched, she couldn't help it. "You want to beware of hubris, Norbert."

Norbert asked, "Who is Hugh Bris?"

Carlotta said, "Hubris is not a who. It's a what. It means 'excessive pride or self-confidence.'"

"Defiance of the gods, Norbert," added Birdie.

"Not," Carlotta laughingly hastened to explain, "that we are gods." She warmed to her work. "But the point is," Carlotta continued with great kindness, "hubris invariably leads to nemesis."

Margaret clasped her hands and said happily, "Norbert, now you are going to ask—where is Nemesis! Go ahead!" The little woman could hardly contain herself. How excited she must be, thought Carlotta, to be in the know and finally have someone else be at a loss in literary allusions.

"No, I know what 'nemesis' means," said Norbert. "You're saying that if I don't accept your direction, I'll find myself in a disaster of my own making."

A hush fell over the Christmas party. Margaret's face fell.

"Let's sing carols!" she suggested, and she was up and passing around sheet music.

The carols they sang were French and English. "Il est né le Divin Enfant," "Joy to the World," "Ding Dong Merrily On High" and "Jingle Bells."

Carlotta sang in a loud and ringing soprano. Birdie waved her arms as she sang as if she could feel the music with her fingertips. Margaret, tone-deaf, sang in a monotone with plenty of gusto. Norbert was a strong tenor. Their voices joining together served to drive away tensions and unite them—mind, body and spirit, as Edith might have said, had she been invited. Which she most definitely was not.

Throughout the evening, Carlotta took on the role of explaining the Club's little in-jokes to Norbert, filling his mug of mulled wine to the brim, and pressing food on him. He needed to understand that if he was included this evening, it was on her sufferance. Even if she *had* tried to block his invitation. He didn't need to know that. She would keep tight control over his sense of belonging. *Next thing you know, they'll be lobbying to make him a member of the Club.* Carlotta made a mental note to be ready to combat that move if and when it should come.

"And now!" cried Margaret. "It's time for the Christmas Grab Bag!"

Everyone had put their wrapped presents in the red-and-gold cloth sack that Margaret had created for the purpose. Carlotta explained to Norbert, "The rules are simple—you pull a present from the bag. When all the presents are pulled, we open them. Then you have an opportunity—but only one—to 'steal' a present from someone else and give that person yours. The only stipulation is, you cannot take back the present you yourself brought here tonight."

"Margaret actually explained the rules to me already," said Norbert.

This man was so annoying. You couldn't tell him anything.

"And it's time to begin!" exclaimed Margaret.

As "Silver Bells" played on Margaret's stereo, one by one the merrymakers plunged their arms into the trove of gifts, turned their heads to one side to show they weren't being influenced by wrappings, and pulled out a selection.

Margaret pulled elegant silver-and-white paper and ribbons off a box that turned out to be concealing a copy of *Reader's Digest*, along with a coupon for a two-year subscription. Margaret lowered her chin and looked over her glasses at Carlotta.

"Yes! You guessed it, Margaret! That's from me! That ubiquitous source of wisdom, written at a ninth-grade reading level. Watch out that Norbert doesn't snatch it from you when we get to stealing gifts." The silence that met her witticism caused Carlotta to reflect. *How annoying, when one makes a joke, and it falls flat because people are worried about hurting feelings.* Birdie and Margaret turned to Carlotta with expressions that showed how humorless they were. Christmas was all about gag gifts, wasn't it? Norbert was the butt of the joke, and *he* was smiling. But then, when wasn't he smiling?

Margaret was leafing through the magazine and actually seemed to be interested in it, and that was irritating, too. What was wrong with people?

"How is *Reader's Digest* a comfort item?" challenged Margaret.

"Margaret, it's *reading* that is our greatest comfort, always," countered Carlotta.

"Huh!" said Margaret. "Look at this. Here's an article about making intelligent jokes: 'How to Be the Wittiest Person in Any Gathering.'"

"What?" said Carlotta, knitting her brows. "Can *I* see that?"

"No way," said Margaret. "It's *my* gift. Thank you, Carlotta."

Birdie was next. Off came plain white paper and a white bow.

"A tea cozy! Oh, how sweet!" she said, turning it around high in the air for everyone to see.

But this was a peculiar tea cozy. It was black and white— and in the shape of a cat—a fat black-and-white cat, just like Myrtle. How hideous. How odd.

"Who is it from?" asked Carlotta and Margaret together.

Norbert spoke up. "Uh, I brought that one. I hope you like it. Or, uh, that someone here will like it."

Birdie and Margaret both said at once, "I like it! I love it!"

Carlotta looked at each of her friends in turn. *Had they all taken leave of their senses? Who would want such a detestable item in their kitchen?*

The real Myrtle had flounced off to try to sleep on Margaret's bed, as if she couldn't stand the infernal racket of Margaret's party, so she was unaware of the compliment of Norbert's gift. No doubt the loathsome beast was lying on top of someone's coat. Myrtle would have selected Carlotta's specifically, from spite. It made Carlotta's skin crawl just to think of it.

"Norbert next!" cried Margaret. Norbert's present was the biggest box. It turned out to be a flannel blanket—patterned with obese black-and-white cats.

Carlotta started at the sight of it. What was going on here? No one was making eye contact with her.

Norbert was enthusiastic about the dreadful thing. "So warm!" he said, rubbing a corner of it on his face. "So soft! I really like it!"

"That was from me!" volunteered Margaret.

"Carlotta next!" said Birdie.

Carlotta tore into the striped paper and opened the box— to pull out a cookie jar. In the shape of a pudgy black-and-white cat.

"That's from me!" said Birdie, eyes twinkling.

"Well, obviously, it's from you, Birdie. There's no one else left, is there? I guess I see what's going on here."

Three pairs of innocent eyes turned to her.

Then Margaret, Birdie and Norbert erupted into laughter, and although there was not a single thing funny, Carlotta forced herself to laugh, as well. Not to laugh would be to show that she was offended, and she would not give them that satisfaction. It was one thing to make a joke at someone's expense. It was quite another to have people make jokes at one's own expense.

"Well," said Carlotta, cutting into the laughter, "I guess it's time for stealing gifts. And *I*," she said, standing and walking to Margaret with her hands out, "am stealing *Reader's Digest*."

"You can't!" chorused Margaret and Birdie. "You can't steal the present you brought. It's the rule!"

"And *I* say, I'm not taking home a Myrtle-themed present— not even to give to Goodwill tomorrow. So we will dispense with the usual rule this year." That was their consequence for ganging up on her. Why some people thought it was funny to make fun of people on Christmas was beyond her.

Norbert and Birdie were more than happy to keep the gifts they had pulled from the bag.

Margaret accepted the Myrtle cookie jar from Carlotta and gave up *Reader's Digest*. The cookie jar was "precious," she said.

Carlotta's thoughts were dark that evening when she returned home to Toutou. Never, in all the history of the Club, had she experienced such treason. Always, she had been the uncontested leader of a compliant group of friends. She was the unchallenged leader because she worked tirelessly to keep her friends intellectually stimulated and happily occupied. This sudden rebellion after so many years of dedication on her part pained her. She was left melancholy and bitter by this evening's experience of being the object of the joke instead of its perpetrator. The humiliating loss of loyalty was due to one factor, and one factor only: Norbert Zelenka. It seemed that Carlotta was out, and Norbert was in. Carlotta rued the day she had taken him under her wing to help him, out of the pure goodness of her heart. For just one dark moment, she wished that he would receive his comeuppance: she wished him ill.

CHAPTER THIRTY-SIX

Ace of Clubs:

Powerful forces for good are at work.
Time spent alone may help you to
align yourself with them.

Christmas day in Norbert's little white bungalow was just the way he and Ivy liked it: quiet and cozy. He'd been grateful to be included in the Club's revelries, and felt that he really had true friends in Gibbons Corner, at last. But a day of tranquil reflection was what he most craved on this sunny and frigid day. He observed to Ivy that even the squirrels remained tucked up in their nests, not caring to venture out in these temperatures.

He thought of the few Christmases he and Lois had had together. How she had loved the lights and the presents! She had always made holidays special for Norbert. Each year, she bought him incredible gifts that he would never have thought of buying for himself, things he didn't even know he wanted until he saw them nestled in sparkling tissue paper under the Christmas-tree lights. A telescope for stargazing.

Bird feeders and birding books. How could she know, before he knew himself, that he would love these things? Or
did he love them because they were from her? For his part,
Norbert had always been perplexed by Christmas shopping.
How could he guess what Lois might want? He'd consulted
his aunt Pearl the first Christmas.

"Women like baubles, Norbert," Aunt Pearl had said.

He went out and put himself in the hands of the first jew-
eler he came to. That was the day he bought the gold locket.
When she opened it and exclaimed it was the most exquisite
thing she'd ever been given, he knew perfect happiness. Even
thinking of that moment now could bring that happiness back.

He wondered what his wife, Lois, would think of his late-
life career. Would she be proud of her husband, the psychic?
She would be very surprised, certainly. And she would be
happy for him: of that, he was certain.

It was strange, reflected Norbert, how a person's life can
change so quickly. It was only seven months before that Birdie
had spied him hurrying home with a box of groceries from
the food pantry, and the Club had interested themselves in his
financial woes. And now he was employed and free of debt.
It felt very good.

It still surprised him to think of himself as a fortune-teller.
He didn't feel like one. He felt more like a—what did they call
it—a "life coach." He helped people see what they were ready
to see and move forward with their lives. He was doing good
in the world. He had never been so gratified in his work life.

The same people who would not notice him as Norbert
Zelenka were respectfully consulting him as "Norbert Z."
His new identity gave him access to people's high regard and
to some of the secrets of their lives. And while he enjoyed his
new sense of importance, he could not shake a sense of foreboding. People, after a twenty-minute conversation with him,

would see their lives in a new light, and turn themselves in a different direction. How could he be sure he was not harming them? Hope saw how he helped people, and how grateful they were to him. But still, how could he know he wasn't "ruining relationships," as the angry mother had accused him of doing?

He was handling a power he did not fully understand.

Christmas Day at Summer's apartment was just as quiet, but not as peaceful, as it was at Norbert's house.

Summer was under a pile of blankets, trying to sleep through the day. She seldom said no to her grandmother, but on this she was unmovable. She would see no one on Christmas Eve or Christmas Day. Carlotta and Hope celebrated the twenty-fifth together, but Summer remained at home, turning off her cell phone and keeping her eyes closed.

Every anniversary of her parents' deaths had been like an electric shock that went on and on, for many days. It started on the days leading up to December 30. It would always be at its worst on the thirtieth itself. And the pain would continue through the days following, blocking Summer from setting any New Year's resolutions or goals, and certainly from attending any parties. This anniversary was the worst one so far, or so it seemed to her now.

She thought with dislike of the school social worker, that silly woman who was always trying to inflict therapy on people who didn't ask for it.

"You know," she had said, "the tenth anniversary can be a big one. Sometimes people don't expect that. You can get what they call an 'anniversary reaction.' Yep, it can be a big one, all right."

Summer had shut her down.

Nevertheless, the know-it-all woman's words were turning out to be prophetic. Summer felt herself shrinking more than ever into her fifteen-year-old self. She was scared and wanted to call someone. But she wouldn't. She couldn't seek support from anyone. If she did, people would sympathize.

I don't deserve it.

She thought then of Gramma's fortune-teller at Hope's café. Ever since she'd heard of him, she'd felt drawn toward trying him out. Maybe he could give her a message from her dead parents. Isn't that what fortune-tellers did? Or maybe he could just tell her that her life would be short, and her sadness would not last forever.

CHAPTER THIRTY-SEVEN

Jack of Diamonds:

A young person at the crossroads.

Some days, Norbert felt drained in his soothsaying role at the Good Fortune Café. He was making a nice amount of money now, but in order to do that, he was seeing too many people. He thought he would talk to Hope about limiting daily appointments to some manageable number, working in more breaks, and even creating a waiting list. Sometimes, at the end of a shift, he felt almost too tired to slide out of his booth and stand up. The burden of the town's problems rested on his shoulders, and it made him slouch forward and wish to close his eyes. People were beginning to depend on him in an odd and unsettling way.

Lolly was a customer who had come for her third reading in as many weeks.

"Ever since my first reading, I have felt so much more confident, like I always know I'm doing the right thing! You're better than a therapist, Norbert Z," she informed him. "I'm going to start coming in for weekly sessions to keep me on the right track."

Lolly had made several changes in her life due to the cards that had shown up in her horseshoe spreads, and Norbert's interpretation of them.

Norbert held the deck away from her outstretched hand and dropped it in his man purse, next to Ivy.

"Lolly, it doesn't work that way. You can't consult the cards—or me—about your every move."

Lolly protested. "*Why* doesn't it work that way? If it's okay to consult the cards once, why not once a week? Why not once a day, once an hour? What harm could it do?"

"No real harm, Lolly, except that you become dependent on someone outside yourself to tell you which way to go."

Lolly folded her arms.

"What do *you* care, anyway? I'm paying you."

"But I *do* care. I care about you—and all the people who consult me. See, you need to connect to your own way of discernment. Make some quiet time—go walking in nature, or listen to music, or doodle on paper. And just ask your questions. And receive the answers that come up. Your intuition is a very practical thing, after all. It's based on all the things you notice, without realizing you've noticed them. Consult your own intuition, and you will see that it gets stronger."

"If you won't give me a reading every week, I'll find a psychic who will."

"Yes," said Norbert, "I foresee that you will."

The young woman called Gigi returned to the Good Fortune Café to give Norbert an update. It was a cold, dry day in the last week of December, and she was warmly wrapped and layered.

"I just wanted to let you know how much your reading did for me," she said.

"So, you've been thinking about it? About moving to a warm spot?"

"I've done more than think about it!" she said, her eyes gleaming under her stocking cap. "Right after that reading, I went home and booked a flight to Albuquerque. As soon as the plane began to descend over New Mexico, I felt this—warm embrace—sort of—come up from the land, and I just felt that at last, I was coming home. And yet it was the first time I ever went there. Now, isn't that a weird thing?"

Norbert nodded. In his months as amateur counselor, he heard weird things every day.

"Well, the sun was shining, and my spirits were so lifted, and I thought, as I walked through the streets and soaked in the atmosphere, I could really do this. This could be my home. Why not?"

"Why not?" echoed Norbert, entranced.

"That's what *I* said! And as soon as I decided, everything just became very easy. I got a job, I got an apartment, and everything just went so fast, as if it were all meant to be. There's no reason for me to get so downhearted every winter. I can have sunshine every day. So, it's done!"

"It's done?"

"Yes! I am just back in town to get the rest of my stuff, and say goodbye to a couple of friends. I had to tell *you*. I don't know if this ever would have happened if not for your card reading."

"Oh," said Norbert, feeling the gravity of his responsibility. "And how did your mother take it?"

Gigi's face clouded.

"She doesn't know."

"You're going to move to New Mexico and not tell your mother?"

"I know. It sounds terrible. I feel terrible. But if I told her..." Gigi's new happiness drained from her face.

"I see," said Norbert. "She'd stop you."

"She knows how to work me. She'd make me feel that I wouldn't be able to manage without her, that she'd suffer so much if I left. In the end, I know I'd just give up. No, I can't tell her. I'm going to send her a text telling her I'm in another state, and that I'm doing well and will contact her as soon as I'm completely settled in. And then I'll block her number."

Once again, Norbert marveled at how quickly a querent had put his suggestion into action. He knew nothing of this young woman. What if he was directing her toward the catastrophe of her life? Why couldn't she think for herself? He suddenly felt very tired.

Gigi hesitated. "Or do you think that's too harsh? You're frowning. So, I shouldn't just disappear on her, right? Even if she is going to try to sabotage me, I still need to tell her where I am."

Norbert smiled wearily. "Now, that's a question only you can answer."

He felt he'd done more than enough for this querent.

CHAPTER THIRTY-EIGHT

Nine of Spades:

Disaster.
You are on the brink of taking an action that will
have far-reaching consequences.
Draw back from the precipice before all is lost.

It was a frigid day at the end of December. An arctic front had plummeted the temperature to five degrees below Fahrenheit, and the town was covered in six inches of snow over a solid foundation of ice. The hardy people of Gibbons Corner were used to this; they covered themselves from head to toe, wore layers over layers, and came out into the glacial air and the blinding brightness of sunshine on snow.

A young girl came into the café, stomping her boots and unwrapping her face. She was greeted by Hope.

"Summer! Come on in! What will you have?"

"Hey, Hope!" Hope hugged the girl. "How about some of that amazing pound cake and a nice hot soy latte? Oh, and I want to see Norbert Z," added the girl, almost as an afterthought.

Hope brought Summer right up to Norbert; there were no

appointments yet on this frost-bound day, and apparently this young lady merited the VIP treatment.

"Norbert, this is my cousin, Summer," said Hope. "Well, second cousin, or cousin once removed—what*ever*—my aunt Carlotta's granddaughter. Give her a good reading, you hear?" With a wink, Hope dashed off to work on Summer's order.

"Don't tell Gramma I came to get my cards read," Summer called after her. "She told me not to bother." Summer turned to Norbert in embarrassment. "No offense."

"None taken."

Norbert realized now that Summer was older than she had at first appeared. Her eyes were blue and flecked with brown, and those brown flecks looked like a continuation of the freckles that speckled her nose and cheeks. He could see her grandmother's strong will in her manner. But she was very different from Carlotta in one way. Her bright inner light was flickering; it was almost out; she was in a dark place. Looking at her, most people would see a pretty young woman, but Norbert's experienced eye saw a person in despair.

It was not a despair that most people would notice, because it was skillfully masked. She approached everyone, including Norbert, lightly, outwardly cheerful. But Norbert, by now, was exquisitely attuned to the feeling-states of the people who came to sit across from him in his booth at the Good Fortune Café.

Over the years, Norbert had observed Carlotta's granddaughter from a slight distance. He had seen that when there was a lull in the conversation, a hood seemed to fall over her eyes. While others noticed her radiant complexion, and heard her merry voice cutting through the chatter, Norbert had always noticed that Summer never allowed silence for more than a beat or two. She seemed to always be expending a great deal of energy, and trying to make it seem effortless. These were things that were easy to notice when he was an unremarkable and unobserved man—before he became a fortune-teller.

As Summer shuffled and handed Norbert the cards, a feeling of confusion and misery came over him. There was also something that made him want to get up and leave. Unceremoniously, with no regard for how strange it might seem. He felt sick to his stomach. Was it the flu? The café seemed to grow dark. If he believed in "energies," he would have said a negative one had just come into their presence. He was slammed by the intensity of it. With all his being, he wanted to take his card deck back and run from this pretty young woman. Some opposite force just as powerful kept him in his seat, taking the cards from Summer and arranging them into the horseshoe spread.

Norbert sighed, looking at Summer's cards. It took effort for him to speak.

He would start with the good cards.

"The Four of Clubs shows that you are loved more than you know." Stalling, he repeated, "More than you know."

Summer's expression was pleasant. She was apparently unaware of the atmospheric change. Maybe it *was* the flu. Hope swept by with the pound cake and the latte. "Looks like a good reading!" she observed, scanning Summer's face and bustling off.

Norbert hung his head over the cards, massaging his temples. He went on. Words flowed from him that didn't come from the card meanings; they were words that forced their way into the air between him and the young woman.

"You have a life lesson and cannot go forward until you learn it. That is why you are blocked. There is a great lie in your life. In fact, you are lying to yourself about something. You have a secret that is ruining your life. Bitterness is poisoning you. If you continue on this path you are on, you will do harm."

"Harm?" Summer's bright mask fell away. She was clearly alarmed. "What harm?"

Now Norbert pointed to the cards.

"There is an older woman, represented by this Queen of Diamonds. Next to her is the Three of Hearts, signaling a broken heart. The Six of Spades signals grief, and..."

"And?" Summer urged him to go on.

"And there is a pair of cards here that I don't like to see together—the Nine of Spades along with the Ace of Spades."

Norbert fell silent. He did not have the heart to go on with the reading. He felt like a machine that had run down.

Summer waited.

"What about the Nine and the Ace? What do they mean?"

"Well, it's a sign that something very bad could happen. You have to be careful. The Nine could signal a disaster of some kind. And the Ace of Spades could be some sort of death."

"A *death*?" Summer's eyes were wide. "Who is going to die?"

"Perhaps no one," amended Norbert. "There are many forms of death. It could simply mean an ending. It could be the end of an illusion or of a chapter of your life. There is a lot of power in this card. It signals a determining factor."

"Wait," said Summer. "First you tell me there will be a death, and then you tell me it could be just an ending. There's a big difference, you know."

"You're right. There is a big difference. The fact is, I can't tell which it is. I can't see it. I can only say that there may still be time to avert disaster. If this loss comes to pass, there will be enormous grief." Norbert felt weighed down as if by some force from outside himself.

"Well, what am I supposed to do?" asked Summer, panic

creeping into her voice. "You say I should be careful. Careful of what? When should I be careful? And this disaster I have to avert—what kind of disaster?"

Norbert looked up from the cards into Summer's distraught face. He was sorry he had begun this reading. He was sorry he had ever begun to read cards at all. The harm he had feared doing, he was doing now, and he saw no way to stop it.

CHAPTER THIRTY-NINE

Queen of Diamonds and
Six of Spades:

A period of great anxiety.
A woman of powerful character takes action.

Hope came out of the kitchen toward Norbert's booth with a look of expectation, followed by confusion.

"Where'd Summer go so fast?"

Norbert was massaging the bridge of his nose, his eyes closed. "She left."

"Norbert," said Hope, "what just happened here? Summer wouldn't just fly out without saying goodbye to me. What did you predict for her?"

Norbert sighed, not meeting Hope's eyes. "It's confidential."

"What? Come on."

"You'll have to ask her. I really can't talk about my querents' business."

The next morning at eight o'clock, Summer did not show up at Carlotta's house to walk Toutou. The temperature was predicted to rise to just above freezing that morning, and was due to plummet back to subzero the beginning of next week. This was the window to enjoy the outdoors. Summer was on winter break from school, and she'd said she would be over at eight to walk Toutou. Carlotta had already put Toutou's boots on her to protect her paw pads from the ice and salt.

Carlotta was more than fit enough to walk her own dog, and she did. These regular walks with Summer were more like playdates for both her granddaughter and her poodle. At eighty, Carlotta felt sure that she had at least another twenty good years in her, but just in case, she had provided for Toutou, naming Summer as Toutou's guardian in her will—along with providing a generous stipend for Toutou's care for the rest of her life.

Carlotta and Summer shared many traits, one of which was a passion for punctuality. When Summer continued to not appear as the minutes ticked by, Carlotta became annoyed and then concerned. She dialed Summer. The call went to voice mail.

Carlotta said, "Summer, dear, it isn't like you to stand us up. Toutou is waiting for you. Please call me back, honey."

After the morning had passed and there was still no call from Summer, Carlotta bundled herself up like a mummy (a stylish one) and got into her burgundy sedan to drive the six blocks to Summer's apartment. Her knock brought no response. On some impulse, she tried Summer's door first to make sure it was locked. It was. She unlocked the door with her emergency key and entered Summer's tidy and tasteful space.

"Yoo-hoo!" called Carlotta.

The stillness there told her in advance that Summer would not be in any of the rooms. She wasn't.

In the bedroom, however, Carlotta found Summer's appendage: her cell phone. It was lying on the bed—which was made. Had Summer not slept in her bed last night? The girl wouldn't leave home without her cell phone. Summer's open purse, minus the wallet, sat on the bed. There were so many coats, jackets and pairs of boots, it was impossible to tell if Summer had left dressed for the weather. But if Summer hadn't left in coat and boots, what would that mean? Carlotta put that thought out of her mind.

Calm, Carlotta told herself. *Cool heads prevail.*

Who might know where Summer had gone?

Hope would probably know something about this. Carlotta left Summer's cell phone on the bed, locked the apartment and drove to the Good Fortune Café.

Smooth jazz was playing on the sound system, and in spite of the Siberian chill, a few customers were scattered throughout the shop, sipping the foam off their lattes, and gazing into their phones, iPads and laptops. One young man sat anachronistically reading a newspaper by the fireplace.

Life goes on while my granddaughter goes missing, thought Carlotta with resentment.

"Hope!" she said sternly, wiping the smile off her niece's face.

Hope left her post behind the counter. Carlotta stepped off away from customers to confer with her.

"Do you happen to know where Summer is?" asked Carlotta, trying to sound casual.

"No!"

Carlotta saw that Hope was already catching her panic.

"It's probably nothing, but I have a little worry. It's just that Summer was supposed to be at my house at eight. It's now eleven. I called her and it went to voice mail. I let myself into her apartment, and her cell phone is there, but she isn't. It just doesn't add up. I've never known Summer to not be where she said she'd be. And I haven't seen her separated from her cell phone since I first bought her one."

"Oh, wow. No, Auntie, I have no idea where she is. But I saw her yesterday afternoon, here. Norbert read her cards. She was smiling, so I thought she was getting good news in her reading. Next thing I knew, she was gone, without saying goodbye. And Norbert looked all worn-out and awful and refused to tell me anything."

Carlotta's eyes blazed.

"Is he coming in today?"

"No, he said he was taking a few days off. What with the cold weather, it's been kind of quiet anyway."

"Okay, here's the plan. You call Summer and leave her another message if she doesn't answer. Tell her she needs to call me immediately. In the meantime, I'll be dealing with our *fortune-teller.*"

Carlotta zipped up Ontario Boulevard a little too fast for weather conditions. Norbert could probably tell her where Summer was, and if he knew what was good for him, he was going to cooperate. She slid dangerously past the stop sign on Harrison Street, but luckily no cross traffic was coming. She parked in the street across from Norbert's little white house and toddled with care across the ice.

Ivy barked insanely when Carlotta pressed the bell, but welcomed her with wiggles when Norbert opened the door. Norbert looked ten years older than the last time she had seen him.

"Norbert, I'll skip the formalities because I need to get right to the point. Do you know where Summer is?"

"Summer, your granddaughter?" asked Norbert.

"Exactly. Summer, my granddaughter. You read for her yesterday afternoon."

Norbert indicated the love seat for Carlotta, and he sank

into the floral armchair opposite. She sat on the edge of the cushion. She had no intention of staying.

Norbert said in his quiet voice, "I wish I'd never started telling fortunes."

"This isn't about *you*, Norbert." Carlotta had no patience for the self-absorbed.

Norbert looked up at Carlotta and prepared to hear some very bad news.

"Summer has been missing for at least three and a half hours."

"Oh, no," cried Norbert. His eyes darted from left to right as he tried to think of a reason that all might still be well. "Carlotta, don't worry. She probably just went to a friend's house."

"You don't know Summer! If she says she's coming over, she comes over. She doesn't forget. She doesn't go somewhere else instead. She doesn't leave her cell phone on her bed and go out."

"You've searched her apartment?"

"I popped in. I didn't search. I'll leave that to the police."

"The *police*?"

"Yes, of course, the police. This is serious. It's not like her to disappear, even for a few hours. She's reliable and dependable and predictable. She doesn't miss appointments. She doesn't go off without telling someone. Something is wrong. I feel it, Norbert! I feel that something is wrong. You talked to her last. Where is my granddaughter?"

"I don't know."

"What did you tell her in the reading, then?"

"That's confid—"

"BS, Norbert," spit Carlotta. Why did this man make her say "BS" all the time?

Norbert gave in. "Okay. I'll tell you. Summer got a very bad reading."

"Norbert, what are you saying?" Carlotta was stricken with horror.

"She pulled the Ace of Spades and the Nine of Spades. You may remember what that means."

"Are you out of your mind? What that *means*? What that *means*, Norbert? What that *means* is exactly whatever you say it means."

"Carlotta, I've learned to read the cards as they come."

"That is ridiculous! So what did you tell her, Norbert? What, exactly, did you tell my young and impressionable granddaughter?"

"I told her the cards showed disaster and even death in some form."

Carlotta cried, "Oh!"

"And I told her that there was still time to avert this, and that she would have to be careful."

"No, Norbert, it's *you*, you are the one who was supposed to be careful. And you weren't. And as for the death—if there's going to be a death, *I'll* tell you whose death it's going to be. If I don't get Summer back, you are a dead man, Norbert Zelenka."

Norbert sat collapsed in his floral armchair as his house continued trembling from Carlotta's fierce slam of the front door. His breath was shallow, and his heart was palpitating. Ivy huddled in his lap, but he didn't even know she was there.

For a person who earned his living through his alleged intuition, he had certainly ignored that intuition all along his way. He'd known from the beginning that fortune-telling was wrong for him. He'd had the persistent late-night alarm-bell feeling that kept going off, telling him to stop the card readings before something disastrous happened. Even in moments of exhilaration, he'd had the ongoing fear that he might cause some harm through a reading. When Summer had sat across from him at the café, his intuition had made him sick with dread. And yet he had stepped around his intuition every single time. And now Summer was missing and he was to blame.

If something awful has happened to that young woman, it will be my fault. How could this be?

I am a quiet person. I am supposed to be living a quiet person's life. I am meant to be a simple man, getting by month to month, just living in a small white house with my white Chihuahua. Why did I try to be more? Was it only because of some silliness remembered from fifth grade about "everyone having a snowflake nature"? I felt good doing the readings, so I told myself it was right. I hadn't felt so happy since Lois had looked into my eyes and truly listened to me. Was the fortune-telling always just about my own need for attention?

What have I done? Oh, what have I done?

Carlotta's next stop was the Gibbons Corner Police Department.

The officer who met with her treated her like an old lady who had lost her mind.

"Wait," said Officer Curry, slowing Carlotta's stream of vital information. "Your granddaughter got a bad reading from a psychic predicting disaster and death, and what? It scared her?"

"Of course it did! It must have!"

"Huh. So you believe in that stuff. Okay," said Officer Curry. Carlotta saw him twist his mouth, trying to hide his amusement.

"What *I* believe is not the point!" said Carlotta, reflecting briefly on the general decay of manners in today's society.

"Right. And she's been 'missing' for—" he looked at his watch "—four hours. Is that right?"

Carlotta said, "Well, four hours that I know of. Her bed was not slept in. She may have gone missing last night."

"But you don't *know* that. She may have slept in her bed, and made it four hours ago. And she's twenty-five years old? Old enough to do what she wants, without reporting to anyone."

The idea! This puppy of a "police officer" was a child himself!

Carlotta looked the officer up and down.

The officer looked Carlotta up and down.

"Carlotta," began the puppy.

"*Mrs. Moon*, if you don't mind, Officer. It would be more appropriate for you to call me 'Mrs. Moon.'"

"I'm sorry, Mrs. Moon. Ya know, I always call my elders by their first names, because calling them by their surnames might make them feel old."

"I *am* old," Carlotta informed him with icy dignity.

"Mrs. Moon, then. Your granddaughter probably just went to Walmart or something."

Carlotta bristled. The idea. Summer would never go to Walmart.

"Or," he continued, "sometimes people just go off for a little while to think, eh?"

"Think? Don't be ridiculous. She's twenty-five years old."

The officer clicked his ballpoint pen closed, as if signaling that he was about done here.

"It's too soon to make a missing-person report. There is no indication of a kidnapping here, from what you've told me. Forty-eight hours is what we require before we consider a person missing, if there's no sign of a struggle, nothing to make us suspicious. If she still hasn't turned up by eight o'clock Monday morning, then by all means, come back and we'll take care of you."

Carlotta bristled again. The very idea of this puppy "taking care" of her!

"You'll see, she's probably fine. She probably just went—"

Carlotta, now that she saw he was not going to help her, had to put him in his place.

"Don't you tell *me* where my granddaughter 'probably just went'! Something is wrong. I feel it in every cell of my body. I know it."

"What?" said Officer Puppy, arching his eyebrows. "Like, a psychic intuition?"

He smiled an irritating smile.

Carlotta didn't break down until she got inside the sanctum of her home on Clarence Avenue. Then, when she composed herself, she phoned Hope to tell her she was taking Toutou to Summer's apartment to camp out there, so she would be the first to know when Summer came home. She asked Hope to use her "Facebook thing" to "announce" that Summer needed to call her grandmother.

"Make it sound not too serious, while at the same time, serious."

"I know what you mean. I'll take care of it… Auntie, I've never heard you this upset."

Carlotta, damning image all to hell, allowed herself to whisper to Hope, "If anything happens to my Summer, I won't be able to bear it."

CHAPTER FORTY

Four Kings:

When there are four Kings in the spread,
the indication is of a gathering of support.

Sunday morning, eight o'clock: twenty-four hours since Summer had failed to show up for Toutou's walk. Carlotta had slept lightly in Summer's bed, waking with every train that rumbled by just half a block west of the apartment. She had checked the clock each time she awoke. Toutou, curled in a circle by her feet, had awakened each time, too, and had looked with compassion into her mistress's eyes.

At last, she gave up trying to sleep, and surrendered to her mind's will to take her back there, back to the worst moment of her life: December 30, 2006, ten thirty at night. A malevolent ice storm; two policemen at her door. She let them in. They stood in her house, dripping, red-faced, hesitating, while ice clicked and snapped against the window behind them.

"Who's been hurt?" she asked, but it didn't sound like her voice. It sounded like a frightened person galaxies away.

One of the policemen said, "Are you the mother of Charles Moon?"

Carlotta sank into her chair, while at the same time, she was standing beside herself watching the scene. None of this could be real. It had to be a nightmare.

They told her that Charlie and Barbara had just been killed.

She didn't believe them for a moment. Charlie and Barbara were alive. They were young. They had years ahead of them. They would bury her someday; that's how it was supposed to be. There was some confusion. Or this was a dream. She wanted her granddaughter. "Summer?" she managed to ask.

"Your granddaughter is fine. She's at the Edwards Cove Police Department. Are you willing to have her brought here to stay with you tonight?"

"Of course," said the voice that was not Carlotta's.

She had no interest in asking any questions; she wouldn't be able to absorb anything they might tell her. She didn't even ask why Summer was at a police station.

By ten o'clock, the Good Fortune Café was crammed full of people ready to form an organized search party for the missing young woman, Summer Moon.

Norbert had roused himself from his depression and horror and joined the town-wide effort. He had left Ivy at home alone. He gave her her favorite stuffed duck, hoping that would ease her loneliness. Something told him that where he would need to go today would be no place for a four-pound Chihuahua.

The café was full to bursting. In spite of the large number of people, there was a sense of united purpose over them all. The teenager Liam from the oil-painting class was pushing a mop around people's slush-spattering boots with the doggedness of Sisyphus. Hope brandished flyers she had printed with photographs and the question "Have you seen her?"

Norbert looked around at so many familiar faces in the crowd: Gloria from the bakery, Roseanne from the library, Summer's friend Marisol Fernandez, Daphne and Stanley from the Center for Deeper Understanding, Birdie and Margaret.

Everyone was seeking a task to assume, to help in the search for Summer. Word had gotten around—Carlotta made sure it did—that Summer's disappearance was precipitated by a frightening reading from Norbert Z. Many friendly acquaintances and even friends seemed to regard him with surprised disappointment, or even reproach.

Norbert thought, *I deserve it. I've caused all these people to be here this morning; I caused Summer to run away. By involving myself in other people's personal affairs, I've been risking creating a calamity like this, and it's finally happened. And why have I done it? So that I could help people? Or so that I could feel so special?*

Wasn't he delighted when he heard back from customers that they had done as he advised, and they were happy? Wasn't his pride inflated when he saw the list of appointments Hope booked for him each day—all the people reserving twenty minutes of his time, and paying good money for it? Was his desire to "help people" something he could trust? Clearly it wasn't, when it led to disasters such as this.

Carlotta's words came back to shame him: "This isn't about *you!*"

Margaret, with Birdie at her side, was briefing Daphne the former nun and Gloria the baker, who were still ignorant of all the facts.

"Summer's been missing since early yesterday morning. She didn't show up at Carlotta's when she was supposed to, at eight o'clock, and it looks like she didn't sleep in her bed the night before. The police aren't interested and won't help us. They say it looks like a 'voluntary' situation, and we should come back to them after Summer's been missing for forty-eight hours."

"Well," said Gloria from the bakery, "it sounds like she might have spent a couple of nights at a boyfriend's, or something like that."

"But what about her not showing up at her grandmother's—or even calling her? Carlotta and Summer are very close. Especially since Summer's parents died when she was in high school. Summer wouldn't disappear on Carlotta. Not in a million years."

Daphne frowned. "What do you think happened, then?"

"That's what we don't know. We can't figure it out." Margaret looked around, and then lowered her voice. "I probably shouldn't be saying this," she said.

The listeners leaned in closer.

"I can tell you that Carlotta has been worried about Summer lately. About her, you know, *mental* state. Her parents died tragically, you see, and this is the ten-year anniversary of their death."

"You mean," said Gloria, "you think she might have— Oh, but no! Summer is the happiest girl anyone's ever seen! She would never—"

Margaret straightened and reassumed her former tone, as if afraid she might have betrayed too much. "What we do know for sure is that something is wrong. We don't want to let time pass while we wonder. The minutes are ticking by. The longer a person is missing, the worse the outcome. Liam goggled it."

"I think you mean he 'Googled it,' dear," corrected Birdie.

Margaret, unconcerned, continued, "Carlotta is calling in a private detective—Birdie's nephew—Reggie Di Leo, from Buffalo. If the police won't help us, he will, we're sure."

The authoritative voice of Marisol Fernandez cut through the din:

"Okay, everybody! Listen up!" The room became silent. "All of you who have internet access right now, get on your Facebook accounts and share the post on Liam's page about Summer. It has current photos, a description, weight, age, hair color, etc. We want this going far and wide."

Heads dropped and fingers tapped away on cell phones.

"Next! We're going to divide you all up into pairs and threes, and send you off to different places. As you go, you'll be putting up Hope's flyers on trees, storefronts, street signs and everywhere you can. We'll need some to go down by the beach, others all through Gibbons Corner. Some of you will go to Edwards Cove. We'll need a few people to go into the forest preserve areas on the outskirts of town."

"What about Black Bear Island?" asked someone in the crowd.

"Yes! We need people to go everywhere. Roseanne—you all know Roseanne from the library—she's over here with a sheet of paper and all the locations. We need you to make a line, and tell Roseanne where you want to go. If you don't know, we'll tell *you*. We're in a hurry. As soon as we get two or three people for one location, off you go. Get in line, and while you do, I'm going to give you my cell phone number. Program my number into your phones *now*. I want you to call me if you find out anything, even the smallest thing."

Norbert was listening and watching, as if he were nothing more than a video camera rooted to the spot. Everyone was taking a role to try to undo the harm he had caused, and he was doing nothing at all. At last, he shook himself. These well-meaning and well-organized people were not going to find Summer. He was sure of that. If the young lady was to be found, it was going to be up to Norbert, and Norbert alone. He would not be joining the search party. An image had come to him unbidden, and was filling his mind. This image insisted on Norbert's full attention.

Norbert had brought about this disastrous turn of events by playing psychic. How could he even think of trusting his so-called intuition again? Yet the vision was clear and vivid. He wished that he could push it aside. It was stronger than he was, and would not be ignored.

Norbert knew where he had to go.

CHAPTER FORTY-ONE

Jack of Spades:

A pompous man; a blowhard.

As Norbert stood to leave, Carlotta rushed through the door of the café, which was held open for her by a fortyish man, short and stocky, with thick black eyebrows under a fur trapper hat. Carlotta made a beeline for Norbert, with the stranger lumbering quickly behind.

"Reggie Di Leo," said Carlotta, "meet Norbert Zelenka, the *fortune-teller* I've told you so much about. Norbert, I'd like you to spend a little time with Reggie. Tell him whatever you know."

Carlotta looked witheringly at Norbert and bustled off to confer with Marisol.

Several people stopped talking and watched the detective take their town psychic in hand, and then they glanced away quickly. They did not want to be seen rubbernecking, even though they all wanted to know what Norbert could have said to make Summer disappear. Norbert led Reggie to the back of the café, to what had become his business booth.

The two men sat down. Reggie took off his hat, and his plentiful hair hung in black chaotic curls, with some graying at the temples. Sitting across from this man whose mission in life seemed to be to track the guilty and recognize the liars, Norbert felt guilty, and as if his lies were about to be exposed. And yet he had not lied. Why did he feel as though he had?

Reggie took a few notes on his phone, but looked intently at Norbert most of the time. After Norbert had given Reggie his full account of his Friday meeting with Summer, Reggie sat back and regarded Norbert for an unnerving moment.

"I get it," Reggie said at last. "So, you—you're a con artist."

Norbert recoiled. The private eye continued, the corners of his mouth turned down in disgust.

"I see right through you, Zelenka. *Fortune-teller.*" He sneered. "You *like* that adrenaline rush of getting away with stuff—and you have your whole life, haven't you? You get high on people believing in your 'psychic powers'—literally shoving their hard-earned money into your hands. It's like they're telling you how smart you are. And Friday, you told Summer Moon a bunch of bull so you could watch the fear in her eyes. You got off on that. And she actually paid you money to frighten her—even better! So you talked to her about death and disaster, and now she's missing. And, hey, if she goes and does something crazy out of her fear—that's not *your* problem. Matter of fact, it works in your favor, doesn't it? You *told* her something bad would happen. So then if it does, well, that makes you look good—you predicted it! You get to just keep on telling fortunes and feeling so damn *special.* Making people believe in you, that's your *drug.* You like getting your kicks this way, don't you?"

Norbert felt himself shrink in the bright light of Reggie Di

Leo's uncompromising stare. An accusing voice within him agreed with the detective's assessment.

"Yeah," Reggie went on, with easy confidence. "You're nothing but a common sociopath. Psychic, my *eye*. You and I know there's no such thing. If you *were* a psychic, you'd know where Summer Moon is."

Reggie turned to find Carlotta and indicated he was "finished with Norbert."

CHAPTER FORTY-TWO

The Joker:

A psychic awakening
The discovery of untapped potential.
Personal transformation.

Before his interview with Reggie, Norbert had had an intense intuitive experience. It was worthy of a shaman in one of his own Peruvian-derivative paintings.

When someone had called out, "What about Black Bear Island?" Norbert suddenly knew with certainty that Summer was there, and no place else. Norbert, standing in the buzz and excitement of the café, had had a spontaneous vision of Summer walking along as the arctic air cut through her gloves and stung her face. He saw tiny ice crystals gathered on her eyelashes; he saw her walking in the bright moonlight, up across the shoreline toward the pines. He saw her find the path and walk along, lighting her way and jangling her keys to warn off the nocturnal animals that filled the island. For that was where she was. Summer was on Black Bear Island.

Norbert knew the island from his youth in the late 1950s

and early 1960s, when he had visited numerous times with his Eagle Scout troop. He hadn't been back since, but he remembered the place as a natural paradise, covered with pine trees and teeming with fascinating wild creatures.

Summer had gone to Black Bear Island, and as if he could see a video in his head of her sojourn, he saw her turn right on the path and walk past a cottage, and forest area, and again, a cottage, and more forest area, and on until she got to the fourth cottage. He saw her light her footsteps in the dark, through the trees, up to the side door of that cottage, and let herself in with the key.

That was the vision.

Was it a vision, or a Sherlock Holmes–style deduction? Did it matter, as long as he knew where she was? In his memory, he heard the voice of one of his customers telling him about some real estate she wanted to buy, a place where she could go and paint. She'd said, *I've thought maybe I could justify it by renting it out sometimes to other teachers.* Logic told him that just because a teacher at Summer's school might be renting out her cottage on Black Bear Island over winter break, and Summer was missing, that was not a sure indication that Summer was there. It would be more likely that the teacher would be using the cottage herself. And yet he knew he would find Summer there. By reading her cards, he had caused her disappearance. The "gift" he had never really believed in was now telling him with certainty where she could be found. As much as he wanted to put an end once and for all to what Aunt Pearl called his "second sight," he would have to trust it, just one last time.

Just as surely as Norbert knew Summer to be on Black Bear Island, he knew that he couldn't tell Carlotta or Reggie Di Leo about this. They would say he'd already done quite enough with his "psychic powers." He couldn't tell anyone with the search-party team, either. Even if they believed him and came with him to the island, their noise and influence would put him off the track.

Norbert slipped away from the crowd, wrapping his green plaid muffler around his face and stepping out into the cloudy winter day. The air was beginning to warm just a bit. The temperatures had been fluctuating uncertainly for weeks now.

A voice called to him: "Norbert!"

Was he hearing voices now, as well as seeing visions?

It was Birdie, wrapped in a full-length green coat, stocking cap and knitted scarf.

"Norbert, I have to tell you," said Birdie, catching up to him. Her eyes were gentle; he had not fallen in Birdie's esteem, at least.

Norbert was anxious to get going, now that he knew where Summer was, or hoped he did.

"I saw Summer's parents this morning," Birdie said in a confidential tone.

That stopped Norbert in his tracks. "But—I heard they died in a car accident when she was in high school."

"Exactly." Birdie's gloved hands pulled up the collar of her coat. "So they dropped by with a message." She looked up and down the street, which was deserted. It seemed the whole town was crammed into the café.

"They said that Summer is safe and well."

Norbert, unsure of what he believed about Birdie's spirit world, felt encouraged nonetheless. "Oh, good. Thank you, Birdie. Thank you for telling me."

"They wouldn't say *where* she is," added Birdie. "I did ask, but they wouldn't say. But she *is* safe and sound..." Birdie stopped to reflect. "Of course, she could be safe and sound on the Other Side, you know. That's possible." She brightened. "But either way! The important thing is, she *is* safe! So there's nothing to worry about!"

Norbert nodded as if reassured, which he most certainly was not.

"Birdie? Would you mind giving me a lift?"

Birdie agreed easily. She betrayed no curiosity about what Norbert planned to do, seeming content with her own thoughts as she drove.

Black Bear Island was situated just a few miles from the mainland. It could be reached by boat from the harbor. Norbert recalled that years ago, there used to be a ferry that ran back and forth regularly in the summer, and that could be boarded not far from where the Center for Deeper Understanding stood currently.

As Norbert got out of Birdie's car, she said, "I'll go back and see what Carlotta needs. Unless you want me to come with you, to wherever you are going?"

"Thank you, but, no, Birdie. I need to do this quietly, and all on my own."

Birdie did not ask what "this" meant. She understood the need to do things quietly, and on one's own.

CHAPTER FORTY-THREE

Ace of Hearts:

Transformative power.
Help comes from an unexpected source.
Above all, trust yourself.

Norbert walked through the snow along Edith's property, to the point where the ferry used to run. There was no ferry there. He stood contemplating the mother-of-pearl horizon as it blended into the lake, far away. He shivered, and waited for his intuition to tell him what to do next.

The snow crunched behind him. He turned.

There was Edith, her eyes bright and watchful.

Anyone else would say, "What brings you here?" or "May I help you?" But odd Edith simply spoke as if resuming a conversation that had recently paused.

"Isn't it beautiful here, Norbert?"

It was.

"It's warming up, eh?" she observed. "I mean, it's all relative." She buried her mittened hands in a muff, creating the general impression of some kind of marsupial animal.

"There used to be a ferry," commented Norbert. He felt an urgent need to get to the island, and couldn't pause for small talk.

"The ferry doesn't dock here anymore. It runs from Edwards Cove now. But not in wintertime, of course. If you want to go to the island, you'll need to find someone with a boat who would take you."

Norbert considered this.

"Edith, there is a young woman missing."

"Ah." Edith seemed untroubled.

Norbert said, looking across at his destination, "I saw Summer go there, in a sort of vision."

Norbert felt no reticence about sharing his vision with Edith. She accepted it as a matter of course. Of course.

Edith topped Norbert's remark: "And *I* saw Summer—or someone—go there, *not* in a vision. So, how do you like that?"

Norbert turned to look at her. As usual, Edith seemed to be enjoying a private joke.

"When?" asked Norbert.

Edith chuckled. "I'm an early riser, Norbert. I have been, all my lives." She pulled her brown knitted hat down farther over her ears. "It was yesterday morning, just before dawn. It was so dark all around, in the woods and on the lake. Full of life. All the night creatures were wrapping up their work, getting ready to go home and sleep. Smoke was coming up from one of the chimneys on the island, like a ghost escaping into the skies, you know? The birds were all just beginning to wake up and start their squawking. That's when I saw a figure—it seemed like it might have been a woman—walking across the ice bridge. She—if it was a she—was using a small flashlight to make a way across in the dark. I thought, *It's a little early in the winter to be using the ice bridge. But then, it's been so terribly cold.*"

The ice bridge.

Norbert had forgotten about the ice bridge.

The harbor between the mainland and Black Bear Island sometimes froze to a depth of four inches or even up to two feet. That expanse of frozen water from shore to shore was called "the ice bridge." When the water froze solidly, people walked across to the island and back. Norbert could remember an Eagle Scout winter excursion from his hometown of Buffalo to this area in 1961. On the frozen harbor, town kids were shouting, "Hey! Look at me! I'm walking on water!" The Eagle Scout leaders warned the young men of tragedies, when kids thought the ice bridge was solid enough to bear them, but it wasn't, and had fallen in. Norbert reflected on how every experience in life eventually seems to become useful.

CHAPTER FORTY-FOUR

Ace of Spades:

There is great power in this card.

It signifies a determining factor.

This is often seen as the "death card."

Try not to be fearful about this.

Death comes in many forms, and many times throughout
a lifetime. It may signal the death of childhood, the death
of an illusion, and so on. Explore possible meanings.

One thing is certain: life is about to change forever.

Alternatively, you might be about to die.

On Friday night, Summer had paced in her apartment, thinking about Norbert's reading.

Was there a great lie in her life? *Was* she blocking her own
path? He had used the word "bitter." Was she bitter? She was
bitter only toward herself. Did that count? Of course, she was
blocked. But how did he know that, just from looking at playing cards she pulled from the deck?

He had said something about her causing harm. She could
not bear the thought of causing any more harm than she already had. Who was that Queen of Diamonds? Could that
be Gramma? But she wasn't doing anything that could harm
anyone, not that she could see. But then, she hadn't seen the
tragedy she was about to cause the last time, either.

When Norbert had talked of disaster and possible death "in
some form," that had sent a shock of terror through her. Was

she about to cause a disaster? Was someone going to die because of her? She began to imagine what those words might mean.

Several hours later, Summer, bundled up so that she resembled a roll of carpet more than a human being, stepped off the snow-covered shore onto the ice covering the harbor. A sign forbade walking on the ice and warned of the depth of the water. She bounced up and down a bit on her boots, allowing herself just for a moment to think of what would happen if the ice were not solid enough. It didn't matter. She was crossing.

The ice stretching out before her had the solemn beauty of a lunar landscape. As she walked, moonlight beamed down on her at first, but as she neared the middle of the ice harbor, clouds covered the sky, leaving her in total darkness. She tried not to think of the deep and frigid water beneath her feet. Tried not to think of the stories of people who had fallen through the ice. In cloud-covered darkness, her small flashlight was enough to light her way, one step at a time. Once she slipped and fell down on the jagged, glassy surface. For a moment, she lay there among the frozen dunes of ice water, thinking about the effort of getting up and continuing her march through the cold. She wondered if she lay there long enough whether she would freeze to death. How cold was it? She rose and pushed on.

It occurred to Summer that for once in her life, if she needed to call for help, she would not be able to. She'd left her cell phone on her bed—deliberately. She'd wanted to be out of reach.

In fact, being chronically out of reach had become her only comfort in life. Holing up in her apartment with her curtains shut, eyelids shut, mind shut against the bright, bewildering world outside. Each day of work required a full evening of "downtime" to recover, and each morning it was a struggle to get up and get dressed for work. Once she was there, she somehow played "Spanish teacher," and no one seemed to notice she was a fake in every way. How could they not notice? And yet they didn't. Her department head had said to her just the week before, "Do you know, you are a very sunny person. Your name, Summer, suits you perfectly. I think you must be the happiest person I know." He probably just wanted to seduce her. If that was his game, he'd lost. She had no interest in seductions, dating, friendships, or any other unnecessary expenditure of energy. There was just barely energy for work and for what was left of her family: Gramma and Hope. In her apartment, the hours slipped by sideways while she stared at the inside of her eyelids. Television overwhelmed her, the internet irritated her, and she couldn't focus on books. She slept a lot. She was halfway through her twenties. Sometimes, she couldn't wait for it to all be over.

It was ten years ago that she had, through one act of teenage rebellion, brought disaster on her family. Through the years, she had rewound and replayed that night so many times, making it end differently. If just one thing had been different, her parents would still be alive. If Rory had found another girl that night and forgot to come pick her up; if her mother had put more authority in her voice; if her dad, instead of standing with his hands on his hips, would have put his hands on her shoulders and stopped her from running out the door; if that fifteen-year-old Summer could have known that what seemed like a game to her would have consequences that would never end.

Summer stepped at last from the ice onto the snow-covered island, letting out her breath in a cloud. It wasn't much farther to the cottage. There was a string of only about twenty cottages on the island, all nestled together along the shoreline. The rest of the island was a protected wilderness. She found where the gravel path would be, beneath the snow, and made her way between the pine trees.

Summer heard the chuckles and screeches of an American marten on the prowl. The marten was one of her favorite creatures. As a kid, she'd written papers about these nocturnal, catlike, carnivorous weasels that lived in the hollows of pines and swung from the tops of trees like acrobats. The island teemed with opossums, raccoons, bats, porcupines and owls. She'd spent summers studying all the wildlife when she'd come to the island with her parents. They'd had a cottage, which was sold after they died, and had since been torn down.

Summer knew this place better than any other on earth. She had explored every foot of this island, and listened to its heartbeat. As a small child, she'd walked along its paths with her dad, trying to not make a leaf crunch—"like Native Americans," he'd said. With her mother, she'd sketched and identified the wildflowers in their botanical illustration sketchbooks. On her own, she'd explored and spent fascinated hours observing the creatures going about their lives. For her, this place was sacred ground. Black Bear Island was the very place she needed to come back to now, to once again put her ear to that heartbeat.

On the island, Summer would be able to find calm. She would be able to reset herself so that she could "avert the disaster" in Norbert Zelenka's reading. Lindsay had told her she would leave a lamp on a timer. Its glow from the window welcomed Summer forward.

CHAPTER FORTY-FIVE

Ten of Spades:

The tearing down of illusions,
to make space for a new beginning, based on truth.

The cottage was simple. It sat slightly apart from the other cottages, which were probably empty. It had two bedrooms, one of which was an art studio filled with easels and Lindsay's works in progress. There was a view of the water from the rustic kitchen table. The living room area was outfitted with thrift-store furniture, which gave a comfy, retro feeling. There was a stone fireplace with, mercifully, some dried-out wood in it. The other cottages on the island were all grander and larger—some were probably too big to properly be called cottages, but this one was homey and cozy like the one her parents used to own, and which had been replaced by a more ostentatious house.

Summer lit the fire, using matches from the stone mantelpiece and newspapers from the iron basket on the hearth. She turned up the thermostat, which Lindsay kept only high enough to keep pipes from freezing when she wasn't there.

The gradual warmth filling the little cottage brought back the circulation to Summer's feet and hands.

She gazed into the fire as it grew into an energetic blaze. At this time of night, she should be asleep, but there was no chance of sleeping now. Her card reading with the strange old man at the Good Fortune Café had unsettled her. He clearly knew things, saw things about her, beyond the facade that everyone else accepted so easily. His deep brown eyes, his hypnotic, soft voice and his air of authority all led her to trust him and his psychic abilities. She felt he was asking her to look deeper into her own mind, and that was odd, because she had spent years of her life ruminating. Summer's thoughts were pulled forward into the flames as she sat curled in a plaid recliner chair. She glanced from the fire to the splendid orange dawn that was springing up within the dark frame of the living room window, and back to the fire again.

I wish they were here. I wish they were here. I wish they were here. If it weren't for me, they would be here.

I never got to reconcile. They died worried about me, probably angry with me, maybe confused about what kind of person I would turn out to be, I don't know. I never got to apologize, or show them that I did turn out to be a decent adult. They would have been proud of me, and I'm sad for them that they didn't get to have that. I would have gone to them for encouragement and wisdom, and I'm sad for myself that I don't get to have that.

Summer's head began to nod. She shook herself awake and stood, and stepped out on the porch with the blanket still wrapped around her. The cold air woke her up and brought her back to life. She stood still. Listening. Allowing. Receiving.

She heard the hoot of an owl and the rustling breeze in her ears. At last, she heard her parents' voices, calm and peaceful, carried to her on the wind.

"We gave you life. Live it."

CHAPTER FORTY-SIX

King of Clubs:

A courageous man, capable of heroism.

It was early afternoon when Norbert stepped off onto the ice bridge. Edith had scampered back into the Center for Deeper Understanding to facilitate her new Tai Chi class, after advising him to take a boat rather than try walking across the harbor. The sun was shining brightly, giving Norbert a bad case of snow blindness. As Edith had said, it was early in the winter for people to begin using the ice bridge. Had the water frozen deeply enough to bear the weight of a person crossing? Norbert, normally cautious, let these thoughts go.

It was his fault that Summer was missing; it was his responsibility to get her back to safety. Now that he was about to take action, his anxiety was abating. Values that he had learned as a boy and believed in all his life told him that when you do something wrong, you must try to make amends.

He breathed in the cold air that was heavy with the fragrance of wood fires. The din of dozens of bird species filled his ears. Even in winter, there were so many birds: the snowy owl, the chickadee, the cardinal and many more whose songs he couldn't identify. Most of the cottages across the harbor looked uninhabited. His heart leaped when he saw smoke snaking up from the chimney of one. Summer was there, he knew it.

He walked with intention across the ice. As he walked, he sensed that the ice might not be quite as thick as he had hoped when he began. That guiding voice within him, the one he had learned to listen to at last, encouraged him to go forward, to find Summer. Was this the Daimon that Birdie had spoken of that day in the art gallery? That Inner Voice that tells you: "Go here," "Do this," the voice that Socrates spoke of?

Some spots were slippery, and he had to take it slow.

Warm spells in winter are the most dangerous times to venture out onto the ice, Norbert remembered from his days in Eagle Scouts and from his dedicated study of *Reader's Digest* articles over the years. Lakes freeze in patches, he recalled, as his feet took him forward. Thinner in some spots than others. How deep *was* this ice? Sudden immersion in ice water can cause cardiac arrest even before drowning, he knew. An Eagle Scout, he thought, would not try this without ice picks to pull himself out of a hole in the ice. If he didn't fall through, he was still apt to slip and twist his ankle. At least he had his cell phone, to call for help. He pulled it out of his pocket.

Under his feet, he sensed a barely perceptible wobble, a slight rocking of the ice. His heart accelerated with fear, as he realized the folly he was committing. He was now past the middle of the harbor, closer to the island than the mainland. He could go forward toward the shoreline of the island—or back toward the mainland. He wasn't going back.

When it happened, it was as if Norbert had expected it all along.

There was a loud *Crack! Boom!* Norbert felt a jolt of pain as his body was engulfed by the frigidity of the lake. He gasped, reflexively covering his nose and mouth against the entry of the icy water. *Step One.* Norbert seemed to hear the instructions from an article read long ago. *Grab for a shelf of ice, and bring yourself over to it.*

He was hyperventilating, and working to slow his gasps.

Step Two. You are in cold shock. Your one and only task right now is to calm your mind. In cold shock, your breathing, heart rate and blood pressure increase. Do not panic; slow your breathing as much as you can. The gasping will stop in a couple of minutes. Then you can act.

Norbert felt a burning agony through his feet, legs and torso, which was immediately followed with numbness.

"The cold shock will pass," he panted into the unfeeling winter scene, and his voice sounded thin and feeble to him. A snowshoe hare hesitated on the shore and seemed to take in the calamity in the harbor, but offered him no encouragement before leaping off into the thickness of the pine trees.

Norbert's clothing, now soaked, had become heavy, and was sucking his weight down toward the depths of the lake, but he kept his arms firmly on the ice shelf.

Nine minutes. Nine minutes to get out, or go unconscious and then drown. He could let his sleeves freeze to the ice shelf, so that even if he went unconscious, he would hang propped there above water and could possibly be rescued. But, no, Norbert was going to rescue himself. He remembered how.

"Do not try to pull yourself up on the ice," he said out loud. He knew that if he did, the thin ice all around would break under his weight, and he would not be able to pull himself out.

Keeping his arms up on the ice, Norbert began to kick his

feet. Later, he could not say how he was able to kick feet and legs that were numb, but all his forces came to his assistance, and he kicked faster, faster and faster, until he made himself horizontal in the ice water, his body parallel with the ice. Then, with just a few really strong kicks, he pushed himself forward on the ice shelf.

"Do not stand up," he instructed himself. He wanted to stand and run from the danger he had just escaped, but he knew that the ice here, being thin, would break if he stood.

Norbert rolled, distributing his weight, and then crawled. Miraculously, there on the surface of the ice was his cell phone, about twenty feet from the ice hole. He had thrown it into the air when he fell in. He grabbed his phone and continued to crawl awhile before he dared stand up and stumble to shore.

Once in the thickness of the pine trees and out of the wind, Norbert, shivering violently, took off all his clothes. He was trembling all over, and his coordination was poor now, and the clothes came off slowly.

"All of them, all of them, you *have* to," he urged himself. The cold wet clothes would have driven him deeper into hypothermia. Everything must come off immediately, and then he must get indoors to warmth within a few minutes, or perish.

He was beyond cold, beyond pain and beyond numbness. His only focus was on survival now.

As if he were a bird with an aerial view of the scene, Norbert saw the pile of soaked and iced clothes lying strewn on the forest floor, and a skinny, nude Norbert, clutching a cell phone and dashing through the trees.

CHAPTER FORTY-SEVEN

Ten of Clubs:

A period of healing,
which may be physical, spiritual or emotional.

By Sunday afternoon, Summer had already run through Lindsay's scant provisions. The island appeared to be deserted. Before the fire in the living room, she sat considering how to get herself home. She wouldn't dare to try the ice bridge again.

Suddenly there was a fierce rattling at the door.

Through the window, Summer saw a naked old man in distress.

It was the fortune-teller.

Norbert sat wrapped in Lindsay Prescott's white chenille bathrobe with his feet plunged into her fluffy rabbit slippers. He was trembling violently, and Summer was frightened for him, but through chattering teeth, Norbert was able to tell her that these physiological reactions were normal and would subside within an hour. In the meantime, a sweet hot drink would be helpful, and no, thank you, it would not be wise for him to sit too near the fire yet—it could cause his blood vessels to constrict too fast.

"Gee, Mr. Zelenka, how do you know so much about hypothermia?"

"*R-R-Reader's-s-s D-D-D-igest,*" Norbert answered.

As Norbert's temperature began to approach normal, and Summer was persuaded that he was out of danger, she realized what he had risked to find her.

"Why have you done this?" She was angry. She had not asked anyone to look for her. It was not even any of his business that she was here. He had very nearly died to find her.

"I had to, Summer. It would have been my fault if something had happened to you."

"*Your* fault if something happened to *me*?"

"The reading. I gave you a reading that upset you."

"Oh." Summer wrinkled her brow, trying to see it from the fortune-teller's perspective. "But it wasn't the *reading* that upset me. It was the clarity that I got. It was like—*truth*—edging in to where I hadn't allowed it before. The truth is what upset me. I saw it all at once."

"Ah, yes. That seems to happen for a lot of people, somehow," Norbert said, humbly. "Knowing the truth about yourself can be upsetting. But it is also empowering. Knowing the truth may not solve all your problems. But it gives you a place to start. That's what the truth can do for you. That is a great thing."

"I think I'd been shutting out the truth—in favor of wallowing in my own guilt. I didn't do it on purpose. I just didn't see any other way. I'd built up this huge wall of blame against myself, for years and years. It seemed reasonable to do it. It seemed fair. I never saw that by doing that, I was only doing more harm than when I committed my original crime."

"Crime?"

"I've always thought of it as a crime. The night my parents died in the accident, they were coming to pick me up, and there was a terrible ice storm. Gramma and everyone in town already knows that. But the part she doesn't know—no one knows—is that it didn't need to happen that way."

Summer hesitated. She could tell this kind man about her guilt. He wouldn't judge her. No one could judge her as harshly as she had judged herself. For the first time, Summer spoke aloud what she had done the night her parents died. As she spoke, the memory returned to her vividly, and it was as if she were living it all again.

"You're not going anywhere with anyone tonight." Dad was trying to sound all authority-like.

"Oh, Summer! There's a winter storm coming in. Stay home with us," Mom was pleading, trying to convince me to stay, as if she didn't realize she was the mom and could stop me. Well, then, she couldn't.

It was four o'clock. I looked out the window, waiting for Rory's old red Dodge Omni to pull in the driveway. The sun was setting dimly in an overcast sky, and ice was beginning to fall in splinters against the house.

"It's just three blocks to the bowling alley. I'll be fine." They always seemed to believe the bowling alley.

Rory honked from the driveway, and my heart leaped.

Dad said, "Don't you go running out there at the honk of a horn. Make him come to the door and shake hands with your father." Dad peered out through the blinds to where Rory's car sat loudly idling. "Hey," he added, "how old is that guy? He looks too old for you."

"Yeah, Dad," I said, trying out my new sarcasm. "He's a senior citizen." I was zipping my jacket and pulling my cap down over my head.

"Don't be smart with me, young lady. Where'd you meet this character? What's his name?"

"The mall," I said as I pushed past my dad, who stood with his hands on his hips, elbows out, legs spread. He was a small and skinny guy, and I thought, "He looks so silly right now." I felt sorry for him. But not sorry enough to stay. Not sorry enough to miss out on Rory.

I stepped out, slammed the door, and ran, slipping and sliding, to the exotic new world of Rory and his car. I thought how easy it was now to defy them I'd never done it in such a major way before. I felt triumphant and guilty at the same time.

It was warm in Rory's car and he had the music up loud. He gave me a knowing look and a smile that made me feel grown up and delicious and just the right amount edgy. He pulled out of the driveway and started cruising. Suddenly I felt shy. As he drove, I looked at him and thought he was better than any of the crushes I had at school. I thought of my dad exclaiming, How old is that guy? And I smiled. It was cool to be with an older guy for once. I didn't know how old he was. Twenty-four? Thirty-five? I wasn't so good at judging ages. But he had long black hair that hung to his shoulders, and dark eyes. He wore an earring. Like Johnny Depp. A pirate.

He was a good driver, I thought, as the ice and snow made patterns on his windshield and he straightened the car out of skids and slides.

From under his seat, he pulled a paper bag and drank from the bottle inside it, and handed it to me with a smile. He had a nice smile. Even, white teeth.

I took a drink and sputtered, and he laughed a friendly laugh, pushing my hair back from my face.

"Aw, you're not used to that, are you?"

And I thought he was so sweet. So I tried again, more slowly this time, just the tiniest sips. It went down burning in my chest, but it wasn't such a bad feeling. It made me think of a cough syrup my mom used to give me when I was little. The effect of the alcohol began to work on me almost at once. So far in my lifetime, I'd barely tasted any.

"What is this—rum?" I asked. I thought, pirates drink rum.

"Whiskey," he said. "It's good for you."

He parked by the beach. We made out while the ice pelted the windows and the wind shook the car. It was different from making out with Noah, a boy my age—my very first boyfriend—who had just dumped me. But Rory kept looking around for cop cars, and when he spotted one rolling down the street, he put his car in Drive and we were moving again. He stashed the whiskey back under the seat until the cop car stopped following.

"I know where I'll take you," he said, as if he had a sudden inspiration, and he turned the car onto Highway 4, toward Edwards Cove.

By that point, I thought I was feeling happier than I'd ever felt, but also strangely divided from myself. It was as if I were at the same time two people: one was a sober witness to all that was happening, and the other was drunk. My face felt numb. I raised my hand to try to feel my cheek and poked myself in the eye. That made me giggle. I felt Rory looking at me, and I hoped I wasn't making a fool of myself. Probably the other girls that he knew were used to drinking.

He pulled into the parking lot of the Fox Point apartment buildings. This was where the Gibbons Corner kids came to buy drugs. Did Rory live here?

Moments skipped, and I was out in the ice storm, holding Rory's hand, and walking unsteadily through the door of a first-floor apartment. I had expected he was taking me to where he lived so we could be alone, but when I entered, I found myself in a threadbare living room where nine or ten listless men were sitting in a smoky haze, as if in a group trance. There was a cloying odor of pot and rancid beer. They all looked up. As they saw me standing in my short boots and leggings, my long blond hair hanging down to my waist, interest began to ignite on their faces.

I stood unsteadily, trying not to lean.

"Whoa, Rory, what did you bring us?"

"Shut up," said Rory, moving into the room to grab the joint that was going around.

I reached behind me for the doorknob, and worked on turning my-self around to face the door. "I'm going. I gotta go now."

I heard Rory's voice saying, gently, "Baby, it's cold outside. Come on in and warm up. No one's gonna hurt you here. What are you gonna do, walk back to Gibbons Corner?"

I heard him moving toward me.

Again, minutes disappeared, and I was running down an icy road, the hail pelting my face. Behind me, I could hear Rory call and then laugh, but I didn't hear the words. I hit the ground hard a few times, and picked myself back up again and again, running on until I got to a gas station. I had run only two blocks, but by the time I burst into the tiny convenience store and woke up the dozing service-station at-tendant, I felt almost sober.

The name sewn on his shirtfront said "Billy," and he watched me dial my cell phone.

"Mommy? Mommy, come and pick me up, please?" What made me call her "Mommy" that night? That's what I used to call her when I was little. I always said "Mom" now. But I felt little again. Little and scared and wanting my mother to come quick and take me home.

She didn't ask any questions; she just took the address and I heard her calling my dad to get his coat.

As the hours ticked by and my parents didn't come, and they didn't answer my calls, Billy finally spoke up.

"I hate to say it, but something mighta happened. It's a bad night out there, eh? I'll just call the police and check if anything's hap-pened, yeah?"

Summer became aware of the old man, focusing his kind attention on her story. She had been right to trust him. He wasn't judging her. He was holding her in his compassionate heart. She could feel it.

"I shouldn't have been out that night in the first place. I pushed past my parents and went out with some creepy older guy because I liked his long hair and his earring or some stupid thing. I was fifteen. Clueless. They tried to stop me, and I disrespected them. Of course, once I was with the creepy guy, I got in trouble." Summer was picking at the blanket that was wrapped around her legs. "My parents had always said, if I didn't feel right in any situation, just call them and they'd come pick me up."

Summer paused, seeing the scene again with regret.

"So you did," encouraged Norbert. "You did what they'd told you to do."

"And their car slid on the icy road and crashed. They died instantly."

Watching the sticks and logs burning in the fireplace, Norbert waited.

"So I'd always felt that I caused it. That I killed them."

"And now?" prompted Norbert. "What do you feel now?"

"And now," picked up Summer, "something has shifted." She looked into Norbert's dark, attentive eyes. "Between the truth that began to hit me during your reading, and the message that I feel now, coming up from the island itself—does that sound crazy?"

"Not at all."

"If I'm quiet here, and just listen, I don't know. There is truth here, too."

"There is truth anywhere you are. The whole thing is the listening part. We don't always listen." Norbert turned the mug around in his hands. He added, as if to himself, "In fact, we hardly ever listen."

Summer nodded slowly. "Maybe I felt, right after it happened, that if I accepted all the blame, my parents would be restored to me. I know that doesn't make sense, but I think I really hoped for that." She tapped her forehead in frustration. "I had a kid-brain."

"Right. You had a kid-brain." The fortune-teller spoke with

energy. "Given the kid-brain you had at the time, who you were then, and your level of development, your blind spots—how could you have done anything but draw kid–conclusions? In fact, with your kid-brain, how could you have done anything differently that night?"

Summer paused, uncertain.

"But I'm sure that when *you* were a kid, you didn't rebel like that, did you?"

"Oh, well, when I was a kid, it was a different time. When *I* was fifteen, it was…almost 1960. No one was rebelling yet. And I didn't have parents to rebel against. I had my aunt Pearl, who I knew had essentially saved me from being sent to an orphanage. So it was entirely different for me, when I had a kid-brain."

"So your aunt Pearl for you was like my grandmother to me."

"I guess so. You and I—we were both orphans, now that you mention it. And we each had a loving woman to raise us."

"You didn't rebel against your aunt, partly because of the times. But maybe there is something special about being raised by that loving person after your parents are dead. I could have given Gramma a hard time. I did think about it. But I was too grateful to her. And sad for her. I lost my taste for rebelling. I just played by her rules. I'm glad I at least did that."

The old man stirred his sugary tea. "Now, what you have been struggling with is self-forgiveness. It's one of the hardest blocks we put in our own path. It's the same for everyone, with self-forgiveness."

"The same for *everyone*?" Summer threw another log on the fire and adjusted it with the poker. "Not many people have guilt like mine."

"Many people do have something they can't forgive themselves for. You'd be surprised how many. When I meet with someone like that over a reading, this is what I tell them. You have basically only two options. One—keep up this grudge against yourself and bring more negativity into the world, make yourself sick physically or mentally and live a life of dark self-absorption."

Summer shivered and looked at him with deep attention. He went on. "Or option two—acknowledge that people do grow and change and do better. Let your apology be a life worth living."

The two sat in a companionable silence for several minutes.

Finally, Summer spoke. "My apology could be a life worth living. That's sort of what I heard my parents telling me a little while ago. I could hear them telling me to live my life. I'd never been able to hear them before, though I'd always tried to. Today, I didn't try. Their voices just floated to me on the wind. It was really them, I think."

The kind old man nodded, and gazed out the window at the snowy branches of the woods all around them.

"Sometimes," said Summer, softly, "I still miss them so much."

"I know," answered the fortune-teller. "I miss my wife, Lois. It's been almost thirty years, and the pain is muted now. But I still catch myself thinking, 'Lois would love Ivy,' or 'What would Lois say if she could see me reading cards in the café?' I think she would think it was funny. She was a person who laughed a lot. Maybe that's what I miss most of all, the sound of her laughter. Yes, the sounds of her laughter and… the beat of her heart."

Summer reached for his hand and held it. He was warming up.

She looked at him clothed in Lindsay's bathrobe and slippers and thought how nearly he had approached death that night.

"I still wish you hadn't crossed the ice. It scares me, to think we could have lost you. The world needs you, you and your fortunes, Mr. Zelenka."

The fortune-teller seemed mildly surprised at this compliment.

"I think the world has actually had enough of my fortunes. I should never have gotten into fortune-telling to begin with. And I've already told you," he said. "I had no choice but to cross the ice bridge. You had disappeared."

"*Disappeared?* I never *disappeared*. I came *here*. I have every right to come here. I love it here."

"But no one knew where you were, and—"

"Oh! Oh, no! I just realized—Gramma!" Summer's mind had been so far removed from Carlotta and Toutou, but now everything came rushing back. "My grandmother is worried, huh?"

"You could say that. There's a huge search party—"

"A *search* party? Oh, no!" said Summer. "Poor Gramma!"

Norbert pushed his cell phone across the coffee table to her.

Carlotta's exclamations blasted through the phone, causing Summer to pull her ear away.

"It's *me*, Gramma! Wait, wait! I'm okay... On Black Bear Island... Wait—let me tell you..."

Norbert smiled as Summer struggled to explain to her grandmother their current circumstances amid Carlotta's outbursts of mixed annoyance and relief.

"Oh, and, Gramma? When the boat comes? Mr. Zelenka? He's going to need some clothes. He left his in the woods... Well, no—not actually naked. He's wearing Lindsay's bathrobe."

When the police boat carrying Norbert, Summer and Officer Curry docked in Edwards Cove that afternoon, the search team was there to greet and cheer them.

Carlotta, after embracing Summer, approached Norbert.

"It appears I will not have to make good on my threat to murder you, Norbert. I'm glad. I am eighty years old and have not had to murder anyone yet. It would be a shame to start now."

Norbert saw that she was fighting emotions that were close to overcoming her. He smiled.

"Norbert, let me start again. What I mean to say is, thank you. You risked your life to bring Summer home. A man your age, falling into that icy water, well, things could have turned out very differently. You are a hero, Norbert."

"Oh, no, hardly a hero," protested Norbert with a frown. "My aunt Pearl always said, when you make a mistake, set things right; make amends. It's just the normal thing to do."

"Normal!" exclaimed Carlotta. "If that's true, then I must say there seem to be very few normal people left in the world these days." She squeezed his arm and turned her attention back to her darling granddaughter.

Reggie Di Leo sidled up to Norbert and tilted his head toward him in a confidential manner. "I don't know how you did it, Mr. Psychic, but you and I both know you're a fraud."

Just then, there was a popping noise in Reggie Di Leo's pocket. He pulled out a cell phone—Summer's. The text was from a "Lindsay Prescott."

Having an amazing time in Rome. Will send pics later. Enjoy the cottage!

"I woulda found her," he said, to no one in particular.

CHAPTER FORTY-EIGHT

Six of Hearts:

You already know the answer to your deepest question.

Carlotta had to hand it to Norbert. He had nearly expired in the attempt to bring Summer back. Of course, her granddaughter was safe the whole time, but the point was, Norbert had not known that. He had shown true heroism.

Naturally, she'd been annoyed with Summer for impulsively disappearing. Summer was suitably embarrassed and apologetic. Young people didn't think things through all of the time. Carlotta was so grateful to have her lovely granddaughter restored safely. After they came home, dear Summer had wanted to talk about that awful night ten years ago, but Carlotta had calmed her down, and they'd said no more about it. Raking over the past was no way to get on with one's living. And the important thing now was to get on with life. With Toutou at her feet, Summer curled up the way only the very young can curl up on her elegant overstuffed chair, and the fire blazing away in the fireplace, Carlotta's heart was filled with peace. And, of course, a New Plan.

That night, Norbert closed the blinds in his little house on Harrison Street. He heard the rumble of a train as it rocked along the tracks downtown. Summer was safe with Carlotta, and she would be reflecting on the lessons that had presented themselves to her in her card reading and during her sojourn on the island. That was her own path to take. Meanwhile, Nobert had some soul-searching of his own to do.

Carlotta had told him that he was a hero. Reggie Di Leo had told him that he was a fraud. Norbert knew that he was neither. He was only a simple man with a desire to be of service to others.

He didn't know if his fortune-telling days were all behind him. What does a fortune-teller do when his readings cause people to do things they wouldn't normally do? Where does a fortune-teller look for answers to his own predicament?

He consults the cards, of course.

Norbert sat down at his table, set Ivy on his lap and the deck facedown before him. No need to do the horseshoe spread. One card was all he needed. One card would tell him: continue or stop. Keep being Norbert Z, the psychic, or go back to being Mr. Norbert Zelenka, respectable retiree and amateur painter. Keep meeting with people, listening to them and advising them… Or live the simple, quiet life of a simple, quiet man.

Taking in a deep breath and letting it go, Norbert fanned out the cards, facedown, before him. He let his hand be drawn to one of the cards, pulled it and read its message. It was the Six of Hearts.

You already know the answer to your deepest question.

CHAPTER FORTY-NINE

Eight of Hearts:

An unexpected meeting brings new perspective.

A Wednesday afternoon in early January. The trees and bushes stood in elegant black outlines, bearing inches of snow, and dangling glittering icicles from their branches. The temperature had risen to a balmy thirty-eight degrees, and the grateful residents of Gibbons Corner were outside in droves, enjoying the promise of thaw while it lasted. A few were out in their boats, some were walking along the snow-covered beach, and a group of kids was sliding on the patchy ice of the parking lot near the pier. Children and their parents were making snowmen in the park adjoining the lake.

Norbert had Ivy in tow in her carrier, where she was bundled in a pink sweater knitted by Birdie. Her chiseled head poked over the top of the bag. No wind blew. There was ice over the pier, and all around were small hills of snow. Norbert stopped just before the sign on the pier: No Admittance.

Pier Closed For Winter Season. He and Ivy gazed off into the horizon—a horizon that was very different from the last time they had been here. The sky and water blended together: green-gray, gray-blue. The beauty of the lake in winter and the relentless shush-shush-shush of the waves calmed Norbert's heart, which had been turbulent.

Norbert considered the message of the Six of Hearts. Was it true? Did he, in fact, know the answer to his deepest question? Should he quit the psychic business, or keep advising customers at the Good Fortune Café?

Gamboling over the snow-covered beach, Carlotta's miniature poodle Toutou appeared. Norbert looked around for Carlotta, but she was nowhere to be seen. A girl of about twelve was following behind the dog, which looped back and ran a few circles around the child and then ran forward again, as if showing off her superior speed. As they approached, Norbert realized that the distant form he had perceived as a child was, in fact, Carlotta's granddaughter, Summer. He waved, and she approached, clipping a leash on Toutou.

"Hello, Mr. Zelenka. Beautiful day! Feels like spring, eh?" Her eyes were covered against the brilliance of the snow with black sunglasses.

"Yes. Warming up," answered Norbert, stomping his feet, which were beginning to feel frozen inside his boots.

She smiled at him and took off her sunglasses, revealing her blue eyes flecked with brown.

"I was going to stop in at the café this afternoon and see if you'd do another reading for me."

Norbert started. "One wasn't enough?"

Summer laughed. "One was enough to put me on a new path. Now I want more directions."

Norbert shook his head. "What do you suppose your grandmother would do to me if she heard I'd read for you again?"

Summer made a dismissive gesture, identical to Carlotta's trademark dismissive gesture. "Oh, Gramma! I can deal with *her*. Seriously, though. Your reading helped me see something I'd been hiding from myself. The self-blame *has* been poisoning my life. I'm trying to change the habit of sinking into that. I don't really know how to do it—not completely."

"It's a funny thing about guilt, Summer. Well. I mean, not funny, really. But the *strange* thing about guilt is that it's the good people who suffer with it. The people who do harm to others repeatedly and never care—they're the ones who are free of guilt. That's strange, isn't it? But the purpose of guilt is only to keep you from making the same mistake again. The point of guilt was never to poison your life."

"How did you get to be so wise, Mr. Zelenka? Every single thing you said in the reading was true."

"Was it?" asked Norbert, frowning. "I'm not so sure about that. Maybe you made it come true because I'd predicted it?"

"What? No! I averted a disaster—just like you said. The disaster was wasting my whole life, making my life be something negative, maybe even hurting the people I love the most with my insistence on blaming myself forever. That was the disaster."

"The disaster could have been you falling through the ice—because of my reading."

"But I *didn't* fall through the ice. *You* did—heroically, I might add… I think I understand now that I need to learn to release the past and live the life my parents gave me. The problem is, I have no idea *how* to do it. I need to write my next chapter, Mr. Zelenka. I just need a little help from you to know how to do all that."

Norbert saw the lake and sky reflected in Summer's eyes. A few snowflakes had begun to fall. Summer caught a cou-

ple of them on her mitten and watched them, before dropping her hand.

"Another reading, eh?" asked Norbert.

Summer nodded.

"Tell you what. Let's do that reading—in six months from
now. In the meantime, listen to yourself. The answers will
come, if you make quiet time and listen. I'm glad to help you,
Summer, if you think I can. But you don't want to depend on
me or anyone else for your answers in life. The fact is, you already know the answers to your deepest questions."

CHAPTER FIFTY

Four Sixes:

A period of equilibrium is restored.
Enjoy it while it lasts.

Carlotta's Club was gathered in her formal dining room, eating *biscuits* and drinking *café*. Brochures on Quebec's Winter Carnival were strewn among the floral china cups, and excitement was popping in the air as twinkling icicles dripped and fell from the eaves outside. Carlotta's New Plan was under way.

Margaret made a brave attempt at using the French she had been batting away at in private lessons with Carlotta and Birdie. The nastiness of the episode of the French tourist was behind them all. Carlotta was back to pretending she was fluent in French, and her best friends were back to pretending to believe her. After all, the Club knew that one day, they would all meet their "tourist from Quebec," in whatever form that might take, so it is best to be kind to their friends when it happened to them.

"I am fatty gay," said Margaret.

"Je suis fatiguée," corrected Carlotta, brightly. "'I am tired' is *Je suis fatiguée.*"

"That's what I said, isn't it?" said Margaret.

"Almost, dear. Very close."

"Well, then," said Margaret.

Birdie soothed Margaret, *"Ce n'est pas grave, Marguerite."*

"Huh?" asked Margaret.

"It's no big deal. It's okay," translated Birdie.

"Well, I'm excited about the *trip!*" sparkled Margaret. "I'm sure there are plenty of people in Quebec who talk regular."

Margaret was such a child, dear old thing. But my, Carlotta reflected, it felt so good to have things back in order in her life.

"Now, let's decide on what we most want to see when we get there. The Charlesbourg Night Parade? The Winter Symphony? The Ice Hotel?"

Brochures went flying from hand to hand and exclamations grew in volume as Carlotta's Club planned their winter vacation. They might have suspected that, regardless of the options they would choose, Carlotta had already finalized their itinerary in her own agenda.

When they did come to realize that their activities were preplanned for them, they would surrender to the power of Carlotta's personality, and Birdie would remark, *"C'est la vie."*

CHAPTER FIFTY-ONE

Nine of Hearts and Nine of Diamonds:

Most favorable.
Because of your humility, you are vindicated.

It was early February and Carlotta's Club was in Quebec. The snow glittered in the sunlight outside the Good Fortune Café, where Norbert sat drinking an espresso and waiting for a customer. Business was slow today, but someone identified as RDL had registered by phone for an appointment at 3:00 p.m.

At 2:58, in walked Reggie Di Leo, the private investigator. The bell on the door jingled merrily and incongruously over his scowling face. Catching sight of Norbert, he nodded once and made straight for the same table where the two men had sat weeks ago, the day that Reggie had "finished with Norbert."

Watching Reggie's approach, Norbert felt strangely calm and self-assured. He saw in a glance a man who had grown mistrustful through his life's disappointments, a man who was in many ways closed off from others and from himself, a man who covered his sadness with hostility. How could Norbert not feel a wish to heal and advise a wounded soul?

"Norbert Z," said Reggie, with less sarcasm than the last time he had said Norbert's professional name.

"Reggie," said Norbert, with a friendly smile.

"Don't get the idea I'm here for a reading," said Reggie, passing a hand through his black locks and emitting a brief, mirthless laugh.

"Ah?" said Norbert.

"I'm here on business. But I'll pay you for your time." Reggie pushed a photograph toward Norbert.

"You did so well with that last missing-person case," said Reggie, smiling with one half of his mouth, as if he were joking, "I thought I'd try you on this one."

"You want me to help you find a missing person?" asked Norbert, puzzling over this compliment from such an unexpected source.

Norbert picked up the photograph and immediately recognized the young woman.

Reggie said, "Her name is Georgina Burns. From Buffalo. She's been missing for seven weeks. Her mother just called me last week, since the police haven't turned up anything. I told her, I said, you waited too long, whadda you think I can do *now*? You shoulda called me right away. Then she— Anyway. You get any feeling about this? You wanna pull some cards out of your deck or something? I mean, at this point, there's nothing to lose. She's gone without a trace."

Norbert looked into the face of his customer, Gigi. Norbert saw her in his mind, soaking up the New Mexico sun.

Glancing back at Reggie, he considered his options.

"Tell her mother," began Norbert, "that she's alive and safe."

Reggie leaned forward, listening respectfully.

Norbert continued, "And she doesn't want to be found."

Reggie sat back. He had expected more.

He said, "That doesn't help me collect my fee, does it?"

"Tell her mother she'll be in touch when she is ready."

"Yeah. Right. My line of work, you don't give people news like that. That's not what they want to hear. 'Where the hell is she?' That's all they want to know."

"She's gone to a place where she can grow into who she is," said Norbert.

Reggie raised his eyebrows at Norbert, then looked out the window and scratched his head. He looked back at Norbert and emitted another dry laugh. He was hesitating between scorn and curiosity.

"What the hell does that mean, Zelenka?" he asked.

"It means, simply, she couldn't grow here."

"She was already grown. She was twenty-seven. Whadda you talking about?"

"This is a young woman who needs just a little space and time. She's finding her life's purpose,"

Reggie said, "Oh! *There* we go. Life's purpose. Well, that's okay, then, huh." Reggie shook his head. "Life's purpose, my ass." He drew his wallet from his coat pocket and pulled out a twenty-dollar bill. "Here's for your time, Zelenka."

Norbert said, "Wait. The twenty minutes isn't up. Do you want a reading for yourself?"

Reggie tilted his chin up and frowned at Norbert.

"You kidding me? Do I look like I go to card readers?"

"Since you're sitting here, I guess you do," answered Norbert.

Reggie hesitated.

Norbert said, "Shuffle."

CHAPTER FIFTY-TWO

Six of Hearts:

A gathering of true friends brings peace.
You are curious about your future.
Begin your plans.

"Ah, greeted by your partner in crime, Norbert," quipped Carlotta as she led her Club through the door of his little white bungalow. Ivy was, as usual, beside herself with joy at the sight of company, wiggling her rear end as she sidled first right and then left, trying to give preference to everyone at once.

Norbert, running a hand over his scant white hair and smiling widely, gestured his friends toward the living room sofa and chairs.

"Oh!" breathed Margaret. "That heavenly scent of lilac coming in through the window—do you all smell that?—oh! It reminds me of the first time we visited you, Norbert."

"'When lilacs last in the dooryard bloom'd,'" inserted Carlotta, not to miss an opportunity to quote Walt Whitman.

Birdie added, "Yes, it was just last May when we brought you our idea. And look how far you've come with it!"

The group sat for a moment in reflection.

It was Carlotta who broke the silence. "Norbert, in this year, you've become a true friend to us—and to no one more than me. I never thought, that sweltering day last year when we came to your assistance, that fortune-telling would ever turn out to be more than just an entertainment for the summer."

Norbert saw them all as they were a year ago, the women urging him to try something he didn't believe in or understand, and he doubting what their motives might be.

"And although you have not accepted our influence as I had hoped, I must admit that you have done rather well. And I have you to thank, Norbert, on behalf of my family. Hope's business has taken on a new life because of you. Hope herself has become a more positive thinker, and she credits your influence. And you uncovered a health problem that she now has under control. And Summer—well—who will ever forget how you fell through the ice to get to her? And the change in her since that day." Carlotta cleared her throat to put a brake on her emotions.

Margaret came to her rescue. "Well, she's just out and about more now, isn't she? As a young person should be. I mean, you see her in town, she's even dropped by the Art League a few times to paint with us, and I understand she's dated a young man once or twice, hasn't she, Carlotta?"

"And therapy," added Birdie dreamily. "She's seeing a therapist in Edwards Cove. Therapy is *wonderful*. I think *everyone* should be in therapy all the *time*. Don't you, Carlotta?"

Carlotta straightened her back. "Well, *you* should, certainly." She smiled wickedly at her old friend.

Norbert didn't know much about therapy. He did know that in the kind and attentive presence of another, we may glimpse our answers, and even better, our questions. He hoped that Summer's therapist, whatever her qualifications, was kind and attentive. Through fortune-telling, Norbert had learned about the power that is unleashed when one person simply pays close and caring attention to another person.

Norbert was a practical and rather orthodox man. For him, it had been a great risk to become a fortune-teller. But it was ultimately a cozy risk: it involved only intimate conversations across a table with a querent while he "held all the cards." This first risk, however, had led to an even greater one that was not at all cozy, when he crossed the ice bridge to find Summer Moon. Since then, he had gone back to the quiet conversations, which were really more in fitting with his temperament and age, guiding people through the cards.

"So what have you learned in this year, through the readings?" asked Birdie. "What new and wonderful revelations have come to you?"

Norbert had been thinking about this.

"I get a lot of food for thought just from customers' questions. For example, once, a querent asked me, 'What is life—all the *striving*—about?'"

The three ladies looked at Norbert with interest, waiting for his answer, but instead, he turned the question on them. "What would all of *you* say to a question like that?"

Margaret didn't pause for thought. She never did. She said, "I would say, just enjoy your life. Make sure you enjoy it. And maybe, don't strive so much!"

Birdie said, "Yes, don't strive. Just *be*. Life is about love."

Carlotta said, "Hmm. Here's the way *I* see it. Each of us is here working on a project—the project of living a Life. A life that is good, that is worth living. And I would say—if I may—that you, Norbert, are doing very well on your project.

"What do *you* think, Norbert? What are we here for?" added Carlotta.

Norbert paused, thinking how to put his thought into words. "I think we are here to be a kind presence in each other's lives." The ladies looked at him expectantly, hoping for more. "I think that is the best we can do."

Carlotta laughed. "Surely not! A kind presence in each other's lives? Why, Ivy does that. Toutou does that. Certainly we can do slightly better than dogs!"

"I must disagree with you," said Norbert, smiling. "I'm not sure that we can."

"Well, Norbert, I am older and wiser than you."

"By seven years," inserted Norbert.

"And *I* pride myself on *learning*. That has to be what it is all about, for the higher animals. Yes, projects and learning. *I* continue to learn every day. And you, Norbert, should you ever tire of the fortune-telling trade, you can always learn a new skill, and we could teach it to you, I'm sure. With all our combined hundreds of years of life experience—"

Margaret interrupted, "Will you stop that?"

"—we can learn anything we put our minds to, and make a new career for you."

"Oh, no," said Norbert. "I am happily settled in my career, thank you. You'll just have to find another project for the Club." Norbert polished his glasses carefully with a white cloth. "I do wonder what is next for you, Carlotta."

Carlotta found herself peering into Norbert's deep, brown, hypnotic eyes, a little longer than she wanted to.

"I wonder what is next for all of us," she said.

★ ★ ★ ★ ★

ACKNOWLEDGMENTS

Norbert, Carlotta and all the rest of the cast of *The Reluctant Fortune-Teller* make their appearance in the world thanks to a wonderful collaboration of many encouraging people.

It is because of my daughter, Claire, that I was able to write this book. It was Claire's idea that I write about "a fortune-teller who doesn't believe in his own fortunes, even though they always come true," and that was the beginning of Norbert's tale. From the very beginning, Claire encouraged and critiqued and added to the gaiety of the making of this story, every step of the way.

My wonderful agent, Danielle Bukowski, believed in Norbert and dedicated hours of skillful editing, which improved this book immensely. I am deeply grateful.

My editors, Liz Stein and Natalie Hallak, asked the questions and made the suggestions that have made this a much better novel. I appreciate your sensitivity, thoroughness and immense gift for story. Thank you, Erika Imranyi, for loving Norbert's story and acquiring it for Park Row, Harlequin/HarperCollins. Thank you also to copy editor Libby Sternberg, who combed through the finished manuscript with precision.

I owe a tremendous debt of thanks to my beta readers: Claire Smolinski, Rosemary Davy, Hilary Ward Schnadt, Fredric Meek, Larry Zoeller, Susan Davy, Judy Davy, Lisa Marquez and my dear husband, Tom Davy, who fueled my writing with soy lattes each morning.

I wish to thank Tom Bromley and the participants in the Faber Academy UK online course "Writing a Novel," and my own local writers' workshop group.

And at last, I keep my promise to my white-haired fifth-grade teacher, Mrs. Dorothy Kean, who told me it didn't matter that I couldn't do math, because I had "a flair for writing and would write books one day." Mrs. Kean, I told you I would thank you in my first book, and here you are.

NORBERT Z'S GUIDE
TO FORTUNE-TELLING

Be guided by your own intuition and common sense, as much as by the card meanings listed here. Have your querent shuffle the cards and hand you the top one, shuffle again and do the same, always shuffling between cards, until you have seven cards. Place them in a horseshoe spread, facing yourself. See if a querent card has appeared in the spread; this would be any face card. Kings are males, Queens are females, and Jacks can be either. If there is more than one face card, one is sure to be the querent, and the others represent important people in the querent's life. Cards to the left of the querent card may signify past events that continue to have an effect now. Cards to the right of the querent card refer to the future. Alternate meanings are listed for some cards; these alternate meanings may seem to contradict the first meaning listed. As the reader, you must use your own intuition to discern which meaning is correct for this querent at this time. Above all, look for encouragement and positive suggestions you can give your querent, because people are very suggestible, and may unconsciously work to make your reading come true.

HEARTS

Ace of Hearts: A transformative power is at work here. You will see that assistance comes from an unexpected source. Above all, trust yourself.

Two of Hearts: You are about to have a fun adventure. Be open to trying something new. Alternate meaning: you have a secret admirer.

Three of Hearts: You may be challenged to defend yourself. Be calm. You are very well able to deal with any difficult person or situation.

Four of Hearts: Be confident in yourself. Another person may feel threatened by your skill and power. Just be kind, respectful and firm.

Five of Hearts: Beware of another's envy. Alternate meaning: know that, ultimately, you are safe. You are flying high, aligned with your inner being.

Six of Hearts: A gathering of true friends brings good times and a sense of peace. Alternate meaning: you are curious about your future. Begin having fun with your plans.

Seven of Hearts: Strife between friends. Focus on common goals. You really are on the same side, truly.

Eight of Hearts: An unexpected meeting brings new perspective. You learn every day and at all times, when you are open. Alternate meaning: a wedding soon. It may be yours or someone else's.

Nine of Hearts: Your deepest wish will be granted. You will receive benefits even beyond your deepest wish.

Ten of Hearts: You have a special gift that you may have not developed. It may even be a hidden gift. Why not begin to use this gift?

Jack of Hearts: A fun-loving person. Possibly a person who parties too much and is irresponsible. Alternate meaning: romance is in your immediate future.

Queen of Hearts: A good-hearted woman, supportive of the querent. A friend indeed.

King of Hearts: A kind and generous man. He will help you in any way he can.

SPADES

Ace of Spades: There is great power in this card. A determining factor. It is the end of one chapter, to allow for the beginning of another.

Two of Spades: We are all carrying our own sorrow. Be kind to everyone. Consider performing a random act of kindness. It's always good karma.

Three of Spades: Health concerns. Do you need to see a health-care professional? Alternate meaning: maintain the blessing of good health that you have by eating well, exercising and getting enough sleep.

Four of Spades: The past must be released. What's done is done. In order to go forward, you must turn your head toward the future.

Five of Spades: A crisis. Help is needed. You or someone close to you needs help. The surrounding cards should guide you as to who, and what kind of help.

Six of Spades: Grief. Loss is one part of life. Allow time to grieve. Grieving is hard work. Be kind to yourself.

Seven of Spades: Your responsibilities require your attention. Alternative meaning: you are taking on more responsibility, and this will help you to grow as a person. The responsibility could be a pet, a child or an elder, or it could be a task at work.

Eight of Spades: You are challenged to withstand criticism. Don't worry. You know who you are. Alternate meaning: let any negative energy just pass you by; it is nothing to do with you. Stay focused on what you love and what makes you happy.

Nine of Spades: Disaster. You are on the brink of taking an action that might have far-reaching consequences. Draw back from the precipice while there is still time.

Ten of Spades: Tearing down of illusions to make space for new beginnings based on truth. You are dedicated to learning and growing. Alternate meaning: you will be signing up for a course of study.

Jack of Spades: A pompous or immature man or woman. A blowhard. This person needs to strut and command attention due to insecurity.

Queen of Spades: A woman who is very perceptive. Don't ever bother trying to fool her! She is a good person to have as an ally.

King of Spades: A serious man with no sense of humor. Critical and closed-minded.

DIAMONDS

Ace of Diamonds: The power of the magician is signified here. Within you there is a powerful force. It is time to tune in to it and let it be your guide. You have great talent.

Two of Diamonds: Others trust you because you are sincere. Great things are coming your way. Look for them. Alternate meaning: a small amount of money is coming to you soon.

Three of Diamonds: Success! Good fortune is building. Gratitude is the secret to happiness. Through a daily practice of gratitude, you will continue to attract even more good things into your life.

Four of Diamonds: Open your mind and allow yourself to explore new ideas. Why not? Alternate meaning: a job offer comes from an unexpected source.

Five of Diamonds: A power struggle or a personality clash. You may be shocked by someone's ingratitude. Whatever the unpleasantness, do not engage. Walk away. You'll be glad you did.

Six of Diamonds: Financial security. Money begins to come to you more easily now. You step into a position of your own power. Honesty is always the best policy.

Seven of Diamonds: Your relationships deepen and grow stronger. Bonds of friendship are emphasized now. You have wonderful people in your life, and they appreciate you. Alternate meaning: you will meet your soul mate very soon.

Eight of Diamonds: There is something good in your life. Do not let it go. It may be a job, relationship or a precious material item. Whatever it is, if it gives you joy—keep it.

Nine of Diamonds: A financial new beginning. Financial reward beckons. Go forward with confidence.

Ten of Diamonds: Your project gains traction. Whatever you have been focusing on is ready to take off now.

Jack of Diamonds: A young person at the crossroads.

Queen of Diamonds: A charming but controlling woman. She can be a strong ally, but beware of falling into her power.

King of Diamonds: A happy and friendly man who will be a positive factor in your life.

CLUBS

Ace of Clubs: Powerful forces are at work. You are creative and artistic. Go ahead and indulge your sense of play. That is where your genius lies.

Two of Clubs: There is yet time to take a different path. What would you really like? Describe exactly where you want to be. Your thoughts will attract what you love.

Three of Clubs: Your business is highlighted. Success is growing, and will grow beyond your expectations.

Four of Clubs: Popularity. You are liked more than you suspect. Your sphere of influence is about to widen.

Five of Clubs: Handle issues delicately or they may explode.

Six of Clubs: A solution is on its way. Beware of the motivations of others. They are not as they seem. Alternate meaning: you will be involved in a legal matter.

Seven of Clubs: Be on the lookout for an important new relationship. Someone would like to know you better.

Eight of Clubs: You are presented with a business opportunity. Consider all sides carefully before responding. Note surrounding cares for guidance.

Nine of Clubs: A period of study and hard work is indicated, if you are to succeed in your aims.

Ten of Clubs: A period of healing now It could be physical, emotional or spiritual. Take the necessary time to recharge.

Jack of Clubs: An unremarkable or dark-eyed man. There are hidden depths here. He has undeveloped potential.

Queen of Clubs: A kind woman. Loyal and open-hearted. She loves others deeply.

King of Clubs: A courageous man, capable of true heroism.

Joker: The reader may choose to leave the joker in the deck or take it out. When it appears, the Joker signifies personal transformation, psychic awakening and a journey into another world.

POWERFUL, SPECIAL COMBINATIONS

Certain card combinations, when appearing in the spread, take on a particular meaning.

Four Kings: A gathering of support. People will come together for your cause.

Three Queens: Strong personalities guarantee interesting company and a good time.

Four Sevens: Don't tempt fate. Be alert to factors that may be hidden.

Four Sixes: Peace and equilibrium are restored for a period of time. Enjoy it.

Ace of Clubs and Eight of Clubs: A job offer or business opportunity carries the power to completely change your future. Stay true to yourself, and you can't go wrong.

Jack of Clubs and Three of Spades: In order to grow into who you are, you need to get away from your early influences.

Jack of Hearts and Ten of Hearts: You need a vacation—or even a staycation.

Ten of Clubs and Four of Spades: How and why are you blocking your own healing? Take care. You are on a path that leads into a dark void.

Ten of Hearts and Four of Clubs: You have people who love you unconditionally, although you may not realize it.

Ten of Hearts and Four of Hearts: Go ahead and have confidence in yourself. If need be, "fake it 'til you make it." You can do this!

Nine of Hearts and Nine of Diamonds: Most favorable combination. Your wishes come true. You satisfy your heart and heal the hearts of others through service.

Nine of Spades and Ace of Spades: Take care to avoid a disaster that has been building.

Three of Hearts and Ace of Spades: Your own recklessness throws you into danger. Try to learn from this.

QUESTIONS
FOR DISCUSSION

1. *The Reluctant Fortune-Teller* explores the possibility of people changing at any point in their lives, of reinventing a new identity and "growing into themselves." Who are the characters you see making these changes? Do you believe that it is true, in life, that we are always able to change? What do people need in order to make changes in themselves?

2. In the book, there are instances of people pretending to be what they are not. How are Carlotta, Summer, Stanley and Norbert all different kinds of impostors?

3. Is Norbert truly psychic? What are your arguments for and against?

4. Consider the roles that jealousy, resentment and envy play in the story. Who are the characters most plagued

by these feelings, and how do these feelings impact their behavior?

5. Why does Carlotta need to be in control of other people? Like Carlotta, how do other characters attempt to control?

6. Norbert finds value in being of service to and helping others. In what ways has he, over the course of his life, fulfilled this sense of duty? Consider how the need to be of service can affect a person's behavior.

7. Discuss Norbert's evolution from the opening scene to the closing scene. How has he grown and changed?

8. Did you enjoy the companion animals and the parts they played? How do they reflect their owners, if at all? What do they add to the story?

9. If you could have lunch with one of the characters, which one would you like to get to know better?

A CONVERSATION WITH KEZIAH FROST

The Reluctant Fortune-Teller tells the story of a retired accountant's second lease on life after becoming the town psychic at the behest of Carlotta's Club. What was your inspiration for the story and characters?

The plot was my daughter Claire's inspiration. We were brainstorming, and she said, "Why don't you write about a fortune-teller who doesn't believe in the fortunes, even though they keep coming true?"

I created Gibbons Corner with the idea of writing about a place where I would like to live.

I really can't say where Norbert or any of the characters came from. Are they all subparts of myself? Are they a mishmash of all the people I have ever known? I don't know. I sat down to write a short story, and they all appeared in my mind and began saying their lines and striking their poses, as if they had always existed. It was delightful for me.

Is there any insight you can give us into Norbert's character? Did you have Norbert's journey mapped out when you began writing? How did his story surprise you and evolve along the way, if at all?

Norbert did surprise me. When I began, I never suspected he was capable of heroism. He appeared in a short story as a minor character, and stepped forward to become the unassuming protagonist of a novel. After getting to know him and Carlotta's Club very well, I did begin to map out the story with index cards and a list of scenes and events. However, the list kept changing as I went along and the story took its own paths.

What was your toughest challenge writing *The Reluctant Fortune-Teller*? Your greatest pleasure?

The toughest was revising. I did revisions with both my agent and my editors. At times, that felt like pulling out blocks from a tower and putting new blocks in the spaces while trying to keep the tower standing. But after a while, I began to see even revision as a creative and fun process, because that work was so clearly making the novel better.

The most pleasurable part is in conceiving the story. It gets revealed bit by bit, day by day, and writing it feels like the most delicious indulgence and my greatest joy.

Can you describe your writing process? Do you write scenes consecutively or jump around? Do you have a schedule or routine? A lucky charm?

I write as soon as I get up in the morning, and for as long as I can. My husband, Tom, thoughtfully brings me a soy latte, and I'm on my way. Depending on what I have to do that day, it may be two hours or it may be five. I usually have Chico, my black Pomeranian mix, on my lap, so he might be my "lucky charm."

I start with the kernel of an idea for a situation, and then some characters suggest themselves. Names will occur to me, and I'll know when I've hit on the right ones. I learned from Alan Watt's book, *The 90-Day Novel*, to really spend time "writing into the characters." I get to know them very, very well: what they want, what they fear, what they are hiding, etc. So much will be based on those early exercises in which I let my characters tell me all about themselves.

I have some scenes that occur to me out of order and I insert them in a document I call "Order of Events," for lack of a better term. Otherwise, I generally start with chapter one and go forward.

Do you read other fiction while working on a book, or do you find it distracting? Is there a book or author that inspires you the most?

It never distracts me from my own writing to read. I read fiction obsessively and couldn't stop if I tried. I love to read many current authors, such as Sarah Waters, Liane Moriarty, Alexander McCall Smith, Rachel Joyce and Rhys Bowen. For inspiration, I go back to the 1920s and '30s: P. G. Wodehouse, D. E. Stevenson, Stella Gibbons, E. F. Benson and Elizabeth von Arnim. Those are humorous writers, and when I read them, I feel grateful to them for the gift of laughter they have left to us all.

How did you know you wanted to be a writer? Can you describe the journey to publishing your first book?

In fifth grade, Mrs. Kean used to call me up to the front of the class to read my poems and compositions. I was afraid the kids would call me "teacher's pet," but they didn't. They had great reactions and cheered me on. That continued next door in sixth grade, with Miss Burns, Mrs. Kean's friend. Every week I was chosen to read my work. I began to see that not only did I get to have the enjoyment of the play that went on in my mind when I wrote these pieces, but I was giving entertainment and happiness to others by sharing my writing. That's when I knew.

I kept writing all through school, and my first master's degree was in English. After that, life led me along many routes and I gained experiences that inform my writing now. I started a couple of novels, but got lost and let go of the threads.

I finished this novel due to ignoring the common advice to not talk about your work in progress with anyone, on the grounds that your inspiration will leave you. That is nonsense! Of course, the people you talk to should be well-chosen, encouraging ones.

I joined my local writers' workshop, which meets at the public library, and I signed up for the Faber Academy UK online course "Writing a Novel." I also had my daughter, Claire, reading along and reacting as I wrote chapter by chapter. I listened carefully to critiques from all of these sources. I know that all that encouragement and accountability helped me to finish writing *The Reluctant Fortune-Teller*.

I found my agent, Danielle Bukowski, through a website called Manuscript Wish List: www.manuscriptwishlist.com.